# IF THE DUKE DARES

## ROGUE RULES
### BOOK ONE

## DARCY BURKE

Zealous Quill Press

# IF THE DUKE DARES

Incorrigible flirt Acton Loxley, Duke of Wellesbourne is in need of a duchess. En route to greet a potential bride, he encounters a most intriguing and captivating widow who completely distracts him from his task. However, she disappears before he can deepen their acquaintance. Acton begrudgingly goes to meet his bride, unaware she and the widow are one and the same.

When Persephone Barclay's younger sister is compromised, Persephone must wed before the scandal spreads. Her parents scramble to present her to the Duke of Wellesbourne; except he's precisely the kind of rogue she has now vowed to avoid. Taking flight to avoid a match, Persephone runs straight into her would-be betrothed and pretends to be someone else. But dash it all, the duke proves to be irresistibly charming! If she remains in his company, she'll end up in the wicked scoundrel's clutches.

Even worse, her second attempt at escape lands her in increasingly poor circumstances. With nowhere to turn and her safety at risk, she may have to accept help from the one man who threatens her resolve—and her reputation.

Don't miss the rest of the *Rogue Rules*!

Do you want to hear all the latest about me and my books? Sign up at <u>Reader Club newsletter</u> for members-only bonus content, advance notice of pre-orders, insider scoop, as well as contests and giveaways!

Care to share your love for my books with like-minded readers? Want to hang with me and see pictures of my cats (who doesn't!)? Then don't miss my exclusive Facebook groups!

Darcy's Duchesses for historical readers
Burke's Book Lovers for contemporary readers

Want more historical romance? Do you like your historical romance filled with passion and red hot chemistry? Join me and my author friends in the Facebook group, Historical Harlots, for exclusive giveaways, chat with amazing HistRom authors, and more!

# THE ROGUE RULES

Never be alone with a rogue.
Never flirt with a rogue.
Never give a rogue a chance.
Never doubt a rogue's reputation.
Never believe a rogue's pledge of love or devotion.
Never trust a rogue to change.
Never allow a rogue to see your heart.
Ruin the rogue before he can ruin you.

# CHAPTER 1

*Weston, England, August, 1814*

*T*he windows of the small sitting room of the Weston Hotel provided a sweeping view of the beach below. Persephone Barclay and her sister, along with their four friends, spent most of their afternoons there, having commandeered it for the month of August for three years running now. They sipped tea, read from books and newspapers, and shared everything.

This afternoon, they were missing one of their number, Persephone's younger sister, Pandora, as she had consented to walk with the Earl of Banemore. Bane, as he was known, possessed a rakish reputation, but he'd proclaimed himself enamored of Pandora, and she was wholly in love with him—or so she'd confided to Persephone.

Persephone knew from experience that infatuation was not love, and only time would tell which of those Pandora was truly experiencing. She'd counseled Pandora to be cautious with the earl, but her sister was so wonderfully giddy that Persephone had also supported her desire to spend time with him.

Their walk would be chaperoned by Persephone and Pandora's mother, the Baroness Radstock. A stiff and demanding woman, the baroness was positively ecstatic that the heir to a dukedom was courting her daughter.

The door burst open, and Pandora hurried inside. Her pretty, heart-shaped face was red, as were her eyes. She looked like she'd been crying.

Persephone leapt up from the settee she was sharing with Min—Lady Minerva Halifax, daughter of the Duke of Henlow. "Pandora, what's happened?"

"Utter disaster." Pandora buried her face in her hands and cried.

As Persephone put her arm around her sister and guided her toward the settee, Min jumped up and closed the door. Helping Pandora to sit, Persephone kept her arm about her, hating the way her sister's shoulders were shaking. Whatever had happened must be truly awful for her to be reacting so poorly.

Min sat down on Pandora's other side, putting her hand on Pandora's back and murmuring words of comfort. With sable hair, delicately arched brows, patrician features, and pale gray eyes, Min was the embodiment of a proper Society miss, though she hadn't yet had a London Season. Her gaze met Persephone's with sympathy and concern.

The entire room had fallen into a worried silence except for Pandora's sobbing. After a few moments, Pandora drew a ragged breath and wiped her hands over her eyes. "Forgive me, I'm completely overwrought."

"Please tell me this isn't Bane's fault," Persephone whispered, though she feared it was. The man, for all his declarations of admiration for Pandora, possessed the reputation of a cad. He flirted with anything in a gown and supposedly frequented a specific brothel in London called the Rogue's Den. It was, apparently, where Society's most elite gentlemen went for their bed sport.

Pandora sucked in a breath and nodded. "I don't understand. He said he loved me."

"What happened?" Min demanded. "It doesn't matter. I'm going to make sure he's out of the Grove by nightfall." The Grove was her father's house situated just outside town. Min, along with her companion, Ellis Dangerfield, spent every August there. Min's older brother, the heir and Earl of Shefford, came and went during the month with various friends, including Bane. This year, they were joined by the Viscount Somerton, cousin to another of their friends, Tamsin Penrose, and Lord Droxford, a surly gentleman who seemed oddly aligned with the more jovial trio.

"He may be packing to leave even now. Or his valet is, probably." Pandora sniffed. "Everything was going so well. Then Mrs. Lawler saw us…together."

Persephone's gut clenched. "Together how?" she asked in a low tone.

Pandora flicked her an apologetic glance. "Embracing. I suppose it was a…compromising position. That's what Mrs. Lawler said anyway."

"What did Mother do?" Persephone was afraid of the answer and surprised she'd allowed Pandora to come here to the sitting room.

"She wasn't there," Pandora murmured, her eyes full of regret. "I didn't tell her about my excursion with Bane."

Persephone stared at her sister. Pandora had lied when she'd said the baroness knew and would chaperone. It had never occurred to Persephone to confirm anything. She trusted Pandora to do the sensible thing. Pandora had not, however, done that. But Persephone couldn't blame her because she knew what it was like to be swept away by emotion and arousal. However, when it had happened to Persephone, she hadn't been caught.

Min met Persephone's gaze over Pandora's head, silently conveying that this was not good. Persephone knew that, but she would hope it wouldn't be a disaster, as Pandora had said.

"I wish my mother were at the Grove," Min said. "I would ask her to speak with Mrs. Lawler."

"Would she?" Pandora said hopefully. But then her face fell. "It doesn't matter since your mother isn't there."

"A compromising situation isn't the end of the world," Tamsin said from the other side of the room. At one and twenty, she was just a year younger than Persephone. However, her youthful appearance—wide blue-green eyes and soft, round cheeks—and her relative isolation in Cornwall made her seem even younger. She spent August in Weston with her grandmother, who lived in a charming cottage near the beach. "My great-aunt was compromised. They simply got married, which had been their intent anyway."

Persephone feared what Pandora would say next.

Pandora's mouth tightened, and anger stole into her expression, lighting her eyes. "Bane will not marry me. After Mrs. Lawler saw us and admonished him for compromising me, then congratulated me for ensnaring a future duke." Pandora twitched and wiped away a tear before continuing. "Bane responded that he was, regrettably, already betrothed to someone else. He apologized to me—profusely, not that it mattered—and I ran away."

Rage ripped through Persephone. She'd never wanted to do harm to another person, but in that moment, she would gleefully have watched Bane suffer any number of tortures.

"If I were a man, I would call him out. If I could shoot, I would call him out."

Min slapped her hand on the arm of the settee. "The scoundrel! He must be forced to marry you. I'm going to speak with my brother at once." She stood, as did Ellis, who was seated in a chair angled near the settee.

Ellis, who at four and twenty was the oldest of their unofficial club, looked to Pandora with sympathy. "I'm so sorry for what's happened. Men can be absolutely awful."

"And yet we are all destined to marry one, whether we want to or not," Tamsin said, also rising. "Why should a reprobate like Bane be allowed to ruin a sweet person like Pandora?"

"Because he's an earl and heir to a dukedom. *He* can do whatever he wishes and likely suffer no consequences." Gwendolyn Price, the newest member of their club, got to her feet as she shook her head. Her brown eyes glittered with outrage as her dark curls brushed her cheeks. "It isn't remotely fair."

"But what can we do?" Pandora asked forlornly.

Persephone clasped her sister's hand and looked into her eyes. "We can vow to not let them get away with their behavior. We can band together and say *enough*. We won't tolerate being treated this way, and we won't play by their rules."

"We'll make our own rules," Min said.

"Starting with 'never walk alone with a rogue,'" Pandora said bitterly. "And never flirt with one either."

Gwen held up her hand. "Forgive me, but what is a rogue exactly? Are all men rogues?"

"Yes," Pandora said emphatically.

Min sent Pandora a sympathetic look. "Not *all* men, but a great many who swan about with their privilege, their poor reputations for whatever transgressions they've committed, and their arrogance."

"I would say rogues pay little attention to Society's rules —or any rules, really," Ellis said.

"That would be their privilege," Persephone added with a nod. "They think they can get away with whatever they want without a care for anyone else. Utterly reckless."

Min shrugged. "Some aren't even that bad. In my experience, rogues can simply flirt too much. They think they're irresistible." She rolled her eyes. "They also tend to gamble and drink to excess. And, of course, anyone who spends time at the Rogue's Den is, by definition, a rogue."

"What's the Rogue's Den?" Gwen asked.

"A place in London where rogues go for their bed sport, and true rogues are not discreet about it," Min said with a sniff. "One must be a member, and it's rather elite."

Gwen opened her mouth to perhaps ask how Min would know, but Min went on. "My brother is a member, and he is most definitely a rogue."

"Your brother's entire set are rogues," Persephone said. "Except perhaps Droxford. I can't say he's exhibited roguish tendencies."

"Not that we've seen, but one must wonder given his company," Min said warily.

Gwen nodded firmly. "I think I understand. I daresay my brother may be a rogue. He is a terrible flirt. He also likes to do risky things—the more dangerous, the better, such as racing in a high-perch phaeton."

"That is absolutely rogue behavior—more recklessness," Min said.

"My mother despises when he does such things, especially since he always promises her that he will stop." Gwen exhaled. "Rogues are likely not entirely truthful."

Pandora scoffed. "Not at *all*. Bane vowed his eternal adoration just moments before he informed me that he was betrothed."

Ellis curled her lip. "That's another rule: never believe their pledges of love and devotion."

"And when you hear of a rogue's reputation, never doubt it," Pandora added fiercely. "They are not to be trusted to change."

"Indeed, once a rogue, forever a rogue," Persephone said, squeezing her sister's hand.

Pandora nodded vigorously in agreement. "Never, ever allow a rogue to see your heart. I wish I hadn't."

Persephone ached for her sister. "Never even give a rogue a chance. I wish I'd given you that advice." She'd hoped Bane was not as bad as his reputation had purported him to be.

Min's eyes glittered with intent. "Most importantly, if given the opportunity, ruin the rogue before he can ruin you."

"Amen!"

"Huzzah!"

Cheers went around the room, and Persephone nearly sobbed at the sight of her sister smiling faintly. It wasn't much, but it was a start.

"I shall record these so we may never forget the rules," Ellis said, whipping a small book and pencil from her reticule. She sat back down and went to work writing.

"Thank you all so much," Pandora said as a few more tears leaked from her eyes. "I fear I am ruined, but I hope you will all remain my friends."

"Nothing could stop me," Min promised. "And I'll do everything I can to minimize the scandal."

Persephone had never loved her friend more and knew that Min would use whatever power she had in Society to help Pandora. Even so, Persephone feared there would be nothing for it, that their family would simply have to remove to Radstock Hall and keep to themselves for the next year. There were worse things that could happen.

Such as the monumental lecture the baroness would most certainly deliver to Pandora—and Persephone. That was going to be painful. How Persephone wished she could take all this away from her sister. Why couldn't it have been her? No one would care if she were ruined, except for how it might affect Pandora.

All the friends took turns hugging Pandora and offering their love and support. Thankfully, they still had another week together before they went their separate ways.

"Finished," Ellis declared. "I'll make copies for each of you and bring them tomorrow."

The door opened again, and this time, it was the Baroness Radstock standing at the threshold. Her vivid blue gaze went directly to Pandora. "Mrs. Lawler has just come to see me," she said softly, but Persephone heard the underlying fury.

Pandora stood shakily, and Persephone helped, rising with her.

"Come, girls, we must pack," their mother said crisply as she pivoted in the doorway.

As it happened, they did not have one more week in Weston. They didn't even have the rest of the day. Within the hour, they were on their way home, and the future, once bright with the promise of Pandora making a brilliant match, had never looked more uncertain.

# CHAPTER 2

*Radstock Hall, Somerset, England*

They'd been home from Weston for four days, and Pandora hadn't left the second floor where their former nursery and current retreat was located except to sleep in her bedchamber on the first floor. Persephone had shared her bed, insistent that Pandora not be alone. Doing so had reminded them both of their childhood when they'd shared a room. It was much easier for them to look back instead of forward. Pandora was certain her life was over.

Because their mother had said so repeatedly.

Now, Persephone had been summoned to the drawing room by her parents. They had, unsurprisingly, found a way to blame her for what had happened between Pandora and Bane. Persephone braced herself for another lecture on how she'd failed her sister and, in so doing, had ruined her family.

She stood outside the drawing room and looked at herself in the mirror hanging nearby. Her face was pale, expectant.

She'd pulled her dark blonde hair into a tight chignon, which her mother found too severe, but what did it matter when they were at home? Mama always found something faulty about Persephone's appearance, whether it was the bump in her nose or the lack of pink in her cheeks.

Taking a deep breath, she jerked her gaze from the mirror and stepped into the drawing room. "Close the door," her mother, who'd become increasingly tense and cold in recent years, said without looking at Persephone. "Sit."

Though she would have preferred to stand in defiance, Persephone did not want to invite even more displeasure. So, she sat. As far away from her mother's chair and the hearth where her father stood as possible.

The baron glanced toward his wife—he typically checked in with her before he launched into any speech. They were a united front in everything.

"Your sister's ruin demands your immediate marriage," he declared. He smoothed his hand down the expensive superfine of his coat, his mouth pursing slightly, which pulled at his cheekbones. The expression drew one's attention to the long, thick sideburns he'd grown about three years ago when the hair on his head had become noticeably thinner.

Persephone's brain latched on to "immediate marriage" with the tenacity of a child gripping a biscuit.

"You are going to save the family," her mother said with deceptive charm.

"With an immediate marriage?" Persephone swallowed a nervous, absurd laugh. She'd had not so much as a whiff of a marriage proposal in three years. According to her mother, she didn't possess the necessary allure or beauty to attract a husband and was likely destined for spinsterhood.

Her mother nodded smoothly. "Yes, to the Duke of Wellesbourne. You remember his mother, the duchess?"

Certainly. She was a prominent member of Bath Society despite living separately from her husband. He was rumored to keep a mistress in London, and that all seemed perfectly normal to everyone. Persephone found it sad. Persephone also remembered that her son ran in the same crowd of reprobates as Bane and possessed an equally abysmal reputation as a rake who was completely unserious about marriage. They were the rogues to whom the rules she and her friends had crafted pertained.

Persephone's stomach sank past the floorboards. They couldn't expect her to wed a man such as he. She wouldn't. She *couldn't*. In fact, she could hardly believe he would actually consent to it, but then he was a duke and probably felt it was his responsibility to finally take a wife. Persephone had no desire to be the fulfillment of his duty.

"I can't imagine a hasty marriage is necessary." Especially since Persephone wasn't the one who'd been ruined. She inwardly cringed to think of her sister being identified that way. "We don't know if there will be a scandal."

The baroness glowered at her. "News of Pandora's improper behavior appeared in the *Bath Chronicle* this morning, without names, of course, but everyone knows the rumor concerns her and Banemore, and it will surely find its way to London." Full lips pursed and blue eyes narrowed, she looked pointedly at Persephone. "You *will* wed. Wellesbourne is an excellent match, particularly for you."

Persephone refused to be bullied into a marriage she didn't want. "Wouldn't we all be better served if Papa forced Bane to wed Pandora?"

"That is not an option," the baron clipped out. He pressed his fingers to the bridge of his long nose, pinching it as if he smelled something awful. "I wrote to the Duke of Wolverton and confirmed what, Bane—*Banemore*—said, that he is already betrothed and will not break that contract because of a foolish encounter with your sister."

Wolverton was Bane's father, and apparently, he would dictate what happened, which was maddening. Dukes and their heirs shouldn't be immune to consequences. But this was what rogues did.

The baroness smoothed her pale hands over her skirts. "I wrote to the Dowager Duchess of Wellesbourne immediately as her most recent letter said that her son is in need of a wife, and he dislikes the Marriage Mart. I explained that my lovely eldest daughter also prefers to avoid the Marriage Mart." She leveled her gaze on Persephone. "She has invited us to come to their home, Loxley Court near Stratford-upon-Avon, to see if you and he will suit."

Persephone hadn't minded the Marriage Mart, just the unrealistic expectations that went along with it. She'd never fit into them, either talking about topics that were deemed uninteresting to gentlemen or saying nothing at all. "You expect me to marry a man I've never met?"

"You *will* meet him," the baroness said. "And then you will wed." She sounded confident, which was laughable given her insistence that Persephone was incapable of snaring a husband. Now she was suddenly going to catch a duke?

Not bothering to disguise her sarcasm, Persephone said, "It seems to me you're placing a great deal of confidence in a situation in which you have until now deemed my attributes inadequate."

Her mother lifted a shoulder. "While it's true you aren't the beauty that Pandora is, you at least possess more sense."

How Persephone hated the comparisons their parents— especially their mother—made between her and her sister. Although, they weren't wrong about Pandora being far prettier on her worst day than Persephone could ever hope to be on her best. Her lips were fuller, her hair thicker and shinier, her eyes more sparkling. Even her laugh was superior. She always sounded as though she were making music, and she looked lovely doing it. Persephone, on the other hand, was prone to snorting. Or even outright guffawing. Because of that, she tried very hard not to laugh. Except when she was with her sister or their friends.

The baroness went on, "I don't expect you'll be caught in a scandalous embrace with Wellesbourne. Not unless it becomes necessary to secure the match."

Did her mother expect Persephone to do precisely what Pandora had done in order to ensure a marriage? "Given that Pandora is not currently betrothed, I would say your logic is lacking, Mother."

"This is not the same situation," the baroness said crossly. "The dowager is my friend, and if her son compromises you, there *will* be a wedding."

Persephone barely kept her jaw from dropping. How awful that her mother was counting on the benefits of her friendship with this woman while also considering trickery to obtain what she wanted. For the first time, Persephone felt an overwhelming dislike for the woman sitting across from her, and it was a horrible sensation. She'd felt inklings of it for years, but she'd always tried to find the good in her, the ways in which her mother truly seemed to want the best for her. But this time, the baroness had gone too far, and Persephone wasn't sure she could think of her mother as anything but an adversary ever again.

"Don't look so horrified, Persephone," her mother admonished. "This is a boon for you. To think that *you* will marry a duke is astonishing."

Persephone wondered how else this might benefit her parents, beyond soothing the scandal Pandora had caused. They'd long commented on how Pandora would undoubtedly secure a match that would ensure they never worried about finances again. "I imagine his fortune is also attractive."

"What is that supposed to mean?" her father asked defensively.

Persephone didn't want to point out the paintings, decorative pieces, or furniture that had gone missing the last few years, or the fact that the constant stream of stylish clothing—primarily for her parents and certainly not for Persephone—had slowed this year particularly. It didn't take a scholar to understand that her father was in debt. He and the baroness had argued for years about finances. Persephone had concluded that her father was not adept at managing Radstock Hall.

Answering her father's question, Persephone dared to say, "It means I suspect you want this marriage for more than just social redemption."

"Advancing the family's prospects is a young lady's responsibility," her mother snapped. "Since Pandora can no longer provide that, you will need to do so." The baroness fixed her with a dark, direct stare. "Whatever it takes."

"I won't trick him," Persephone said in a low voice, her brain scrambling to come up with a plan to avoid this scheme.

Her father made a sound in his throat. "You won't need to, my dear. Your mother is right. You are more sensible than your sister, and I imagine a duke who dislikes the Marriage Mart will prefer someone older and more sedate." He pinned his gaze on Persephone and smiled faintly. "Like you."

Older and more sedate. A prize catch indeed.

Persephone's mother nodded. "That's precisely why Wellesbourne will endorse this match."

The idea of marrying one of Bane's sordid friends was completely odious. "There has to be someone else who will meet your requirements for this immediate marriage," Persephone said, though she could see her mother was set on this plan.

"Why look elsewhere when you can have a duke?" Her mother sounded exasperated. "Really, Persephone, I thought you would be more excited about this. Who could have thought you would have this opportunity?"

Who indeed.

Persephone felt as though the walls were closing in around her. She tried to recall what Wellesbourne looked like. He had auburn hair and an easy smile, and she supposed he was objectively handsome. "Just because he's a duke doesn't mean he'll make an excellent husband. He has a reputation as a rake and is a friend of Bane's. Think of Pandora. I would rather not consider him."

"He could be whatever he wants and friends with whomever he chooses, and you will manage to accept him. You will be a *duchess*." Her mother's enthusiasm wasn't surprising. She'd married above her station when she'd become a baroness. However, Persephone's father's title wasn't prestigious, and his fortune was lacking. And now that Pandora wasn't able to carry them up the social ladder, that duty had fallen to Persephone, the spinster-in-waiting.

"Only if he accepts me, which I find hard to believe." A duke would want someone loftier than Persephone, even if she were staggeringly beautiful and possessed an excess of charm.

The baroness made an inelegant sound. "We are out of options, Persephone. Your sister's ruin could be the ruin of us all. Is that what you want? I expect you to do whatever it takes to ensure this match is successful. If you can't do that, then perhaps you shouldn't be a member of this household. It's not as if we hadn't already planned to send you somewhere after Pandora was settled." Her mother sniffed. "But all those plans are ruined now. This is a magnificent opportunity for you. I know you'll come to see it that way."

Persephone swallowed the emotion rising in her throat. She wouldn't cry. It was already bad enough that her cheeks felt hot. They were likely ablaze with color. The message from her mother was painfully clear: she either married this abhorrent duke or she would be sent into spinsterhood. Which had apparently been the plan all along.

Her mother stood. "We're leaving for Loxley Court tomorrow morning. There is much to organize. We'll need to send Pandora to Aunt Lucinda's in Bath, if Lucinda will agree to it. She won't want to jeopardize her standing in Society, and it may be that Pandora's presence would do that." The baroness bustled from the room.

Persephone needed more time to plan. She wasn't ready to be led to the slaughter, which was precisely how this felt.

"Chin up, my girl," her father said, ambling toward her. He placed a hand gently on her shoulder and gave her another lackluster smile. His blue eyes were dull. Bored, even, as if he could hardly be bothered to conduct this conversation. "You'll save this family yet. Won't that be satisfying?"

Then he was gone too, leaving Persephone to wonder how she'd ended up in this impossible position. It wasn't that she didn't wish to wed. After years of hearing that she likely wouldn't, she just hadn't allowed herself to indulge the fantasy.

And now to hear that she must marry a blackguard to save her family's reputation and fortune—for that was what seemed to be at stake—was beyond the pale. She wasn't sure what was worse—that demand or the discovery that her parents had planned to send her somewhere after Pandora was married. Where was that, a nunnery?

If they wanted her gone, perhaps she should disappear entirely.

With leaden feet, she trudged upstairs to the second floor where their former nursery was located and which she and Pandora now used as a retreat. Pandora would listen to these new developments with sympathy and would share in Persephone's outrage.

Contrary to what their parents thought, Pandora was quite clever. She'd simply misjudged Bane and had listened to her heart instead of her head. It could happen to anyone.

As expected, Pandora was snuggled into the window seat, a book in her lap. She was, however, not reading. Her gaze was trained outside as Persephone entered.

Not bothering with preamble, Persephone closed the door and stated, "They want me to wed. Immediately."

Pandora turned her head. Unfortunately, the sparkle in her eyes that Persephone had thought of earlier was still absent. It had disappeared after Bane had compromised, then rejected her.

"Oh, Persey, I am so sorry." Pandora grimaced, and Persephone began to worry that the stress and sorrow Bane had caused would permanently damage her beauty—not on the exterior, but inside. Pandora had always been vivacious, and her joy was contagious. It was difficult to be in her company and not feel good. But all that had changed.

"This is my fault," Pandora continued.

"It absolutely is not," Persephone said. "I encouraged you to determine your feelings for him, and I too believed what he told you." She couldn't bring herself to repeat what they now knew were lies—that he admired Pandora greatly and couldn't imagine life without her. What nauseating drivel.

Pandora shook her head as she swung her legs to the floor from the window seat and set the book on the cushion at her side. "I will not allow you to accept any responsibility.

I was foolish, and I knew better. Bane's reputation well preceded him. I stupidly trusted him when he begged me not to believe everything I'd heard."

The bitterness in her tone renewed Persephone's desire to seek vengeance. "How I wish there were a way to punish him for what he's done to you."

"How I wish we'd come up with the Rogue Rules before I met him." The barest hint of a smile curved her lips. "I do think I'm going to embroider them and hang it on the wall in here."

Two written copies of the rules had arrived yesterday along with a letter from Min and Ellis. Min had said that her brother and his friends had left the Grove before she and Ellis had returned from the hotel. Then she'd called them cowards.

Pandora straightened her shoulders and fixed her gaze on Persephone. "Tell me what Mama and Papa said."

"I'm to accompany them to visit one of Mama's friends—the Dowager Duchess of Wellesbourne. Her son, the duke, is in need of a wife, and Mama insists that will be me."

Pandora wrinkled her nose. "Wellesbourne? He's one of Bane's friends. Bane mentioned him several times. He said he's a good sort, amusing, charming, but I'm sure those are lies too. Bane wished he was in Weston to meet one of my friends."

One of her friends. Not Persephone. She focused her irritation on the man who deserved it—the scoundrel who'd broken her sister's heart. "I shall take any recommendation from Bane as a black mark against a person."

"That is probably for the best," Pandora agreed. "I suppose you tried to tell Mama that you did not want to be forced into marriage."

"Of course. That went as well as you could expect. Worse, actually. She said if I couldn't ensure a betrothal, going so far as to suggest that I entrap him in a compromising situation, I may as well leave."

Pandora gasped. "She didn't say that!"

Persephone nodded, keeping the hurt and anger at bay. "She did." Persephone didn't want to add that the plan had always been for her to be sent somewhere. Pandora didn't need to hear that on top of everything else she was suffering. Persephone could carry the pain of that revelation and of what felt like an awful betrayal by their parents on her own —at least for now. "Mayhap that's what I should do. Leave, I mean, not force a compromising situation." That her mother would even want to risk another scandal after what had happened to Pandora was appalling.

"I think you should," Pandora said firmly. "In fact, you should go to Aunt Lucinda's. Then she can talk some sense into Mama. Or Papa at least."

Moving to join her sister on the window seat, Persephone perched on the edge. She gave her sister a sympathetic smile. "Mama hopes to send you to Aunt Lucinda's." Persephone didn't want to mention the possibility that their aunt would say no. Pandora was dealing with enough after having her heart trampled upon by that rogue.

Pandora slowly nodded. "That is understandable. I couldn't possibly go along with all of you to meet Welles-bourne." She looked down at her lap. "In my state, I can't accompany you anywhere. Perhaps Aunt Lucinda won't even want me."

"Nonsense!" Persephone grabbed Pandora's hand, and her sister met her gaze. "Aunt Lucinda will go out of her way to eviscerate Bane as soon as she hears what's happened. She will be your staunchest ally."

"Yes. Probably," Pandora murmured.

"She will," Persephone said firmly, giving her sister's hand a squeeze before releasing it. "In any case, I can't go to Aunt

Lucinda. You need her more than I do, and it's the first place Mama and Papa would look for me. It's probably best if I just go with them." And do her best to ensure the duke wanted nothing to do with her. She'd been unmarriageable for three years without even trying, surely she could avoid the parson's trap if she put in some effort.

"It's unconscionable that they expect you to marry Wellesbourne." Pandora's brow furrowed. "I'm so sorry to have caused this, Persey. I hope you won't hate me."

Persephone gave her sister a warm, love-filled smile, desperate to ease her sister's guilt. "I could never do that."

"You won't have to marry him," Pandora insisted. "They can't force you."

No, but they could make her miserable. She saw no way to avoid accompanying them to Loxley Court. The only way to circumvent their plans was to make sure the duke wouldn't want her as his wife.

Her mother's words repeated in Persephone's head. The baroness had never explicitly said Persephone was nearly worthless when compared to Pandora but threatening to throw her out of the household told Persephone exactly what she needed to know—that her parents didn't value her as a daughter or even as a person. Persephone had never felt so horrid. Or so alone. She was simply a means to an end: saving the family.

Spinsterhood away from them couldn't possibly be worse.

"I need to think about it," Persephone said, trying not to let her sister see the turmoil inside her. "I'm sure the answer will present itself." She could only hope.

# CHAPTER 3

*A*cton Loxley, Duke of Wellesbourne, stepped into the common room of the New Inn in Gloucester after washing the day's travel from himself and taking a respite. Tomorrow, he would arrive home at Loxley Court, where his mother was expecting him.

So that he could meet a potential bride.

This was a monumental shift in his behavior. He'd spent the last several years avoiding even the discussion of marriage, preferring to enjoy his youth, which his father had always encouraged. Then, a couple of years ago, he'd begun to suggest it was time for Acton to do his duty and take a wife. His father's death had prompted Acton to accept that it was time to wed.

Acton did wonder if there was something else prompting him to seek a wife *now*. He'd cut his annual visit to Weston, which he made with his closest group of friends, short in favor of traveling to Wales to spend time with another friend who was more serious minded. Did that mean Acton was growing more serious?

He wasn't sure, but he probably ought to if he was going

to be a husband and a father. Hopefully, that would come when he met the right person, and mayhap that would be the young lady he would meet tomorrow.

The table nearest him was occupied by a young couple who were staring deeply into each other's eyes. They appeared to be in love. Perhaps they were newlywed. Would Acton and his bride behave in such a way? He'd yet to make the acquaintance of a woman who inspired him to such fancy, but that was likely because he wasn't made for such emotions. His father had always explained that men such as they had too many responsibilities to harbor sentiment. They needed to be focused and strong—and leave love and romance to poets and artists.

"Good evening, Your Grace," the innkeeper said, interrupting Acton's thoughts, which Acton appreciated. "The private dining room is just this way."

As Acton followed the man, he cast a lingering glance around the warm, inviting common room. Perhaps he'd spent too much time in taverns or gaming hells with his friends, but this environment was far more enticing than a dim room with no one in it.

Except there was someone in it. A solitary woman with dark gold hair swept into a simple, almost severe, style sat at one end of the rectangular table.

"I apologize that I do not have a separate table for you, sir," the innkeeper said with a faint grimace. "We are over capacity tonight, and this was the best I could arrange."

"It's quite all right. Indeed, I would prefer not to dine by myself in here." Acton stood near the table but didn't sit. His place had been set at the opposite end from the woman, and he much preferred to move it to sit across from her.

The innkeeper nodded. "I'll fetch our finest Madeira for you, as well as your dinner."

"The bottle, if you don't mind," Acton said with a smile. Perhaps he could tempt the lady to share it with him.

"Very good, sir." The innkeeper bustled from the room, closing the door behind him.

Acton eyed the young woman, curious as to why she was alone. "Seems silly for us to dine at opposite ends of the table," he said, picking up his utensils and moving them to the place across from her.

She lifted her head, and Acton took a few steps toward her so he could see her more closely. The moment her gaze met his, a ripple of awareness swept over him. Her eyes were a lush, vivid blue that reminded him of the sky in early autumn when the air was crisper and the colors more vibrant. An intriguing bump marred the line of her nose, and dark gold brows arched over her stunning eyes. Her pink lips parted—barely. Acton held his breath in anticipation that she would speak.

"Does it?" she asked, sounding uninterested.

"To me, yes. But then I rather dislike dining alone. Do you mind if I sit here?"

She took just longer than a moment to respond. "What if I said yes?"

Was she joking? Flirting? Or did she really not want him to sit there?

Bah, of course she wouldn't mind him sitting there. She had to be flirting.

Acton slid into the chair.

She eyed him warily. "I'll be finished soon."

He sent her his most provocative gaze. "When you finish, perhaps I'll persuade you to keep me company. Unless you need to dash upstairs for some reason?" Such as a husband or children. Perhaps she was only alone here in this room.

"I do not. Though, I am tired from traveling. Aren't you?" she asked before picking up her wineglass.

"I'm quite refreshed after a hot bath. The innkeeper has taken very good care of me. You are traveling alone, then?"

She snorted, then wrinkled her nose before she lifted her hand to briefly cover her mouth. "That is a presumptuous question."

"That you found amusing, I think. Or perhaps that was a sound of offense. If so, I offer my deepest apologies. I confess I am embarrassingly curious about you."

Once again, her stunning eyes met his. "Why?"

He shrugged. "A beautiful woman traveling alone is curious."

Her eyes had widened the slightest degree when he'd called her beautiful. Did she not like to be complimented? He'd met a woman like that once. She'd found flattery empty and preferred when a man showed what he thought of her instead of telling her. Acton had worked hard thereafter to demonstrate his soaring opinion of her attributes.

"It oughtn't be. I'm a widow on my way to visit family. Since you're being unabashedly inquisitive, I'll do the same. Where are you going?'"

"Home, actually."

"And where is that?"

He narrowed one eye at her. "Are you equally curious about me, or just giving as good as you get?"

"Probably the latter." Her mouth tried to smile, but she wouldn't let it. Why not? Perhaps she was newly widowed and didn't think she ought to show amusement. That would explain the laugh that had come out as a snort. She'd tried to stop it. "You're avoiding answering my question."

"Not on purpose. Home is near Stratford-upon-Avon."

A serving maid brought Acton's dinner and the bottle of wine. She poured Madeira into his glass and deposited the bottle on the table before dipping a brief curtsey on her way out.

"A curtsey for you?" Acton's companion asked. "And the innkeeper called you 'sir.' Are you nobility?"

"Er, yes." He usually proudly proclaimed his title, as his father had taught him to do, but in this private dining room alone with this beautiful woman, he wanted to be just a man. He picked up his wineglass. "To making new friends."

She gave him a dubious look as she plucked up her glass and gently tapped it to his. "Friends? It's a trifle early to make such pronouncements, isn't it? Perhaps we won't get on at all."

Acton laughed before sipping his Madeira. "I'm confident we shall." He gave her one of his most dazzling smiles. "So confident, in fact, that I'd make a wager on it."

She arched a brow. "How would that work?"

"I'll wager a pound that by the end of the evening, we'll be laughing and jesting so much that our cheeks hurt. That will mean we are friends."

"A pound?" she looked at him as if he were daft.

Acton realized that was excessive. "A shilling?"

She shook her head. "No wagers."

Was that because she didn't like to gamble, or because she couldn't afford it? Acton took in her simple costume, a dark brown traveling dress buttoned to her throat, and her lack of adornment. She wore no jewelry, not even a comb in her hair. No wedding ring either. Didn't widows typically wear those?

"Who awaits you at home?" she asked. "Your wife?" There was an edge to the question, as if she expected an affirmative answer and had therefore judged him a cheat.

Acton swallowed a bite of roast beef and took a drink of wine to wash it down. "She might be, actually. Not that she's my wife. Yet. I'm to meet someone to see if we will suit."

He thought of the woman who would be waiting when he arrived at Loxley Court. She was the daughter of a baron, and the baroness was a friend of his mother's. Because Acton had rarely seen his mother during the past twenty-three years, he didn't know these people at all. That the dowager had taken an interest in helping him find a bride was both surprising and, if he were honest, unsettling. She'd never bothered with him before. Not until his father had died.

Acton missed him. In the year his father had been gone, Acton had realized all the things he hadn't learned, things he'd taken for granted thinking his father had decades before him. But an attack of his heart had stolen him swiftly, and Acton had spent the intervening days and months trying to be the duke his father expected.

He was fairly certain he fell short. Marrying and providing an heir would go a long way to fulfilling his duty—and making his father proud.

Noting that she was watching him intently, Acton realized he'd been woolgathering. He stuffed a bite of parsnip into his mouth.

"You're on your way to meet a potential bride?" she asked, sounding far more interested than she had yet.

"Yes." He didn't really want to discuss it with her. He was enjoying their conversation and preferred to leave his potential duchess where she resided—in the future. "Where are you headed?"

"Pardon me if I don't say. I find it's better for a woman on her own to guard her secrets."

Secrets. That single word provoked Acton's curiosity like none other.

"I can understand that, but I promise you are safe with me," he vowed intently.

She gave him a look that said she didn't believe that in the slightest, but said nothing. Had he done something to offend her? Was it the mention of a potential bride? Had she felt an instant connection with him that made her feel...jealous?

That seemed absurd. And yet, Acton couldn't deny that something about her intrigued him. He'd called her beautiful, but that wasn't exactly right. She was singular—it was those eyes. Yes, those eyes held a wealth of secrets, and he wanted to learn every single one of them.

She tapped her finger on the base of her wineglass once. Twice. "What will you do if you meet this woman and she's not to your liking? I mean, if you determine you won't suit."

"Then we'll go our separate ways with nothing lost." Acton took another bite of the beef. After swallowing, he asked, "Have you been widowed long?"

"About a year." She set her utensils down. Oh no, was she done eating? He didn't want to lose her company.

"I'm sorry for your loss. No children?"

She shook her head. "We weren't married long."

"I wouldn't have thought so. You seem young. I'd wager not even five and twenty."

"You do like to wager," she said, perhaps with a hint of reproach.

That was how he and his friends talked to one another, and there was a stupid amount of wagering between them. Not all of it was for money. They wagered silly antics or to obtain things they wanted. Once, he lost a bet with his friend Bane and had to attend Almack's with him. *And* he'd had to ask three wallflowers to dance. It was bloody awful.

"Bad habit with friends, I suppose." He wished he'd wagered with her after all. If he'd won—and they did seem at least friendly—his prize could have been her staying with him until he was at least finished eating.

She set her napkin on the table, another signal that she was finished with her meal. And her wineglass was almost empty.

"I hope you aren't going to leave," he said. "I'd be honored if you'd remain here, at least until I'm finished."

"Do you really dislike being alone?"

"Somewhat. But it's more than that. I like you. I feel as if we are on our way to being friends. I should like to deepen our acquaintance." Acton was torn between wanting to be done with his dinner so he could focus entirely on her and prolonging the meal to ensure she stayed.

Her brow arched in that saucy fashion once more. He liked it. "Deepen it how?"

Was she using a seductive tone? Or was he just hoping she had?

"However we like," he said casually, despite the increased speed of his heartbeat.

She batted her lashes. "I see." Now she sounded demure. But perhaps she really was flirting with him. God, he hoped so. He had a sudden image of whiling away what could have been a perfectly boring evening with this thoroughly tempting widow.

"You should finish eating," she murmured, jolting him from his lurid waking dream.

Acton took a large bite of the beef while glancing at the door to ensure it was closed. Too bad he couldn't lock it.

He watched as she finished her wine. "Would you care for Madeira?"

"I would, thank you. Why don't you tell me what qualities you hope your potential bride will possess?"

Filling her glass, he refilled his own while he had the bottle. "My father always said the perfect wife would be clever, well-spoken, dutiful, and, above all, beautiful."

She put her hand around the wineglass, her fingers stroking the stem. It was most distracting. In a thoroughly erotic way. Was she doing that on purpose? "What an interesting list. Which of those are most important to you?"

"Er—" His mind was arresting on the movement of her fingers. He nearly said, "Sexual prowess," but that was not something he'd mentioned. It was also not something he ought to say to someone he'd just met who wasn't an employee of the Rogue's Den. "I don't think I would enjoy being married to someone who wasn't clever."

She licked her lips, and now he had to think she was arousing him on purpose. She'd been a widow for a year. It was not unrealistic for him to think she might be interested in the same thing he was—a night to remember.

"You're not eating," she said. "Are you finished?"

"I might be. But please don't leave."

"How can I when you've just refilled my glass?" She held up her wine and took a sip, her lips curving into the barest of smiles.

She did seem interested. Acton's pulse picked up more speed as a heady desire rushed through him.

Setting her glass on the table, she looked over at him, her dark lashes framing her sultry gaze. Acton was fast becoming enchanted.

"I think I'm finished with my dinner," he said. His throat had gone dry as his body hummed with anticipation. "I'd like to see what dessert will be."

Her lips parted. "What do you desire?"

He leaned toward her, breathless with want, "You. Draped across this table like a feast. Or upstairs in my bed, your limbs tangled with mine." Apparently, he'd thrown caution completely away. More accurately, it had been demolished by his raging lust for this enticing woman.

Her nostrils flared as she inhaled quickly. "What lurid suggestions."

Damn, had he gone too far? He typically said such things to his lovers, and they liked it. And she was a widow, not some green girl. Like the woman he would consider marrying.

*Do not think of her right now.*

"I hope I didn't offend you. I find myself utterly captivated." He found himself pushing his dishes aside and leaning over the table toward her. "I should like to kiss you."

"I'm sure you would. However, I am not so easily seduced." She moved quickly, plucking up her wineglass once more. Before he could ascertain what she was about, his face and chest were dripping with Madeira. Blinking, he saw that she'd tossed the contents of her glass on him.

He sputtered. "What the devil?"

"The devil indeed," she spat, rising. "You think you can smile at me and charm your way under my skirts? And because you're a duke, you think you can get away with it. Not with me, you can't. In fact, you shouldn't try it with anyone. Preying on a solitary widow... Have you no shame? Men like you are a menace to women everywhere."

With a final snarl, her tempting lips twisting, she strode to the door and departed the dining room.

Acton stared after her, wondering what in the hell had happened. He'd clearly misread that entire situation.

But she'd stroked the stem of the wineglass and licked her lips! She'd looked at him provocatively and asked him what he desired. She'd done everything but invite him upstairs.

Or so it seemed.

He frowned, irritated with himself and hating that he'd offended her so deeply without even realizing it. She'd been glorious in her anger, though. It was a shame he'd never see her again, for he was somehow still as entranced as he'd been before she'd doused him with wine.

As he used his napkin to wipe his face, he conjured the things she'd said, thinking they'd be forever emblazoned on his brain. Then he froze.

How had she known he was a duke?

# CHAPTER 4

$\mathcal{P}$ersephone carried her small valise downstairs
early the following morning. As with the day
before, she was leaving before dawn even broke over the
horizon.

Yesterday, however, she'd been fleeing from her parents.
She'd traveled with them to Cirencester, where they'd stayed
the night. Over dinner, she'd had to listen to the baroness
instruct her on how she might entrap the duke into marriage
—should that become necessary. Even if the duke hadn't
been an utter rogue, her mother's machinations disgusted
Persephone. She would do anything to ensure Persephone
married this man, regardless of Persephone's wishes.
Distraught, Persephone had determined she couldn't
continue with them to Loxley Court.

She'd gone upstairs before them and quietly packed a few
things into her valise. Then, she'd used her letter-writing
supplies to scratch out a short note informing them that she
was returning home. After barely sleeping, she'd roused
herself from her narrow bed in the corner of their chamber,

removed her bedclothes, which she might need, and stolen away.

The first mail coach had been going west to Gloucester, and while that wasn't the direction Persephone wanted to go, she'd taken it with plans to depart at Gloucester, where she would take a coach south to Bristol.

It was too late to go to Weston. All her friends would have gone by now as it was the first of September. Min and Ellis were on their way to Bedfordshire, and Tamsin would be journeying to Cornwall. Gwen, however, lived in Bristol. That was Persephone's destination by default. Persephone only hoped the Prices would give her shelter, at least for a few days.

Persephone wondered what her parents had done when they'd found the note she'd written. Her mother was likely outraged and would make sure her father felt the same. They'd probably arrived at Radstock Hall yesterday after-noon only to find that Persephone wasn't there. That would have made the baroness practically apoplectic. Persephone didn't feel even a little badly.

But here she was in Gloucester, having had to spend the night and take the coach to Bristol in the morning. Which was how she found herself once again departing an inn at dawn.

It was good that she'd had plans to leave early. That way, she would avoid seeing Wellesbourne. She was sure the man she'd met last night was him. When he'd confessed to being nobility, then told her he was traveling home to meet a potential bride and that home was near Stratford-upon-Avon, she'd deduced that he had to be the duke she was supposed to meet. Then he'd behaved like an arse, and she'd been absolutely convinced.

Perhaps she shouldn't have baited him, but she wanted to know if he was the rake that she'd heard him to be. He was that and more. To try to seduce a widow when he was on his way to meet his potential duchess was abominable.

She'd broken two of the Rogue Rules by being alone with him and flirting with him, though the flirting had been fake. The moment she began to suspect his identity, she focused on the most important rule: ruin him before he can ruin you. She'd decided dousing him with Madeira was as close to ruin as she could bring him given the circumstances. She was sure as hell not going to allow him to ruin her.

Recalling his surprised features drenched in Madeira brought a smile to her face. She oughtn't take pleasure in his discomfort, but after what his friend had done to Pandora, she concluded there was no harm in it. Men like the two of them deserved a splash of wine in the face now and then.

Persephone made her way through the common room and departed the inn. The sun was now up, casting a milky light over the yard. Glancing about, she nearly stumbled as she caught sight of the duke walking out of the stables. She did not want him to see her!

Heart pounding, she hastened across the yard away from his path. She didn't dare look back as she rushed toward the mail stop to catch the coach to Bristol. The last thing she needed was to have to speak with him after last night. Hopefully, she would never encounter him again.

She barely made the coach in time. Indeed, it was loud and confusing, and there were multiple coaches. She was just glad to have made it and that she was able to sit inside the coach, since it was chilly. Her valise had been strapped to the back.

The sun was now visible above the horizon as the coach started forward. Persephone closed her eyes and tried not to think of how tightly the woman beside her was pressed into her side. At least it was a woman and not some man with wandering hands.

Persephone imagined Wellesbourne sitting beside her. He'd try to engage her in conversation, then he might attempt to lean closer or even touch her. He'd certainly proposition her with more lewd language.

Well, perhaps not after she'd tossed her wine at him.

If Persephone were honest, and she didn't really want to be, she would admit that his attention to her had been initially flattering—before she'd known who he was. He'd seemed to find her genuinely attractive. For the first time in years, and only the second time ever, she'd felt desirable. Now that she knew his identity, she rather hated that he'd been the one to make her feel that way.

He probably hadn't even found her that alluring. Men like him said and did whatever was necessary to achieve their goal. And his goal had, without question, been to seduce her into spending the night with him.

There was no point in wasting any more time thinking of him. She was never going to see him again.

Unless her parents continued to insist that she marry him. She could only hope that if they ever met, he'd recall she'd thrown wine on him and immediately declare they did not suit.

Persephone wondered what her parents were doing now. Were they looking for Persephone upon discovering she hadn't actually returned home? Not because they cared for her, but because she was apparently intrinsic to their desperate plan to save the family.

More than anything, Persephone wanted to believe that. However, she couldn't, not after the demands they'd placed on her along with the revelation that she was to be cast aside as soon as Pandora married and elevated the family. She realized her panicked flight was about more than avoiding marriage to a scoundrel. She didn't want to just be her parents' pawn; she wanted to be their daughter. Whom they loved.

Heart aching, Persephone turned her thoughts to someone who *did* love her: Pandora. Hopefully, she was feeling better being with Aunt Lucinda. After staying in Bristol with Gwen for a few days, Persephone determined she ought to join them. In Bath, at Aunt Lucinda's, she could come up with a plan for her future. More and more, she expected it would not be at Radstock Hall.

Feeling sad and tired, Persephone allowed the movement of the coach to lull her to sleep.

The sun was much higher in the sky when she jolted awake. And the coach was half-empty.

The older man across from her was leaning toward her. "Is this your stop?"

Persephone blinked several times. "Are we in Bristol?"

He stared at her as if she were daft. "This is Worcester."

Worcester! She'd gone completely in the wrong direction! In all the fuss that morning, she must have boarded the wrong coach.

Clambering down, Persephone stumbled as she hit the dirt. The coach wouldn't stop for long, so she hastened to the back to fetch her valise. There were several trunks and other pieces of luggage, but her small gray valise wasn't where she'd seen it stowed. It wasn't there at all.

Panicking, she rushed to the front of the coach, where the coachman was just settling onto the box. "Pardon me," she said. "My valise isn't on the back of the coach. It's gray and about this size." She held her hands up to approximate the valise.

"Haven't seen it," he said. "Need to be on my way now, though."

"You can't leave!" She couldn't be this far from her destination and without her things!

He gave her a sympathetic look. "I'm afraid I must. And you said your valise isn't on the coach, so there's no point in staying. Best of luck to you."

Persephone had to back away quickly as the coach started forward. She gaped as it moved away from her. But the man was right—what difference did it make since her valise wasn't on the coach? And staying on the coach made no sense as she would only continue in the wrong direction.

How had she made such a horrid mistake? And what had happened to her valise? She'd seen it on the coach—the wrong coach, apparently—before they'd departed Gloucester. Someone had to have stolen it. Someone who'd been in or on the coach. Turning in a circle, Persephone looked about for anyone familiar, but she didn't recognize anyone.

What was she going to do without her belongings? Thank goodness her money was sewn into her undergarments. But it was already a fast-dwindling sum, and now she would have even less as she booked passage to Bristol. Tears stung her eyes. She didn't even have an extra handkerchief.

She would not capitulate to misfortune. Things could be far worse. She could be betrothed to that jackanapes Wellesbourne.

Straightening her spine and lifting her chin, she moved forward. She would book passage on a coach, hopefully leaving today and if not, she would find an inn that was both affordable and acceptable. Nothing too fancy and nothing too…rough.

Things would improve. They had to.

~

*I*t was still late morning when Acton arrived home at Loxley Court after departing Gloucester. The butler informed him that their guests had arrived the day before. Knowing he would be expected to have an audience with them, he washed away the dust of the road and met his mother in the drawing room.

Even after spending time with her over the past year, she seemed like a stranger to him. Her dark red hair had only a few strands of white even though she would be fifty the year after next. She was thin with a warm, welcoming smile and a collection of freckles that were somehow endearing. They made her...approachable. She wasn't at all what he'd expected. His father had rarely spoken of her, but what he had said made it sound as if she were cold and unfeeling. On the contrary, she went out of her way to be attentive to Acton and tell him—almost daily—that she was glad to be with him.

He found it awkward. And he could hear his father saying it was the excess of emotion that bothered him.

"Wellesbourne, how do you look so handsome after riding all the way from Gloucester?" she asked with a light laugh.

"I'm always this handsome, Mother," he said, smiling. "I understand our guests are here?"

She clasped her hands before her. "Yes, but not everyone we expected. Lord and Lady Radstock are here; however, Miss Barclay is not. She has taken ill."

"I rode home for nothing?" Acton could have stayed at his friend's house in Wales. They'd been having a brilliant time making plans for the next Parliamentary session. He was an MP, and together, they worked to effect change in their respective branches.

"Lord and Lady Radstock believe she will recover quickly. They didn't want to forgo the appointment with you, so they've come to meet you."

What a waste of time. Acton had agreed to meet a potential bride, not her parents. "I hope you told them they needn't have bothered."

The dowager moved toward him, her expression concerned. "Come now, you can be pleasant and still meet them, can't you?"

Acton gritted his teeth. "I'm always pleasant. You would know that if you knew me well, which you do not." He immediately regretted his words, especially when he noted the flash of hurt in her gaze.

"I realize I can't replace the years I wasn't with you," she said softly. "But I try every day to be the mother I wasn't."

"I know, and I appreciate that." He'd allowed her to move into the dowager house because he'd been delighted— surprised but delighted—to learn she wanted to be his mother. Still, he couldn't forget the fact that she'd abandoned him at a very young age. He'd barely known he had a mother.

Her gaze moved beyond Acton, and he realized they were no longer alone. He turned to see the Baron and Baroness Radstock standing at the doorway. She was attractive, with blonde hair and piercing blue eyes. His dark hair was thinning, yet he sported impressive sideburns. What was most notable about them was their clothing. They were dressed in the height of fashion, and their garments were made of rich materials. London Society would welcome them on appearance alone. However, he thought his mother had mentioned that Miss Barclay's dowry was rather small. The baron and baroness didn't look as if their daughter would have a limited settlement.

And here they were without her. Which was just as well. Acton was feeling somewhat moody since the widow had doused him with Madeira. What he'd thought had been a wonderful encounter had gone completely and horribly wrong.

His discontent wasn't entirely because of her actions. He

was questioning himself as he'd completely misread the situation. He'd thought she was flirting, that she reciprocated his interest. And he'd been utterly mistaken.

The dowager pivoted so that she could see both their guests and Acton. "Lord and Lady Radstock, allow me to present my son, His Grace, the Duke of Wellesbourne."

The baron and baroness moved into the drawing room. He executed a bow while she dipped into an impressive curtsey. Acton would wager they'd been presented at court.

But of course they had. The man was a baron.

Thoughts of wagering brought the widow to mind. And not his friends with whom he wagered. How odd.

"It is our great pleasure to make your acquaintance, Duke," the baroness said smoothly. Given that she spoke first and the baron was eyeing her expectantly, Acton deduced that she exerted a great deal of influence in the marriage.

"I was hoping to meet your daughter," Acton said. "Though I'm pleased to meet you too."

Pleased was perhaps a bit of an exaggeration. He was disappointed to have wasted his time in coming if the potential bride wasn't even going to be here.

The baroness frowned slightly. "We deeply apologize for our daughter's absence. I'm afraid she took ill with a cold just before we departed. We thought it best if she rested for a day or two. She will join us soon, however."

She would? Acton supposed he could wait.

He forced himself to take a breath. This was his future duchess—or could be, anyway. He should not be thinking of meeting her as an inconvenience. Damn, but the episode with the widow had upset him. He felt as if he'd been knocked off his horse after a consistent record of winning races.

The dowager gestured toward the nearest seating area. "Let us sit. While we are sorry Miss Barclay was unable to join you, it's good that you've come." She took a chair and the baron and baroness sat together on a settee.

Acton couldn't bring himself to join them. He moved to stand next to a vacant chair.

"I'm glad you think so," the baroness said with a smile that wasn't nearly as pleasant as his mother's. "We thought it important to visit as planned and at least tell you"—she flicked a glance toward Acton—"about Persephone."

Persephone. Queen of Hell. Acton wondered how well the name suited her. Perhaps she was a hellion, and that was why she'd been left at home.

"I would like to meet Miss Barclay," he said.

The baron nodded. "Of course. In the meantime, we could negotiate the marriage settlement?" He said the last part slowly, as if it were difficult to get out. Acton hoped so since it was an incredibly presumptuous suggestion given that he hadn't even made the acquaintance of the proposed bride.

Acton forced himself to smile faintly. "I don't think that's necessary. Not until we decide if we will suit." He slid a look toward his mother to ascertain her reaction to the baron's proposition.

"I'm confident you will suit," the baroness said before looking to her husband. "Show him the miniature."

A miniature would answer the question of whether they would be compatible? Acton wouldn't choose a bride on looks alone. Could he even trust that this painting accurately depicted Miss Barclay?

The baron pulled a framed oval miniature from his pocket and handed it to Acton. "See how pretty she is? She'll make you an excellent duchess. She's clever and accomplished with a needle as well as at the pianoforte."

Clever. One of the words his father had used and the one he'd told the widow was his primary requirement in a duchess. Was it a coincidence that Miss Barclay's father described her in the same way?

"And she'll be a marvelous hostess," the baroness put in. "She's been very helpful to me with planning dinners and the like."

Acton took the miniature, and as soon as he lowered his gaze, he sucked in a breath. Staring back at him was the widow he'd met in Gloucester.

What the devil was going on here?

"I knew you'd find her attractive," the baroness said, sounding pleased but also relieved, which Acton found peculiar. He'd already deduced that the Radstocks were slightly disagreeable and now he wondered if they might be genuinely unlikeable. They might even be the sort of parents who raised a daughter who flirted with a duke and then threw wine in his face.

This was a bloody mystery. Still, he bit his tongue before he acknowledged that he'd already met their daughter.

Miss Barclay. Who wasn't a widow at all. What was she about? She wasn't sick, and she wasn't at home. Did her parents even know where she was?

Acton frowned slightly. "I find it odd that you would come here without Miss Barclay if, in fact, she only has a cold. Why not wait until she recovered? That would surely have been the better course of action."

He looked down again at the miniature. Miss Barclay wasn't smiling, but there was a vivacity to the way she held her head—a slight tilt that seemed to convey her energy. Or perhaps it was her gaze that had so captured him in person. In the painting, her lids dipped the barest amount, making her look as though she were hiding something, such as a delicious secret. Hadn't he thought that about her last night? That she possessed a secret? And he supposed she did. She was gallivanting about western England pretending to be a widow when she was purported to be sick at home.

It was entirely likely that he was seeing things in the miniature that simply weren't there, that he was attributing the charming and seductive characteristics of the widow he'd met to the image in his hand. Charming and seductive…right up until she'd reprimanded him and soaked him in Madeira.

In hindsight, mayhap he'd deserved it. He'd propositioned a young, unmarried woman. Yes, he'd thought she was a widow, but did that give him leave to say the things he'd said?

Perhaps he'd spent too much time in London with courtesans.

Acton looked from the baron to the baroness, wondering if either would answer his question about why they hadn't waited for their daughter to recover.

Finally, the baron spoke. "We, ah, didn't want to miss this opportunity."

It sounded as if they were afraid that he would have moved on to another candidate. Acton settled his attention on the baroness. "You are a friend of my mother's. I would have waited to meet Miss Barclay." Though, he recognized that his initial reaction was irritation at having to wait. But now that he knew the identity of Miss Barclay, he wanted to get to the bottom of this conundrum—if he could. "Is there perchance any reason she may not have wanted to come?"

Enough color drained from the baroness's face that Acton had his answer. Miss Barclay *hadn't* wanted to come. So much so that she'd likely run off. What a reckless chit. What could she hope to achieve?

Acton meant to find out. "As it happens, I need to leave to attend to some business. Perhaps when I return, Miss Barclay may have recovered and will be here to meet me." He knew that wouldn't happen. "There will be no marriage settlement until we both agree that we will suit." He looked toward his mother. She appeared stiff, her back straight as an arrow.

"That seems reasonable," the dowager said, though her gaze was clouded, and her brows pitched down slightly.

With a final nod, Acton departed without saying anything more. He was nearly to the top of the stairs when his mother caught up with him.

"Wellesbourne, are you angry?" she asked from behind him.

Pausing, Acton turned. He glanced toward the drawing room and kept his voice low. "I'm not angry, but I am confused. It seems odd that they would come here without their daughter." And lie about what was happening with her, but Acton kept that to himself for now. The baron and baroness had to know their daughter was gone. They'd lied about her whereabouts.

Though he was tempted to go back and ask them for the truth, he much preferred to hear it from Miss Barclay first. He'd return to Gloucester and speak to her—if she was still there. Hell, she could be anywhere. He'd start in Gloucester and not rest until he found her.

Once he determined what the devil was going on, he'd alert her parents. Probably. He couldn't shake the distasteful sensation he'd had in their presence.

"It *is* strange that they came without her," the dowager allowed.

"And that they wanted to agree on the marriage settlement without my having met her. You can't have thought I would consent to that."

His mother's features tightened into a faint grimace. "I did not know that was their intent."

"It doesn't recommend them."

"You *are* angry," she said, her hands fidgeting together.

"No. Well, perhaps a little. I just find it obnoxious. Is there some reason they didn't bring Miss Barclay and then wanted to rush into a marriage agreement? I find it suspect."

Except he knew Miss Barclay was not at home. Why was she in Gloucester by herself?

Acton shook his head. "Mother, I need to go."

"But you only just arrived. What business could you have when you knew you would be spending time with Miss Barclay?"

"Business I put off because of this meeting and can now attend to," he said.

"I understand. I'd hoped to see you for longer. Will you return in a few days to meet Miss Barclay?" She spoke tentatively, which she often did. She said it was because she didn't know him and didn't wish to overstep. While he appreciated that, since their relationship was new to him, at some point, he hoped she would just relax and say what she wished without worrying about his reaction. Did she think him a beast?

"If she even comes. I confess I'm skeptical."

She went on, "Shall I invite the baron and baroness to stay or recommend they go home to their daughter?"

It wasn't at all up to Acton what the Radstocks decided to do, but he was torn by the question. If they went home, it would not be to their daughter. "There isn't a point in them staying if they don't absolutely expect their daughter to arrive, and their comments on that matter seemed vague. Please do as you see fit."

"You didn't like them, did you?" she asked.

He was surprised by her direct question. "I confess I found them...I don't know, almost annoying?" He gave his head a light shake. "My apologies. I know she is a good friend of yours."

"She was very supportive of me in Bath," the dowager said softly. She'd resided in Bath with his younger sisters after leaving when Acton was five years old. His father had rarely spoken of her, saying only that it was best if they lived in separate households. Until Acton went off to school, he saw her for a fortnight every year when she came to London to oversee the annual ball they held at Wellesbourne House. Even then, he didn't really see her. He spent most of his time with his governess.

"It's all right," the dowager added. "You don't need to like my friends."

Allowing his exasperation to get the better of him, Acton exhaled. "You don't have to be fine with that. You don't have to like everything I do."

Her brown eyes rounded for the barest moment. "I don't, actually, but I don't think it's my place to share that."

"You're my mother. At least, I'm told you are." It was a snide comment, and he immediately regretted it. "You *are* my mother." Just one who hadn't wanted him for a very long time and now suddenly did. Acton assumed she felt guilty after his father had died so unexpectedly.

"I am, but I deserve your wariness and your disdain. I am trying to make up for the time we lost. Sometimes, I fear it's too late." She gave him an earnest stare, and there was so much emotion shining in her eyes that it almost made him uncomfortable. "You've only to ask me to leave, and I will. I never wish to cause you upset."

*Then why did you abandon me?*

The question hovered on his tongue, but he didn't let it out. What would be the point? That was all in the past. She was here now, and she was trying.

"I don't want you to leave," he said. Besides, she resided in the dowager house. It wasn't as if she were underfoot or meddling in his business. Except for this marriage nonsense —which he'd agreed to in order to avoid suffering the Marriage Mart. "Please apologize to them for me. Say I am tired from my journey and preoccupied with the business to which I must attend." Neither of those things were a lie. Acton was a trifle fatigued after rising so early and now he would leave again. And he was also fixated on finding Miss Barclay.

"There is no need to apologize. Perhaps this wasn't the best idea." She gave him a sheepish smile. "I just wanted to help you."

"Which I appreciate. Perhaps the match with Miss Barclay will work out yet." He nearly laughed. The woman who'd tried to drown him in Madeira would surely not become his duchess.

That didn't mean he wasn't going to try and help her. Because whatever the reason, she shouldn't be traipsing about by herself pretending to be a widow. She might very well encounter someone who wouldn't be put off by the contents of a glass of wine to the face.

He would help her, whether she wanted it or not.

# CHAPTER 5

The spartan room at the Black Ivy Inn in Gloucester began to close in on Persephone. She'd kept to her room with the exception of fetching her dinner the previous night and breakfast that morning, then walking to catch the mail coach to Bristol. Only to find out it had been canceled for some unknown reason.

So now she was stuck for one more night in her pitiful room with its incredibly lumpy mattress and ill-fitting lock on the door.

Groaning, she stood up from the chair and went to the window. It was in desperate need of cleaning.

How had she come to be here?

Because she'd encountered a string of bad luck after deciding to flee from her parents and their awful marriage scheme. Perhaps that was fate telling her she'd made a mistake.

No, she didn't believe that. This was still better than marrying a reprobate, even if he was a duke.

Yesterday, after arriving in Worcester, she'd discovered she'd missed the mail coach to Bristol. Weighing whether she ought to spend money on an inn or on a private coach, she'd decided on the latter. However, the only thing she could afford was someone who was already going to Gloucester and would take her that far.

She determined it was better to get there and spend the night than have so far to travel tomorrow. Except, she hadn't calculated her funds correctly and once she arrived in Gloucester, she could not afford to stay at the New Inn where she'd lodged the previous night.

She'd been forced to move away from the High Street and managed to find an acceptable, albeit shabby, inn, the Black Ivy, with a monosyllabic innkeeper and a pair of pretty maids whose costumes revealed more than Persephone would have thought necessary for the employees of an inn.

"Blast it all," Persephone muttered. She turned from the window and grabbed her hat and gloves before leaving the chamber.

After setting her hat atop her head, she pulled on her gloves as she walked down the stairs. The two maids were cleaning the common room, which it desperately needed. Persephone had come down to dinner last night only to take her plate right back up to her room upon finding the inn too crowded and the boisterous men too many. That morning, she'd warily descended for breakfast only to see that the common room was in dire need of repair after last night's activities. She'd once again plucked up her meal and retreated to her room.

Becky, with pale blonde hair and the younger of the two women, was wiping down the tables while Moll, who was older than Persephone by a few years and sported wispy brown hair, swept.

Pausing in her task, Becky called over to the other maid. "Moll, did I tell ye the cathedral is looking fer a cleaning woman? I thought I might try fer the job."

"They'll frown on yer evening work," Moll said with a laugh. She glanced toward Persephone. "Do ye need something, Mrs. Birdwhistle?"

Persephone had adopted the surname of her governess, whom she still missed. The woman had guided her and Pandora with a firm but kind hand. When Persephone thought of a mother's love, Mrs. Birdwhistle came to mind.

"I don't, thank you. I thought I might go for a walk."

"It is a nice day," Becky said. "I'm going to try to get out meself for a bit."

"To the cathedral?" Moll asked with a teasing smile.

Becky shrugged. "Why not? It might be better than working here."

"But not as fun, I'd bet." Moll swept the detritus she'd amassed into a neat pile.

Departing the inn, Persephone made her way toward the High Street, where the nicer inns were located. She'd inquired at two of them before realizing she needed to look elsewhere for lodging within her budget.

As she turned a corner, she saw a woman sweeping a stoop and noted the sign above the door, "West Gloucester Day School for Girls."

The woman was young, perhaps in her early thirties with neatly pinned hair and a faint smile lifting her mouth. Moving closer, Persephone heard she was humming. But she looked up as Persephone approached.

"Good afternoon," the woman said.

"Good afternoon." Persephone glanced toward the sign. "You work here?"

Nodding, she said, "I'm the headmistress."

Did that mean she owned the school? The day school Persephone and Pandora had attended was owned and overseen by a married couple.

While in her room at the inn, Persephone had pondered

her future. She had to think her parents were furious and that they might not want to welcome her back. In that event, she would need to find employment. She'd thought of becoming a governess, but a teacher at a school would also be tolerable.

"I hope you won't find me impertinent," Persephone began. "I wonder how one becomes a teacher."

"It can be difficult for a woman, and we're only allowed to teach girls, of course." She leaned toward Persephone and spoke in a low tone as if she were imparting a secret. "Between you and me, we're better off. Teaching boys is much more difficult."

Persephone laughed. "I can imagine." Particularly since a great many of them grew into terrible men.

The headmistress straightened and held the broom handle. "If you're looking for a position as a teacher, I'm afraid I don't have any openings, but if you'd like to leave your name and direction, I could write to you if that changes."

Her direction. How could she communicate that when she wasn't even sure where she'd be tomorrow? Persephone felt a flash of fear, but she still couldn't bring herself to regret fleeing her parents and their asinine scheme.

"I don't know that I'm quite ready for employment, but I may be. Er, my parents are hoping I will wed, but I'm not interested in their choice."

The headmistress's green eyes narrowed slightly as she nodded. "I certainly know what that is like. When I turned five and twenty and was still unwed, my father gave me my modest dowry and encouraged me to find a position as a governess. And that was what I did for five years. I lived quite frugally and used my meager earnings and my dowry to buy this school from the gentleman who retired. That was four years ago."

Four and thirty and living independently! "And you never married?"

"I didn't have to," she said with a broad smile. "Do you live here in Gloucester?"

Persephone shook her head. "I'm just passing through."

"If you're by yourself, please be careful."

"I'll do that, thank you."

"And write to me when you're ready for a teaching position." The headmistress extended her right hand. "I'm Rachel Posthwaite. We'll see if I can take you on."

Persephone took the woman's hand and shook it gently. It was the first time she'd ever shaken someone's hand. "You don't even know my qualifications."

Miss Posthwaite sized her up, her gaze moving over Persephone with studious care. "I daresay you come from a landed family, perhaps even nobility. Your speech and diction are excellent and your carriage that of a lady who has been taught to walk with elegance."

Persephone blinked at her. "You gathered all that?"

Miss Posthwaite laughed. "You remind me of myself. Take very good care, miss? Lady?"

"Miss Barclay." Persephone realized she'd forgotten to use her alias, but supposed it was all right with this obviously kind woman. "Thank you for your generosity."

They exchanged nods, and Persephone went on her way. Her step felt lighter, and her shoulders stood straighter. Smiling, she glanced back toward the school and saw that Miss Posthwaite was no longer outside.

Because she hadn't been paying attention and had arrived at the corner of the High Street, she smacked directly into someone else.

"Careful there." Hands gently clasped her upper arms to hold her steady.

That voice...

Persephone snapped her head up and gasped. It couldn't be. Why was *he* here?

His dark brown eyes fixed on her, and the edge of his mouth ticked up. "I know you," he said, smiling more widely.

And she knew him—the bloody Duke of Wellesbourne.

"You do not," she said sharply, pulling away from his grasp.

"But I do, *Miss Barclay*."

Persephone gasped even louder, then slapped her hand to her gaping mouth. How on earth did he know who she was? And why wasn't he at Loxley Court meeting her parents?

"We've much to discuss," he said, one of his dark brows arching with…was that amusement? Of course he would find her situation a matter of humor.

"We've nothing to discuss. Please excuse me." Heart thundering, Persephone tried to move past him.

The duke gripped her forearm—not painfully, but firmly.

Swinging around to face him, Persephone glared at his hand and then at his face with its superior *I am a duke, and you will do as I say* expression.

His eyes narrowed, and he didn't let go, despite her trying to pull her arm away. "You've a great many things to explain, Miss Barclay. And I am not letting you leave until you do."

~

*A*cton could not believe his fortune in finding her. He'd traveled to Gloucester and questioned the innkeeper at the New Inn, who'd told him she'd taken a mail coach somewhere. He'd tried to determine where, but no one had recalled seeing an attractive woman in a drab brown dress.

With no notion of where to go in search of her, Acton had stayed at the New Inn last night, hoping today would offer some revelation. He'd slept late and now found himself strolling along the High Street, where he'd run straight into his quarry.

Who was not nearly as pleased to see him as he was to see her.

He should not have found her attractive while she was so obviously furious. But she was glorious in her outrage, her blue eyes spitting contempt and her upper lip curling with distaste.

"Unhand me," she demanded.

"Only if you promise not to run off. I will only follow you and catch you, and we can go through this entire endeavor again."

She gave him a defiant stare. "I will scream and call for help. I'll say you're accosting me."

"And I will say you are my betrothed and behaving badly. When I mention I'm the Duke of Wellesbourne, no one will intercede." He didn't enjoy threatening her in this manner, but he wasn't going to let her run off, not after miraculously finding her just now.

She snarled at him, and he still found her absolutely stunning. "You're a beast."

"I'm concerned for your welfare. If that makes me beastly, then I'm an absolute monster." In response to her snarl, he growled then bared his teeth, as if he truly were an animal. Her reaction—eyes widening and lips parting—nearly made him smile.

"I don't want your concern."

He looked her over. She wore the same dull brown gown as when he'd met her, and the garment looked as though it needed some care. There were dark circles under her eyes, and her hair wasn't as glossy as he recalled. "I'd say you *need* my concern and my help. It's good that I've come for you."

"Come for me? I am not your betrothed, nor am I your responsibility in any way."

"That may be true, but you have my concern even if you don't want it. I'm going to release you now, and you are not going to run. Agreed?"

She pursed her lips, and he wasn't sure she would stay.

"Please?" he asked. He thought of her obnoxious parents and the lie that she was home sick while she was really running around western England. She was in flight and needed to believe that she didn't need to keep running. "I only want to know what you are about. I am not going to make you do anything you don't wish to do." He released her arm and held up his hands in surrender before dropping them to his sides.

She eyed him warily as she rubbed her forearm. "Good, because I refuse to marry you."

"That is fortunate since I've no wish to marry you either." He'd honestly not given it much thought, but decided that was the thing she most needed to hear.

"How do you know who I am?" she asked, folding her arms over her chest as if that would keep him at bay.

Acton was just glad she wasn't running off. He allowed himself to relax, though not entirely, for he needed to be ready to snatch her again if she bolted. "Your parents showed me a miniature, and I recognized you immediately."

"They didn't." She groaned softly as she rolled her magnificent eyes.

"I do believe your father thought I would decide to wed you on the spot."

"Did he say that?" she asked, appearing horrified.

"No, but he seemed most eager for that outcome. They told me you were ill and had stayed home. Do they even know where you are?" he asked, wondering what sort of scheme this family had concocted to entrap him.

She pressed her lips together. "None of this is your business."

"It is when our parents are trying to bind us in matrimony. As your potential betrothed, I am meddling. It seems someone must. You should not be gallivanting about by yourself. There are many bad things that could—"

Miss Barclay sliced her hand through the air in front of him. "Stop. Please. I don't need to be lectured by *you*, a peddler of bad things."

Acton gaped at her. "A what? I don't sell bad things."

"You offer them willingly enough. I am *quite* aware of your reputation, *Duke*."

"I'm not a bad person," he said defensively.

A couple that looked to be in their sixties stopped near them. They were both smiling broadly. "You sound like us," the man said with a laugh.

"But the best arguments always lead to the best reconciliations," the woman added. She gave them a suggestive look. "Especially in the bedchamber."

The man giggled along with her as he patted her arm, which was linked through his. "Saucy minx." He looked to Acton and Miss Barclay. "May your marriage be as long and happy as ours has been." Touching his hat, the man led his wife away.

Miss Barclay turned her head to stare after them. "They thought we were *married*?"

Acton tried not to laugh. "The look on your face when she mentioned the bedchamber was the best thing I've seen in ages."

She returned her attention to him. "You cannot say such things and claim you are not a beast. Nice gentlemen don't laugh at young ladies who are in distress."

"Are you in distress?" he asked, sobering.

Her color was high, and her lips were parted. Indeed, he

could imagine her looking like that in his bedchamber, but for wholly different reasons, of course. "Because of me or what that woman said?" he clarified.

"All of it! I am trying to mind my own business and avoid the parson's trap." She definitely did not want the marriage, then. If there was a scheme to unite them, she was not a willing participant.

He exhaled with exasperation. "There is no trap."

"I'm confident my parents would disagree."

That made sense to Acton. Her father had been eager to conduct the business of marriage, even without Acton having met the bride. "Why are they so insistent you marry me?"

Her eyes rounded, and she looked at him as if he were incapable of logical thought. "Why wouldn't they be? You're a duke." She said the last word as if it were an epithet. "For most people, that is more than enough. Your personality, sentiment, or reputation matter not."

"But those things matter to you," he said softly.

"I've no wish to marry a rake." She turned from him and started down the side street from whence she'd come.

He hastened to walk alongside her. "I met your parents, and while our acquaintance was short—I left as soon as I realized who you were and that you are not, in fact, at home, sick in bed—I sense they may be…difficult."

She sent him a skeptical look. "You deduced that from a brief interview?"

"Your father was keen to discuss the marriage settlement. I found that distasteful since you and I hadn't even met. Well, we had, but they don't know that."

Pausing, she turned toward him. "Please tell me they still don't know that."

"They do not."

Her eyes narrowed. They were such a spectacular blue and so full of life. He doubted he could ever be bored by her, even if he just sat and watched her. "Why didn't you tell them we'd met and where?"

He shrugged. "Since they were lying about where you were—and why—I determined something was afoot. It occurred to me that you may be running away from them. And that they didn't seem overly concerned." He frowned. That bothered him, and while he knew what it was like to have a parent who didn't seem to care for him, he'd had one, his father, who had.

"I traveled with them to Cirencester. I'd intended to accompany them to Loxley Court, however, I realized I just couldn't be forced into marriage, so I left. The earliest coach leaving Cirencester came here to Gloucester."

"But you hadn't even yet determined if we would suit."

She looked at him as if he were a slug sliming its way across her beloved garden. "I know enough about you to be *quite certain* we will not. In any case, I left them a note that I was returning home."

"But you did not."

"No," she said hesitantly. "I had some...mishaps."

"I see." He didn't, but decided pressing her about those now would be a mishap of its own.

What he did see was that her parents had continued on to Loxley Court after she'd departed their company. They likely expected her to do what she'd said and return home. Even so, they ought to have followed her there. One just didn't let an unaccompanied young woman travel about alone. Which was why Acton had come looking for her.

She abruptly pivoted and started walking once more. "I don't know why I'm telling you any of this. It's none of your affair."

"I maintain it *is* my concern since my mother asked me to consider taking you as my duchess."

She snorted. "I am *not* considering you as anything other than an unpleasant memory."

"I gathered that after you doused me with Madeira," he said wryly. He looked about as they walked. "Where are we going?"

"Also none of your business."

"I'll just accompany you, so I'll find out eventually." He watched her jaw clench.

"You're a tyrant." She turned the corner onto a street with several older, run-down buildings.

"I'm not demanding you marry anyone," he said affably.

"No, only that I suffer your company." She stopped again and gave him a weary look. "Can you please leave me alone?"

Without waiting for him to answer, she looked up and down the street, then crossed. Acton hurried to join her on the other side. "No, I cannot. You may not believe that bad things can happen to you, but what if they did?"

She cast him a hooded glance. "Bad things such as a rogue trying to seduce me at an inn?"

"Worse. A degenerate assaulting you and not taking no for an answer."

She walked a few more feet, then stopped in front of a dilapidated inn. A sign with black ivy hung crookedly over the door.

He wrinkled his nose. "Is this where you're staying?"

"Not all of us are wealthy dukes."

"The New Inn on the High Street where we met is very nice. You were able to afford it before."

She bristled. "Well, I can't now."

Now he was more curious than ever about her "mishaps." "I'll pay for your room there—your *own* room." He was fairly certain she would have accused him of trying to compromise her. Wasn't that what rakes did?

Not Acton. At least he hadn't yet. Hell, perhaps he really

did need to stop being so forward with women. Most of his interactions were harmless—stolen kisses or touches and nothing more. That didn't include his escapades at the Rogue's Den. Which weren't the best-kept secret.

Could his reputation prevent him from obtaining a bride? Perhaps he should reconsider his behavior.

He recalled the first time he'd heard someone mention his rakish reputation. He'd been in London for the Season when he was twenty-two. When he'd asked his father if he should try to curb his behavior, the duke had laughed and said, "You're the heir to a dukedom. No one can dictate your behavior except me, and I see no problem with your activities, provided you are *discreet*." The message had been clear: do what you like, just don't let anyone catch you doing anything untoward.

Acton suspected his father would tell him to stop worrying about Miss Barclay, that she wasn't his responsibility. While that might be true, he couldn't just turn his back on her. Perhaps that was because he understood what it was like to have a parent who didn't seem to care.

While he'd been woolgathering, Miss Barclay had set a hand on her hip and was staring at him in disbelief.

"You don't approve of my offer?" he asked.

"I wouldn't accept anything from you even if I'd spent my last tuppence. Men like you always expect something in return."

"*I* don't," he said firmly, disliking that her opinion of him was so low.

"Will you please just go home and leave me in peace?" She flung her arm in a vague easterly direction.

"If I go home, I will likely encounter your parents again." He didn't know if that was true. Perhaps they'd departed after he'd turned around and left Loxley Court after meeting them. There was one way to find out—he would dispatch a letter to his mother asking. He'd do that shortly, but first, he went on, "And if I see your parents, I'm afraid this time, I'll have to tell them where I saw you. It's just not prudent for you to be here alone." He glanced toward the derelict inn. "Especially *here*."

"I will only be here for the night," she said.

"Then where will you go?"

"That is none of your concern," she snapped. "Stop acting as if you have some responsibility or right to manage me."

Acton wiped his hand over his face. "We can continue like this, or you can accept that you need help. You can't have a great deal of funds if you're staying here instead of the New Inn. The place looks as though it may fall down or is teeming with rats. And, frankly, you look as though you could use some…care." Still, he found her absurdly captivating—acerbic tongue, bedraggled gown, and all.

Her jaw dropped. "You can't think to criticize my appearance? Truly, your ability to cause offense knows no bounds." Turning on her heel, she stalked into the inn.

Acton followed her inside and watched as she strode across the common room and started up the stairs, disappearing as she reached the landing and went around the corner.

"May I help you, sir?" a feminine voice asked from Acton's right.

He looked in that direction and saw a pretty barmaid, at least he assumed that was her position. Her pale blonde hair was pinned atop her head and her eyes were pitched in a seductive gaze. Her costume was neither demure nor overly revealing, but it certainly accentuated her curves.

"I'd like to take a room, if one is available," he said.

She perused him with surprise and unabashed interest. "Here?"

"Yes."

"I'll fetch the innkeeper, but I do believe our largest room is available." She batted her lashes at him before turning.

"Wait, before you go, I have a question."

She faced him once more and moved closer to him. "Yes?"

"The woman who just came in—she's staying here."

"Mrs. Birdwhistle?"

*Mrs.* Birdwhistle. Was she playing the widow again? And where had she come up with that ridiculous name?

"Yes, Mrs. Birdwhistle. How long has she been here?"

"Just since yesterday."

Acton wanted more information than that. He took a step toward the maid and summoned his most flirtatious smile. "And what can you tell me about her?"

The maid put a hand on her hip, drawing his attention to the indent of her waist. "She keeps to herself mostly, takes her meals up to her chamber. Arrived without a thing, not even a small bag, which I found odd. Moll and I think she's running from a nasty husband. Poor thing."

"That is unfortunate." And also untrue, but he didn't disabuse the maid of her suspicion.

"Moll is the other maid," she said brightly, apparently moving right past whatever darkness she thought might be affecting "Mrs. Birdwhistle." "And I'm Becky. Let me know —*personally*—if ye need anything." Her expression bordered on a leer, making it absolutely clear what she would be willing to help with.

While Acton wasn't interested in her physical favors, he always appreciated help. "Thank you, Becky," he drawled softly. "I'll be sure to seek you out when I require assistance."

She giggled before taking herself off.

Acton surveyed the common room. With its low ceiling and blackened hearth, the space felt rather close. It was tidy, however, which filled him with relief. He could only hope his chamber would be the same. At least he traveled with his own bedcoverings, even if he had left his valet at home, as he did from time to time. He'd need to fetch his horse and valise from the New Inn. Pity, for it really was much nicer. In fact, he would leave his horse stabled there.

When he returned, he'd ask Becky or Moll to make up his bed. Damn, he wished he had spare bedding for Miss Barclay.

*Mrs. Birdwhistle.* Who traveled with no luggage. What was that about?

He had so many questions and so far, very few answers. Miss Barclay was not enthusiastic about his presence. He would need to work harder to gain her trust. She couldn't keep on with whatever she was doing.

A thought occurred to him, and he couldn't believe he hadn't thought of it before. Perhaps she wasn't running away from her parents or from him. What if she was running *to* someone?

It wasn't outrageous to think she might wish to marry someone else. Someone of whom her parents didn't approve.

But if that were true, where was this gentleman? Had he been caught up somewhere, and she was now alone, fending for herself? If so, he didn't seem good enough for her. If Miss Barclay had consented to meet Acton for an assignation or any other reason, he would bloody well show up.

He needed to get to the bottom of her situation. Hopefully, without irritating her further. An idea came to him, one that he thought could improve her disposition.

But would she accept anything? Only if she didn't know it had come from him.

# CHAPTER 6

*A*fter leaving the duke in the common room, Persephone had shut herself in her bedchamber and seethed. She didn't know what was worse, that her parents had gone and attempted to settle the marriage without her or that the would-be groom had come after her.

At least he hadn't told her parents that he'd seen her. It was…odd. Especially given his ongoing prattle about her safety and how she needed his help. If he were that concerned, shouldn't he just have informed her parents that he'd encountered her in Gloucester?

Still, she was glad he had not. She wasn't eager to face her parents after running away from them.

She was still mulling the duke's arrival and the news he'd shared when the innkeeper's son arrived with a tub.

"I didn't ask for a bath." Persephone couldn't afford that. But oh, how wonderful it sounded!

"I was told to bring it up," he said, pushing into the room and depositing the metal tub in front of the fire. "I'll be right back with the water."

"But I can't pay for this," she called after him as he stepped over the threshold.

"Already paid for," he called back before disappearing down the stairs.

Persephone frowned even as her insides cartwheeled with joy at the prospect of washing all the travel and frustration away. The tub wasn't large, but it would do nicely.

A short while later, as she lounged in the cooling water after scrubbing herself clean—soap had also been provided, which she also couldn't pay for. It occurred to her that Wellesbourne had to be behind this. Apparently, he couldn't stomach her bedraggled appearance.

It grated to accept this gift, but she reminded herself that she didn't need to see him again. Presumably, he'd arranged for her bath then returned to his *nicer* lodgings at the New Inn.

A knock on the door made her sink deeper into the tub. "I'm busy!" she called.

"It's Moll," came the feminine voice in response. "I've packages for ye. I know ye're in the bath. I won't peek. I'll just drop them on the bed and be on my way."

Packages?

"All right," Persephone responded.

Moll slipped into the chamber and, true to her word, didn't look in Persephone's direction as she deposited two paper-wrapped packages on the bed. Persephone stayed submerged, which meant folding herself up, until the maid left.

Curiosity drove Persephone from the tub earlier than she would have left it. Grabbing the toweling that the innkeeper's son had brought, she ignored the frayed edges and rough texture. She dried herself enough to keep from dripping, then wrapped the towel around herself before making her way to the bed—it wasn't far since the room was so small.

She untied the string on the first package and folded back the paper. It looked to be bedclothes. Made from a soft, smooth cotton, they were covers for a pillow and the mattress. There was also a blanket of fine gray wool. Persephone finished drying and dropped the toweling to the floor in favor of bundling herself in the blanket.

Sighing as the soft wool caressed her freshly cleaned skin, she turned her attention to the other package. Inside was a traveling gown made of light wool dyed a vibrant blue. It reminded Persephone of the miniature iris that bloomed at Radstock Hall in the spring.

There were also undergarments, which should have shocked her. Or offended her. The man was a known rake, and she ought not accept gifts from him. The bath had been far too much. But the thought of dressing in her travel-worn clothing after the refreshing bath made her want to weep.

Her gaze lingered on the bedclothes. Surely, she could keep those? Just for the night, then she could return them to him at the New Inn.

Exhaling, she turned to the hook near the door and froze when she saw it was empty. What had happened to her gown? Persephone had hung it there before slipping into the bathtub. Had Moll taken it when she'd come in? Persephone hadn't noticed, but with the door ajar, the maid could have grabbed it on her way out without Persephone seeing.

Now she would *have* to wear the new gown. Since her undergarments were still on the bed, she decided she would don those. That way she wasn't accepting *everything* Wellesbourne had offered. *If* it was indeed the duke who had arranged the bath and purchased these items.

By the time her hair was dry and she'd dressed, noise from the common room was already filtering upstairs. It sounded as though it would be another busy, boisterous evening. The innkeeper's son had come to empty the tub and remove it, and he'd said they were expecting as much.

As with last night, she would go down only long enough to request her dinner on a tray so she could dine here in her chamber. Alone with her pair of candles.

Using the cracked mirror on the wall, Persephone pinned her hair up and admired what she could see of the pretty new gown. She would hate to return the garment, for it fit rather well despite being slightly short. Alas, she could not keep it. Unless, she learned it hadn't come from the duke.

But who else would have given it to her? Persephone doubted she would like the answer to that.

She covered the bed and pillow with the new sheeting and had to credit Wellesbourne's consideration. It was one thing to want her to look nicer—she could see him desiring that for himself if not for her—but to ensure her comfort when she went to sleep? That was not something she would expect from a rake such as he.

Perhaps he truly did want to help her without expecting anything in return. Or, more likely, he'd purchased the bedding because he hoped to continue his seduction and wanted to be sure the bed was clean and comfortable.

That would certainly align with him not telling her parents that he'd met her. That puzzling fact lingered in her mind. Why keep that from them? Unless he'd planned to seduce her. She just didn't understand his motivation.

She recalled what he'd said about her parents. He seemed to find her father's discussion of a marriage settlement premature and annoying. That had to recommend him, didn't it?

Or, mayhap he wasn't remotely interested in a possible marriage and had only agreed to the meeting to appease his mother. That was something a rogue like him would do.

The reasons for his behavior mattered not. She was done with the Duke of Wellesbourne. For good.

She left the chamber for the common room. The scent of dinner, specifically of whatever seasonings were being employed, wafted from downstairs, and her stomach growled in response. Last night's meal of lamb stew had been surprisingly tasty.

Rounding the corner on the landing of the stairs, she surveyed the room. It wasn't as crowded as last night, but that could very well change. She caught sight of a pair of gleaming Hessians jutting out from under a table. Lifting her gaze, she inhaled sharply.

Wellesbourne had returned.

He lounged near the hearth, gripping the handle of a tankard sitting atop the table. His lips were spread in a wide, engaging smile as both Becky and Moll stood nearby. They stood in such a way, slightly leaning toward him, as to encourage him to view their bodices, which were cut lower than anything Persephone had ever worn. But then, Persephone's wardrobe was universally demure. In fact, now that she thought about it, the gowns that Pandora wore were more enticing than Persephone's. She'd always attributed it to Pandora just being more appealing but perhaps their mother had purposely dressed them differently.

And why wouldn't she?

Persephone shook away thoughts of the baroness and watched as the duke flirted with both maids. Didn't they have work to do? Persephone wanted her dinner, but didn't wish to interrupt them. She hoped to avoid speaking to the duke at all.

Except, she ought to thank him.

Or should she? There was nothing to indicate he was behind the bath, the gown, or the bedding. He was just the most logical answer.

If he wasn't going to be open about what he'd done, why should she bother showing her gratitude? They could pretend none of it had happened. Yes, she preferred that.

The maids finally took their leave of him, and Persephone continued down the stairs. Naturally, another woman, very attractive, with red hair and dark, sultry eyes, sidled up to the duke as soon as they left. The man was a magnet for women. But not for Persephone.

Staying on the opposite side of the room, she made her way to where Becky was currently speaking to a table with a trio of men. One of them slid a glance toward Persephone and gave her a suggestive smile.

Persephone pivoted so she could see Becky from the corner of her eye, but not the men at the table. When Becky was finished with them, Persephone intercepted her and asked for her dinner.

"I'll fetch it for ye in a bit, dearie. We're very busy tonight, as ye can see. Why don't ye find a place to sit, and I can bring ye an ale or a glass of wine?" She bustled off before Persephone could say she had no intention of sitting anywhere. If she did that, she had to expect the duke would consider it an invitation to join her.

Or, he'd just approach her as he was doing now.

Persephone stiffened as he came near. He was almost unbearably attractive, with a heartrending smile that made her want to giggle like a green girl. His features were superbly chiseled, as if he'd been created from the work of some ancient master sculptor—strong jawline, enchanting dimples, a provocative set to his mouth. He looked as though he was always on the verge of smiling, as if his good humor simply could not be contained. Was he never sad or bored or angry?

She knew he could appear surprised. He'd displayed that

quite wonderfully both when she'd tossed wine at his face and when she'd run into him on the street.

He looked slightly surprised now, in fact. "Good evening, Miss Barclay. I wasn't sure if I'd see you. Moll said you prefer to dine in your chamber."

"Please call me Mrs. Birdwhistle."

"Oh yes, I'd heard that was your alias." He leaned closer, and she caught his scent of sandalwood and amber. "Where on earth did you come up with that name?"

"Mrs. Birdwhistle was my governess. I hold her in the highest esteem."

"Then it is a grand name, indeed."

Persephone didn't want to have pleasant chitchat with him. "Why are you here? Shouldn't you be at your *nicer* inn?"

"So droll of you, but no. I'm lodging here now."

She was surprised he would exchange his certainly well-appointed suite at the New Inn for whatever they'd given him here. "Are you spying on me?"

"I'm watching over you. There's a difference." He sounded smug.

"I'd rather you didn't. Why don't you watch over the maids instead? You seem to have become quite friendly with them."

He lifted a shoulder. "I'm friendly with everyone. It is my amiable nature."

She thought of the red-haired woman who'd taken the maids' place. "One might even call it flirtatious."

Aha! He could look discomfited! He shifted his gaze from her briefly, and the end of his mouth ticked barely down. "Er, yes. I've been called that a time or twenty."

She arched a brow at him, murmuring, "Only twenty?"

His gaze moved over her. "You look lovely this evening."

"There you go flirting again." She couldn't help thinking of one of the Rogue Rules: never flirt with a rogue. They made it difficult by constantly flirting themselves, but Persephone would not bend.

"Can't I offer you a simple compliment?"

Was he hoping she would acknowledge his gifts? If he wasn't going to make it clear they'd come from him, she wasn't going to bring them up. "Thank you."

"The color makes your eyes shine even more vividly."

Was he just saying that to be flirtatious, or had he chosen the gown to complement her eyes? Given his thoughtfulness with the bedding, she had to wonder if he had indeed given the task more consideration than she would have expected from a scoundrel. Or perhaps matching gowns to eye color was *exactly* what scoundrels did. She had no idea.

He went on, "I was hoping I could persuade you to dine here in the common room with me."

"It's…too noisy." She'd been about to say too risky, but didn't want to invite another offer from him to pay for her to lodge elsewhere.

"It is rather riotous. I could join you upstairs?"

She cocked her head to the side, recalling the rule to never be alone with a rogue. "That's forward of you. Anyway, I only have one chair." And the table was barely large enough for her dishes, let alone his too.

"I have two chairs at the table in my chamber. We could dine there," he said with a great deal of charm and far too much assumption.

"No, thank you." She was not breaking that rogue rule either. Again. She'd already spent enough time alone or mostly alone with him.

He moved closer to her and fixed her with a provocative stare. Then he pursed his lips into a faint pout. Good Lord, did this work with other women?

"Please reconsider," he asked, somehow managing not to

sound as though he were pleading. He seemed quite earnest, actually. Perhaps the pout wasn't an act.

Of course it was! She could not afford to be swept away by his undeniable allure. "You can stop that," she said more coldly than she'd intended. "Your flirtation won't work with me."

His pout pitched into a frown. "Not at all? People, women in particular, generally find me engaging. I thought you did too—when we first met in Gloucester. I felt an immediate connection to you, and I would have sworn you did too."

"Not at all. I only pretended to be interested in you."

"Is that true?" He shook his head. "I completely misread that—and you. I confess that troubles me. I pride myself on discerning people."

She felt a little sorry for him, for he seemed genuinely surprised and mayhap even a little wounded. "I can't believe I'm the first person who is impervious to your efforts."

"You might be, actually." He appeared to be considering that. Persephone worked to not roll her eyes. Blinking, he refocused on her. "Why did you dump wine on me?"

"I should think it was obvious. I didn't want to marry you, and that was the best way I could think to deter you."

He laughed. "That doesn't make sense. I didn't even know who you were. In fact, we hadn't introduced ourselves at all. Honestly, I found the mystery provocative." He paused, studying her intently. "How did you know who I was?"

"You said your home was near Stratford-upon-Avon, and when you said you were going there to meet a potential bride, I deduced that you had to be the man I was supposed to meet. I also knew the Duke of Wellesbourne to be an over-confident, swaggering rake, and you certainly fit that description."

He put his hand to his chest. "You strike a dagger directly into my heart."

Persephone did not stop herself from rolling her eyes this time. "On second thought, I will dine with you. I shall request a bottle of Madeira so that I may pour the entire contents over you."

The corner of his mouth ticked up, and she wanted to laugh with him. This was an entirely ridiculous conversation. Except she didn't laugh. And in this situation particularly, she couldn't encourage him. It was why she continued to treat him so poorly. She needed him to leave her alone.

"Then I shall also ask for a bottle," he said. "We can circle each other and try to land our respective drenchings on our targets."

The image provoked a small snort to leap from Persephone's nose. She immediately brought her hand to her face and looked away.

"I like it when you snort," he whispered. "It's endearing."

She shot him a look of surprise. Was he serious? She couldn't tell. "Now I know you're being insincere and merely trying to charm me. Or seduce me. I can't think of another reason you would come looking for me without telling my parents we met." And yet, she still couldn't reconcile him wanting to do that—she was not the sort of woman a man like him seduced. She attracted overeager curates or second sons with nothing better to do on their school holiday than dally with a naive bluestocking. Those being the first and second men she'd kissed.

"I promise, I did not seek you out for seduction." His tone was completely sincere, and she was actually disappointed by that. It might have been nice if he'd wanted to, even if she had no intention of surrendering to his advances.

"I want to be sure I understand," he continued. "As soon as you determined my identity, you feigned interest—you quite provoked *my* interest—then soaked me with Madeira. And this was because you knew of my reputation and had already decided we would not suit because of it. Is that why you didn't accompany your parents to Loxley Court?"

"Yes, that is a fair summation."

"And here I wondered if you were perhaps meeting a gentleman for an assignation. I should have realized that didn't make sense. A woman who dislikes rakish behavior would certainly never participate in a scandalous situation." He noted the slightest flare of her nostrils and wondered at the cause of it.

"I am not meeting anyone. I am trying to avoid marriage to *you*."

He straightened. "You should not believe everything you hear about people. I am not the rake I'm purported to be. It is unfortunate that you didn't care to at least meet me, for I believe we may actually have suited. You possess an admirable spirit."

She batted her lashes, copying the way the maids had gazed at him. "To think you might have chosen me! I may swoon." She pressed her hand to her forehead.

"Go right ahead. I will catch you," he said with considerable cheer, as if he hoped she would faint into his arms.

With relief, Persephone noted Becky coming toward her bearing a tray. "Dinner for Mrs. Birdwhistle," she said, handing it to Persephone before winking at Wellesbourne.

Persephone expected her to stay and bat her eyes some more, but she carried on, bustling to a table with three men who roared with approval when she arrived. Clutching the tray, Persephone inclined her head toward the duke. "I'll bid you good evening, then."

He exhaled in a distinctly disappointed fashion. "I suppose I shall have to dine alone."

"I doubt that. I'm confident Becky or Moll or that pretty red-haired woman would love to keep you company."

"I'll dine alone. Near the stairs, so I can make sure you aren't bothered."

Persephone hadn't considered that. "You won't have to look after me much longer. I'll be on my way in the morning."

His brows rose. "Oh? Where are you going?"

"Home."

"That's just east of Bath, isn't it?"

She saw no point in keeping it from him. He likely already knew where she lived. "Radstock Hall. Er, thank you for caring enough to ensure I was safe." It was more than her parents had done. That realization made her stomach sink and threatened her appetite.

"It has been my pleasure. I must tell you that I dispatched a letter to my mother earlier asking whether your parents had returned home or planned to remain at Loxley Court until you arrived after recovering from your illness. While I was there, they indicated you would be joining them upon your swift recovery."

He'd written to his mother? "You didn't tell her you'd found me?"

"I did not."

She might never like him, but she certainly appreciated his handling of this situation. "Thank you."

"I wondered if you might care to wait until we receive a response from my mother before departing?" he asked.

Perhaps it would be better to know what her parents were doing. Did it really matter? They were going to be furious with her regardless of what she did next. The only way they would likely welcome her home was if she walked in on Wellesbourne's arm and introduced him as her betrothed.

They would be ecstatic. Not because she'd secured an excellent match for herself or that she may even have fallen in love. They would be relieved that the family would be saved—both socially and financially. There were so many debts to be settled, all of them to do with the baron and baroness presenting themselves as though they were members of the wealthy elite. Persephone was surprised she had any dowry left at all.

"Have you come to a decision?" Wellesbourne asked. "I assume you are pondering my proposal that you stay one more day."

In truth, Persephone wasn't entirely enthusiastic about facing whatever came next, whether that be returning to Radstock Hall or forging an independent life of spinsterhood.

She could endure one more day. Particularly since she had clean bedclothes.

"All right. I'll stay. One more day."

"Excellent. Enjoy your dinner!" he said amiably.

Persephone murmured, "Good night," then turned and climbed the stairs. At the landing, she looked down to see he was still watching her. She wondered if he would indeed sit at the base of the stairs.

As she went to her chamber, she reluctantly acknowledged that it was comforting to have someone watching out for her. Too bad it wasn't going to last.

# CHAPTER 7

*A*cton awoke early because sleeping on the abysmal mattress in his chamber at the Black Ivy was nearly impossible. While he did not regret moving to the dilapidated inn so that he could ensure Miss Barclay's safety, he absolutely regretted the bed. There wasn't a bedcovering in the world that could improve its quality. Even so, Acton was glad he'd brought his own bedclothes.

The rest of the room wasn't much better—a rickety dresser with drawers that stuck, a square table with water marks on the top, two wooden chairs for that table, and two cushioned chairs near the blackened fireplace. The fabric covering the chairs had once been red, but was now a faded dark pink with stains and a few holes. He hadn't particularly wanted to sit in them but told himself he was being haughty. His father's voice sounded in his brain: "As you should, you're a duke!"

His father would be horrified to see Acton's lodgings. He would perhaps even be frustrated by Acton's behavior. Why was he wasting time with a young woman who didn't want his help?

Because he couldn't leave her to the wolves—or whatever else was out there. That included her parents. He still couldn't fathom why they hadn't returned home to follow their daughter.

Who hadn't gone home.

The whole thing was a mess. Acton was completely at a loss as to how this situation would conclude. And he had to admit he was rather invested at this point. Miss Barclay might not like him, but he found her surprisingly intriguing. Even after she'd pretended to flirt with him, then doused him in wine. She was not afraid to call him out nor was she intimidated by his title.

After performing his morning ablutions in very cold water from the jug on the dresser, he donned his clothing and made his way downstairs. He hoped to run into Miss Barclay but suspected she would break her fast in her chamber. He'd kept close watch on the stairs last night. No one had gone up. He'd confirmed with Moll that he and Miss Barclay were the only people lodging at the inn.

What he really hoped to do was convince Miss Barclay they should relocate to the New Inn. They would be far more comfortable there.

As luck would have it, Miss Barclay was downstairs, perched at a table near the hearth. Indeed, it was the only unlittered table in the common room. It appeared the maids had not yet tidied after last night's revelry.

Miss Barclay looked in his direction, and he noted she was wearing her dark brown traveling gown instead of the one he'd purchased for her. Had something happened to it? At least her gown looked fresh and pressed, which it should after he'd paid the maids to take care of that. "Good morning, Mrs. Birdwhistle."

"Good morning." She eyed him warily as he approached. "You're up early."

"Am I?" he asked as he approached her table.

"I thought dukes slept until afternoon."

"In London during the Season, perhaps." He'd done that more times than he could count. "I must confess my mattress did not promote comfortable rest."

"I would have thought a duke's accommodation would be superior to mine."

"Well, I do have one more chair at my table," he quipped. "Does your dresser list to one side and rattle horribly if you attempt to open a drawer? I say attempt because they stick and are rather difficult to pry open."

"My dresser is *missing* a drawer." Her features were impassive, but her eyes held a hint of mirth.

"Well, then, it seems we are somewhat equally matched. We could still move to the New Inn. I don't mind paying for your lodging."

"I know you don't, but I can't accept that from you."

"You accepted the other things I purchased for you." He'd hoped she might mention them last night. She'd clearly taken the bath, for her hair had regained its shine and she'd smelled of some indistinct but intoxicating floral scent. And she'd obviously worn the gown he'd bought. He couldn't imagine she'd forgone the bedclothes. She might be stubborn as hell, but he didn't take her for a fool.

She blinked at him, appearing nonplussed. "What things are those?"

She really didn't know? He hadn't included a note or anything, nor had he asked anyone who'd delivered the items to inform her who'd paid for them. That had seemed gauche.

"I paid for a bath to be delivered," he said. "I also purchased sheeting for your bed and that lovely gown you were wearing last night."

"Oh, that was you? I did wonder. Did you also arrange to have this gown laundered?" She glanced down at herself. "I do appreciate that, because I hadn't wanted to accept the blue gown, but since the maid took mine, I had no choice. I did wish to return the gown and the undergarments from whence they came. I did not wear the latter."

She hadn't? He'd chosen the items with care and discernment. "Was the sizing wrong?" He frowned.

"The gown was short, but perhaps you didn't notice last night amidst the cacophony down here. I have no idea if the undergarments fit." She pursed her dainty pink lips at him. "It's awfully presumptuous of you to purchase any of that, particularly something so...intimate as underclothing."

"I was trying to help. You are incredibly stubborn."

"I don't wish to accept gifts from a man who isn't related to me. If that makes me stubborn, so be it. I think it makes me smart to avoid potential scandal."

He gaped at her. "You are gallivanting about western England unchaperoned, and you want to congratulate yourself on avoiding scandal?" He couldn't help it; he laughed.

Becky came to the table bearing a tray. "I've yer breakfast, Mrs. Birdwhistle." She turned to Acton immediately. "Good morning, Mr. Loxley. Can I bring ye some eggs and mayhap a steak?"

He smiled broadly at her. "Whatever you have would be divine, thank you, Becky."

"Always flirting," Miss Barclay muttered.

As the maid moved away, Acton looked over at Miss Barclay. "I'm being kind and polite. You twist everything to be a mark against me. Not that flirting is a bad thing."

"Ask your future duchess what she thinks about that."

He flinched inwardly. His wife might, in fact, feel slighted if he continued to flirt with women. But should he care? His father had told him from a young age that wives were necessary, but he needn't be faithful. Acton had known his father wasn't loyal to his wife, but why would he be when she'd left him to live separately? What Acton didn't know, and honestly hadn't thought of, was whether his mother had been faithful. The fact that she'd dressed in mourning for six months following his father's death seemed to indicate she may have been, but he didn't think he would ever ask her.

"Your point is taken," he said softly. He flicked a glance at her covered tray. "I presume you're taking that upstairs? Is there any way I could persuade you to break your fast here with me? There's no one here but us, and you won't have to carry that upstairs."

She hesitated, then cast a look toward the stairs. He could have sworn he heard her stomach rumble. When she pulled the cover off the tray, he wondered if that had been the deciding factor—her hunger had won out. He doubted it was the lure of his company.

As she took a few bites of her eggs, her brow furrowed. Swallowing, she gave him an intent look. "You seem to think I enjoy the situation I find myself in. I didn't choose my current predicament. I took the first coach I could from Cirencester in order to get away from my parents before they could awaken and stop me. It just so happened to go to Gloucester. Then I took the wrong coach, which put me completely out of the way *and* my valise was stolen."

She'd been through more than he'd realized. "It's just as well you have someone to help. A friend, even."

"We are not friends." She poured tea from the pot on her tray into the cup. "I shouldn't be confiding in you at all."

"I'm glad you are as I have appointed myself your personal protector."

She splashed tea over the side of her cup. "My *what?* I am not, nor will I ever be your mistress."

Acton grimaced, hating that he'd said something so stupid and caused her to spill her tea. "'Protector' was a poor word choice. My apologies. I am ensuring your safety."

Using her napkin, she wiped her hand, then dabbed up the spilled tea. "You are also ensuring my eternal irritation."

"That is not my intent. I am only seeking to help."

She stirred sugar into her tea. "You keep saying that. The only help I'm willing to accept from you at this juncture is whatever information your mother can provide about my parents."

Acton hoped her response would come today, but it was more likely to arrive tomorrow. He was just going to have to convince Miss Barclay to stay one more day. Really, two more days because they wouldn't be able to book passage anywhere until the following day, probably.

Ugh, that meant two more nights in that bed. At least the food here was good, far better than he would have anticipated based on the inn's appearance.

"Then I shall be glad to help with that," Acton said. "As well as look after you. I'm afraid that aspect is not negotiable."

"I'm well aware that you are as autocratic as any duke." She sipped her tea and tipped her head toward Becky, who'd just arrived with Acton's breakfast.

"The steak would have taken too long, so I brought ham," the maid said, smiling expectantly at Acton.

"Thank you, Becky. I'm sure it will be as delicious as it was last night."

The maid turned her attention to Miss Barclay. "I hope ye're happy with yer dress. My aunt does the laundry."

Miss Barclay swallowed a bite of toast. "It's wonderful. Please express my gratitude to your aunt."

"I do like that blue dress more, though," Becky said. "Makes your eyes look pretty."

"Er, thank you."

"Call if you need anything else," the maid added brightly before returning toward the kitchen.

Acton poured his tea. "It seems to be unanimous—you should keep the blue dress."

"Unanimous among whom?" she asked. "I don't recall hearing any sort of question as to whether I should keep anything. I cannot accept that or the other garments from you."

"What about the bedclothes? We are staying here at least one more night. Surely you want to keep those?" He had her there.

Her mouth tightened.

"But I suppose I can take them back if you'd rather not keep them," he offered.

"Fine. I will keep those for the duration of our stay. They are on loan to me, agreed?"

He gave her a single nod. "Then consider the dress and other items a loan too."

She picked up her toast. "What will you do with them when I am finished? Give them to your next paramour? Or perhaps you have a current one?"

Acton thought of his friend Droxford, who was perhaps the best scowler in England, and wished he'd learned to do that. Next time they were together, Acton would ask for scowling lessons. "I do not have a current paramour, and I would never gift something I bought for you to any of my, ah, female friends." He'd been about to say lovers but decided that would be inappropriate as well as invite Miss Barclay's censure.

He wondered if she was just being proper or, worse, if she was a prude. If she was the latter, they might not have suited after all. Acton couldn't see himself wed to someone who didn't enjoy the physical aspects of marriage.

"That gown is probably too modest for your female friends, anyway," Miss Barclay noted.

She was correct, but he didn't say so. He would hope that

the "loan" would turn into permanence, but perhaps the gown's insufficient length was a problem. "I could ask one of the maids to do whatever they do to make the gown longer. Would you keep it, then?"

"I think you mean they would let the hem out," she said. "And no, I wouldn't keep it."

He sighed with resignation. "All right. I just thought it was the perfect color for you. And I thought it might bring you joy during this trying time." He scooped some egg with his fork. "I didn't even realize how many challenges you'd faced." To have her valise stolen on top of everything else was horrible. He froze before taking a bite. "Your money wasn't in your valise, was it?" That would explain why she'd been able to afford the New Inn a few days ago, but now could not.

She narrowed her eyes at him. "Do you think I'm stupid? My money was and is always on my person."

Now, *he* felt foolish. "Very sensible. I don't think you're stupid at all. I'm impressed by your resolve in the face of adversity."

"Thank you," she said with a hint of uncertainty, as if she wasn't sure what to say to him. She really didn't know what to do with his kindness. She seemed convinced that he was a villain.

"Honestly, you deserve the gown and much more. You are owed recompense for the loss of your things."

"Not by *you*. Unless…you didn't steal my valise, did you?"

"Of course not. But since you believe me to be a corrupt individual, why not make me pay for my sins?"

She opened her mouth, then snapped it closed. After a moment, she spoke slowly. "There is a certain logic to that, I suppose. It would help me come to terms with having accepted the bath and the bedclothes." She gave him a sheepish look. "I'm afraid I couldn't bring myself to refuse them. Once I saw the bed in my chamber here, I was distraught to not have my sheeting."

"Well, I hope whoever stole the valise needed the contents more than you."

She laughed, but there wasn't much humor in it. "What a charitable thought."

"I do try to find the positive in things," he said. His father had always told him to turn his back on sadness and disappointment, that those emotions only weakened a man.

"Which I find bewildering." She picked up her tea for a long sip.

"Why is that?"

"Because you are a consummate rogue." She set her cup back in the saucer, then arranged her utensils to indicate she was finished with her breakfast. "I hadn't thought you would be cheerful or…pleasant."

"I must ask how you define a rogue."

"Men who prey on women and who take great advantage of their station and privilege as gentlemen. Men who aren't… serious or genuine."

"I see. Well, some may think a rogue is simply a man who enjoys life. Indeed, rogues are *quite* pleasant. No one would find us attractive if we were beastly." Actually, Droxford could be exceedingly unpleasant at times and managed to be incredibly popular with women. They seemed to like his gruff nature, as if they could somehow warm him where all others had failed. He frowned at Miss Barclay. "You seem committed to your dislike of me."

She shrugged. "I'm sorry, but I can't trust you. Or like you."

"Why?" he pressed again. Her animosity was making him self-conscious. He didn't think he was a bad person, and he'd already decided to stop being so rakish.

Several moments passed as she seemed to consider what to say. He braced himself for something truly awful.

"What have I done?" he asked.

"It's nothing specific *you've* done. Although, your reputation is bad enough. And you surround yourself with people—your friends—who possess even worse reputations."

That was probably true. He thought of his friends, and they were, for the most part, as libidinous as he was. A few were well known for their sexual prowess, one or two for their penchant for high stakes whether it was wagering or some other sort of competition, and they were all probably guilty of using their position to their advantage in a variety of ways. Acton had been delighted when his father had secured him an invitation to join the Rogue's Den, and he was also a member of White's, Brooks's, and the Phoenix Club. He sought sanctuary in those places rather than attend Almack's or many of the many balls and routs to which he was invited. He had the luxury of delaying marriage, of doing whatever he damn well pleased, really.

Her definition of a *rogue* came back to him. Perhaps he hadn't been particularly serious. But, he was genuine—or tried to be. And he did, now, genuinely want to find a wife. Still, it was possible he was not taking it quite seriously enough.

"Did I make you stop and think?" she asked, jolting him.

She had, actually. He recalled what she'd said before that. She'd indicated that he'd done nothing specific to warrant her distrust while also pointing out the poor reputations of his friends. "Did one of my friends harm you in some way?"

"Not exactly." She answered very quickly and didn't meet his eyes.

Acton wasn't certain that all his friends were as cautious as he was. He knew some of them probably took things too far with young ladies and were most unserious in their attentions. They stole kisses without any thought toward marriage. Hell, they all did—Acton had kissed many a young lady back when he'd suffered entire Seasons on the Marriage Mart and, more commonly, at house parties. It was time for him to have more consideration for his actions and the consequences of them.

Miss Barclay set her napkin on the table. "I'm going to cease this conversation now. You have a frustrating way of needling things from me when I wish you would leave me alone."

"I really need you to get past that notion," he said, also feeling frustrated. "I am not leaving you alone. What sort of cad do you take me for?" She shot him a look of wry surprise, and he nearly laughed. "Don't answer that, for I already know: an exceptional one. Still, I am the cad who is watching over you until you return home. Won't it be easier if we just become friends?"

She stared at him. "A young lady *cannot* be friends with a known rake."

"We can out here on the edge of England, where it's unlikely anyone knows who we are."

"You think because you called yourself 'Mr. Loxley' that no one will realize who you are? Especially since you used your real name over at the New Inn?"

"No one from the New Inn is going to speak to anyone here and vice versa." Except the stable master at the New Inn knew he was lodging here because Acton's horse was there. Damn. Still, it probably didn't matter.

Probably.

She leaned back in her chair and studied him a moment. "I don't understand your motivation here. A rake suddenly behaving like a gallant knight?"

"I am a duke," he managed to whisper the last word. "It is my duty to care for those—" He stopped himself before he said beneath him. Good God, he sounded pompous. And privileged, just how she'd described a rogue. Honestly, he reminded himself of his father. Had he been a rogue? Most probably. "To care for others. Besides, you aren't a stranger— our mothers are dear friends."

Her nostrils had flared when he'd abruptly cut himself off. "So, you feel beholden?"

"Must you take everything and turn it into a negative?" He immediately wished he could take that back. Given what he knew of her parents, negative might be the norm for her. "My apologies. I can't begin to know what has brought you to this point where you feel as if you've no choice but to run into danger."

"You really think my behavior is dangerous?"

"It certainly isn't *safe*, not for a young lady."

"How would you even know? Have you ever put yourself in the position of one? I daresay you may have caused potential 'danger' to any number of young ladies. Am I wrong?"

She had him there.

"Er, no. I confess there have been times when I have treated…romantic encounters as more of a game, which the Marriage Mart tends to be, in my opinion."

"I assure you, trying to make a good marriage is not an amusement for most young ladies. It is a matter of family pride, duty, and, in many cases, necessity."

He did realize that he ought not be officially on the Marriage Mart if he wasn't intending to immediately wed, which was why he'd kept his activities during the Season to a minimum the past couple of years. "I am trying to do better. You are showing me the ways in which I can, ways I had not even realized, I'm somewhat ashamed to say." He hoped he was a man of integrity and hearing that he might not be was a blow.

"Am I your self-improvement project?" Was that a whiff of humor?

Acton smiled, grateful for a lighter path of conversation. His roguishness, both past and present, was beginning to weigh on him. "Why not? Think of it as us helping each other."

Her gaze turned wary once more, and he feared he would lose this battle too. "All right. I'll *keep* the gown. But that is all the help—along with the bath and the bedclothes—that I will accept from you."

It was the smallest of victories, but he would take it. "I don't suppose you'd dine downstairs with me tonight?"

She arched a brow. "I think this breakfast was more than enough time spent together."

Did she? Then she definitely wasn't going to like it when he insisted on accompanying her home.

She rose, and he leapt to his feet. "Will I see you later this afternoon perhaps?" he asked.

"Probably not," she responded as she approached the stairs. "I'll be busy as I've a hem to let out."

He couldn't keep from smiling as he watched her round the corner on the stairs. He'd finally made some progress with the world's most disagreeable young lady. No, that wasn't fair. She was fleeing the prospect of being forced into something she didn't want. She'd felt there were no other options. How he wished he could learn why. While she might think she revealed too much to him, there was far more he was desperate to know.

He wanted to discover what she truly wanted, beyond just avoiding marriage to him. Then, perhaps he could help her achieve it.

And why did he care so much? Was this truly an effort to improve himself, to better his reputation?

Perhaps a little. Acknowledging that it had taken a chance

meeting with his potential bride for him to realize he needed to change his behavior and his attitude made him uncomfortable.

Except she wasn't his potential bride. She was a woman risking a great deal to avoid marrying him. If all he did was ensure she didn't marry him, that was the least he could do.

# CHAPTER 8

*P*ersephone had borrowed sewing supplies from Moll after breakfast in order to take out the hem of the blue gown. The needlework took her into the afternoon, but when she was finished, she grew bored. The two books she'd packed in her valise were sorely missed.

Compounding her boredom was the knowledge that Wellesbourne was nearby, and spending time with him would almost certainly alleviate her ennui. He might be irritating, but he was also entertaining. He possessed a fine sense of humor. She'd actually enjoyed sharing breakfast with him that morning. It seemed the more time she spent with him, the less she disliked him.

Which was foolish. She could not afford to forget that he was, at his core, a scoundrel, else she could end up like Pandora.

No, not like Pandora. Persephone would never allow herself to fall in love with someone such as Wellesbourne. Except…was he really as bad as Bane? He hadn't ruined anyone as far as she knew. She could accept his help without exposing herself to his roguishness. She just had to remember the rules, and so far she wasn't doing the best job of that.

Accepting his help was the smart thing to do. If her valise hadn't been stolen, she wouldn't have needed his assistance at all. Additionally, his point that he was paying for his sins by helping her was inarguable.

Anyway, that was what she was going to believe.

Would he come to her room if he received a letter from his mother? She had to assume he would.

Persephone hoped it would arrive today. She found she was growing more anxious about her parents' reaction to what she'd done and what would come next.

Perhaps she ought to dine with Wellesbourne. She at least wanted to find out if he'd received a letter.

After an interminable afternoon, it was finally time for dinner. Persephone left her chamber eagerly and made her way downstairs where the common room was once again busy. Noise and heat greeted her.

Looking about, she noted the duke seated at a table on the other side of the room. And he wasn't alone. He was sharing a table with the woman he'd been speaking with last night—the red-haired beauty. They were deep in conversation, their heads tilted toward one another. Their expressions went from intent to smiling. Then they laughed. She touched his sleeve. He didn't seem to mind.

Why had Persephone thought for even a moment she should spend time with him? He was a callous rogue, always flirting with the next woman he saw.

Deciding to avoid him—surely, he would have notified her if he'd received word from his mother—she picked her way along the periphery of the room toward Moll, who was wiping a table. When she finished, Persephone intercepted her and asked for her dinner.

"I'll go and fetch it." Moll gave her an apologetic look.

"But you may need to wait a bit. The cook burned herself earlier, and things are behind."

"I understand, thank you." Persephone moved to the wall and flicked a glance toward Wellesbourne. He and the gorgeous woman were still laughing and talking. It grated on her. But why should it? He wasn't anything to her. Just a nuisance who insisted on helping her.

"Evening, pretty lady." A man moved close to Persephone's right. Too close.

His breath reeked of ale, and the rest of him just reeked. He leaned his face toward her. "Ye've got a room here, don't ye?"

"Excuse me," she mumbled and took a step forward.

The man grabbed her arm. "Don't be uppity now. Let's have some fun." He leered at her before taking a drink from the tankard he held in his other hand.

Fear moved through her as her heart began to race. "No, thank you." She pulled her arm from his grip, then shoved at him so he couldn't grab her again. He stumbled, and his tankard tipped, covering him in ale.

Persephone didn't hesitate. Nor did she care about her dinner any longer. She moved quickly toward the stairs.

Before she could reach them, Wellesbourne intercepted her. "There you are. I somehow missed you coming down. Is everything all right?"

"I'm fine," she lied. She was still quivering with agitation —and fear that the man she'd just pushed would come after her. "I'm just going back upstairs. It's too crowded down here."

He frowned. Since he didn't say anything about what had happened, Persephone presumed he hadn't seen it. And why would he when he was focused on his tablemate?

"What about your dinner?" He glanced toward her empty hands. "I presume you came down to fetch it?"

"I think they're too busy. I have some food upstairs." She had a crust of bread. "Go on back to your lady friend." Persephone looked toward the woman who was watching them with interest.

"She isn't my lady friend," he said. "What if I bring your dinner up to you?"

"No, thank you." Persephone was growing more upset. She needed to get out of there! And she wanted to look to see what the man who'd grabbed her was doing, but she didn't dare for fear of making eye contact. "Please excuse me."

"Here comes Moll," the duke said.

Persephone made herself wait while the maid navigated the common room. When she arrived with the dinner, it was all Persephone could do not to snatch the tray from her grasp and race upstairs.

"No waiting after all," Moll said with a broad smile.

"Thank you," Persephone managed with a forced smile as she accepted the tray. Then she whipped around and hurried upstairs.

Once she was in her room, she set the tray on her tiny table and went back to the door. She set the lock, which had felt loose since she'd arrived. Now, she worried it wouldn't stay locked.

Nervous, she positioned her chair so she could stare at the door. There was a knife on her tray. That could serve as a weapon, if she needed one.

What was she doing suffering this unnecessary fear? She ought to go home first thing tomorrow.

That she'd had to resort to running away to avoid her parents' demands and doing so had brought her to this was the real concern. She might be safer overall at home, but for how long? What did her future hold?

It turned out, Persephone didn't actually want her dinner after all.

*A*cton kept watching the stairs even after Miss Barclay disappeared around the corner with her dinner. Though he hadn't observed what had happened to her, he could tell she was shaken. He'd seen her making her way along the edge of the room and had transferred his attention back and forth between her and Charity Staunton, the charming red-haired siren who'd joined him at his table. Apparently, he'd been just distracted enough by Charity to miss seeing what had transpired.

What he *had* seen was Miss Barclay rushing away from a man who was brushing at his clothes which appeared sodden. He'd noted Miss Barclay's distress and immediately excused himself from Charity while cursing his inattentiveness.

Moll had moved away, but Acton followed her. "Moll, did you see anything happen with Miss…*us* Birdwhistle?" He'd almost called her Miss Barclay.

The maid shrugged. "No. Mayhap I saw her talk to a gent over there." She gestured toward the man with the wet garments. "Can't be sure, though. Blasted busy in 'ere tonight."

Then she was gone.

Acton frowned, then glanced toward the stairs and frowned some more. He looked back at the man Miss Barclay might have been speaking to and decided to keep an eye on him.

In the meantime, he returned to Charity, who gave him a pout and asked why he was gone for so long.

"Just checking on a friend," he said before sipping his port.

"That mousy thing?" Charity asked.

Mousy? "I wouldn't describe her that way."

Granted, Miss Barclay was still wearing her dull brown gown instead of the pretty blue one he'd bought her. Had she not been able to lengthen it?

Charity gave him a broad smile, but didn't reveal her teeth. That was a telltale sign there was probably something not worth seeing behind her lips. "I'm glad she's gone on her way."

Becky delivered their dinner, and Acton ate with one eye trained on the rough-looking man. Moll had brought the ruffian a fresh tankard when their dinner arrived, and while Acton was still eating, the man finished it and obtained another. The man had to be quite drunk.

"Did you hear what I said?" Charity's question drew his attention, and he reluctantly peeled his gaze away from the man across the room.

"Er, no. I'm sorry."

She pursed her rouged lips at him. "You've been distracted since that chit pulled you away from me. I just asked if you wanted to go up to your chamber after dinner, but I wonder if she's your bed sport." Charity sounded peeved. Jealous, even.

Acton didn't have time—or patience—for such nonsense. Watching over Miss Barclay was his priority. Indeed, what the hell was he still doing sitting with Charity? He should have abandoned her and put his entire attention on the ruffian.

Angry with himself, Acton looked back toward the drunken man, but he was gone.

A surprising panic filled Acton's throat. He snapped his attention to the stairs and caught the shape of someone just as they turned the corner. Was it him?

Acton wasn't going to take the chance that it was. "You'll have to pardon me," he said, rising. "Your meal is paid for.

And drink all you like." He didn't spare her a glance as he hurried from the table to the stairs.

He took them two at a time and looked down the corridor toward Miss Barclay's room just in time to see her door slam. Barreling in that direction, Acton heard her shriek. He sprinted faster, throwing open her door just as she fell back onto the narrow bed in the tiny chamber.

The man from downstairs stood over her, but turned his head to glare at Acton. "Ye're interruptin'!"

"I am." Acton moved toward the man and grasped him by the upper back of his coat. Hauling him away from the bed, Acton drove his fist into the man's gut.

The man grunted as Acton silently thanked Gentleman Jackson's establishment for training him in pugilism. Acton kept ahold of the man and dragged him to the door. "Get out and don't come back. I've no problem taking you all the way to the magistrate and seeing you prosecuted. Do you understand?"

Lifting his head, the man looked up at him with bleary, reddened eyes. He nodded.

"Say you understand so I know you comprehend me, or I'll hit you again."

"I unnerstand. And I'm goin' to flash the hash." The man clapped his hand over his mouth.

Acton threw him into the corridor. "Not in here, you won't."

Without waiting to see what happened next, Acton slammed the door closed and threw the lock. Right away, he could feel that it wasn't catching. "This is broken."

"Apparently."

"You can't stay here." He turned toward her and saw that she'd stood. She'd wrapped her arms around herself, as if she were cold.

"No."

Acton was surprised she didn't argue, but then he could see she was pale and frightened. And why wouldn't she be?

He wanted to comfort her, to take her in his arms until she stopped shaking. But he had to think she wouldn't want that, especially from him.

"You said this would happen," she whispered in a ragged voice. "That a degenerate might assault me."

It almost sounded as if he'd predicted it, which he hadn't. He'd just been trying to talk sense to her by pointing out things that *could* happen. "I certainly didn't hope for that."

"That would make you even more terrible than you are," she murmured.

"I don't think I'm terrible." Why was he defending himself in this moment? She needed his care, not conflict.

"No, you aren't. I can see you are actually trying to help. However, I can also see that you are still a libidinous rake. Do you need to get back to the woman downstairs?"

"No."

"Because she's going to meet you in your chamber?"

"Absolutely not." In the past, hell, a fortnight ago, he would have arranged that. But not now while he was watching over Miss Barclay. "I admit I was distracted by her, and for that, I am deeply regretful. I hope you can forgive me. You are my primary concern. I only want to keep you safe," he said firmly, taking a step toward her so that a foot or so separated them. "I just did that, didn't I?"

"Yes, and I am most appreciative."

He could see her pulse moving in her throat, and her cheeks were now flushed. "I'm so sorry that happened."

"I should go home first thing tomorrow." She hesitated and took a stuttered breath.

"You sound uncertain."

"It's just…I'm not sure I can go home. Not unless I agree to marry you. Or someone else of my parents' choosing."

Acton had never seen her so vulnerable. "Did they threaten you somehow?"

Again, she seemed reluctant to answer. "I am their least favorite daughter."

That didn't really answer his question, but it gave him insight. "You have a younger sister. Any other siblings?"

She shook her head.

"She is at home?"

"No. I can't—" She looked away from him. "I don't want to discuss this with you. It's…private."

It was also obviously upsetting. "I'd like to comfort you. If you'd let me."

Her gaze shifted back to meet his. "How?"

"I could hold you until you feel better?"

One of her dark gold brows arched slightly.

He held up his hands. "I swear, it will be a platonic embrace meant to soothe your unrest."

It took her a moment to respond, and then he was shocked by what she said. "All right." She lowered her arms to her sides.

Moving tentatively, Acton stepped closer to her. He put one arm around her, then the other. Instead of pulling her to him, he simply held her like that for a moment.

"This is awkward," she said to his neck, for the top of her head came to his mouth. How easy, and satisfying, it would be to press a reassuring kiss to her forehead.

"Shall we stop, then?" He held his breath, realizing he didn't particularly want to.

She tipped her head down and tucked it beneath his chin as she pressed herself against him. Her hands came to his waist, and she leaned into his embrace. Acton wrapped his arms about her more tightly and closed his eyes. She was warm, and this close, he could at last discern her floral scent: lily of the valley.

His body began to react to having her against him. He felt her curves and listened to the steady sound of her breathing as she settled in his arms. He nearly kissed her then. The need to brush his lips against her temple was overwhelming. Not to arouse her, but to show her she was safe and protected.

She pulled back slightly and looked up at him. "Thank you. I feel better now."

He felt something more than better. He felt...awake. Alive. As if he'd been sleeping in the silent dark and the curtains had been thrown open to reveal a bright, exciting day that he couldn't wait to begin.

Her gaze remained locked with his, and her lips parted. Acton nearly groaned. Now, he wanted to arouse her as he was.

Was she inviting his kiss? How he wanted to press his mouth to hers, to show her that not all men—and not all rakes—were beasts.

He moved his hand up her back and splayed his palm at the base of her neck. His pulse pounded in his ears. He'd never been so focused on a single thing. Kissing had always been second nature. But this was different. This was something he wanted with his whole being, something he was certain would be life altering.

Before he could lower his head, she removed her hands from him and took a step backward. There would be no kiss.

Acton had never been more crushed.

# CHAPTER 9

*I*f Persephone hadn't moved away from him, they would have kissed. She could see it in his eyes and sensed it in the response of her own body. She wanted to feel his lips on hers, to lose herself and forget the horrible attack she'd just endured.

But she just couldn't allow it—not with him. Which was unfortunate because she was fairly certain her past kissing experience would pale in comparison to Wellesbourne's kisses. If she wagered, she would put all her money on him kissing like an absolute champion.

Shaking, and not from the man who'd stormed into her chamber, she brought her hands up and clasped them in front of her chest. "I am grateful that you managed to come upstairs when you did." She was also surprised since he'd seemed most engaged with the red-haired woman.

"I wish it had never happened. I can see you're still upset." His brow furrowed, and his concern was evident.

Except, she wasn't still troubled from that—well, she *was*. But he was noting her reaction to nearly kissing him, not that she would correct him. It was best if he believed she was still flustered from the ruffian.

"You should sleep in my room tonight," he said.

"With you?" She wanted to refuse but knew it was the only way she would feel safe, even if it did completely break several Rogue Rules.

"Yes, of course. I'll sleep in a chair, and you can have the bed. In the morning, we can discuss what to do—either waiting for my mother's letter or just leaving for Radstock Hall as soon as possible."

*We*, as if they were a pair. "The chair can't be comfortable."

"It can't be worse than the bed. I don't know about your mattress, but mine has more lumps than a rocky field."

"It is similarly uncomfortable," she said with a faint smile.

He stared at her mouth. "Is that a smile?"

"A very small one."

"I'll take it. You are an extraordinary woman, Miss Barclay. Shall we gather your things?"

Persephone went about collecting the few items she had. Nearly all of them, she realized, were things he'd given her, including the bedclothes, which the duke was pulling from the bed. It was a strange sight to see a man of his station performing such a mundane task. She wouldn't have thought a duke or a rogue would do such a thing. But then Wellesbourne continued to surprise her.

He also met her expectations by exhibiting a strong interest in a woman he'd just met.

The man was a conundrum, and not one she needed to solve. She only had to get through tonight and make a decision about her future tomorrow, preferably after receiving a letter from his mother about her parents.

This was all their fault. If Persephone hadn't felt as though she had to flee their household, she never would have found herself in these circumstances. And that was her answer—she could no longer trust or rely on them. She would need to forge her own path, which likely meant a future as a paid companion or a governess.

She could not return to Radstock Hall. The realization was both terrifying and oddly liberating. But mostly terrifying.

"Miss Barclay?"

Blinking, Persephone realized she'd been standing clutching her things as she stared off into nothing while her mind churned. "Yes, sorry, I'm ready."

Wellesbourne moved to the door and held it for her. She stepped out into the corridor, then stopped short before she put her foot in a puddle of sick. "Looks like he did indeed retch," she said.

"Charming." Wellesbourne's tone dripped with sarcasm. "This way." He walked around the mess and led her to the opposite end of the corridor. His room had a key, which he fished from his pocket and inserted into the lock.

"A locking door. How lavish."

He looked back at her and waggled his dark brows. "Wait until you see inside." He held the door.

"I can hardly wait to see your wobbling dresser with the sticking drawers." She moved past him into the chamber. The space was more than twice the size of hers, as was the bed. And there were four windows since the room was set into the corner. Still, it was as shabby and dull as her chamber, only with a working lock.

Persephone was shocked that he would stay here, even to look after her. "You can't have stayed anywhere like this before." She set her things on the dresser beside a chipped basin and a jug.

"No, I haven't." He'd closed the door and now locked it

before depositing the bedding he carried on the table. "Have you?"

"No," she admitted, hoping she would never have to again.

"It's not so bad. I would lodge in the gutter if that's what I needed to do to keep you safe."

Persephone whipped her attention to him. Had he just stated he would follow her into a gutter? "I'm sure that's not a line you've used in your past flirtations," she said with a half smile.

He grinned. "I can say with confidence that it has never entered a conversation."

She looked about, wondering which chair would be his bed. There were two situated near the hearth. Faded red fabric covered the cushions, and one featured an oval-shaped discoloration. If he used them both, stretching his legs from one to the other, it might work. They could add the two wooden chairs from the round dining table near the window. That would give him a bed-like support. But it would be woefully uncomfortable. Though, he said it couldn't be as bad as the bed. What was worse, lumps or a hard surface beneath one's backside?

Now she was thinking of his backside, which she'd glimpsed through the tails of his superfine coat on occasion and tried fervently to ignore. His clothing was impeccably fitted, covering the contour of his well-formed body to perfection. She reasoned it was acceptable, if not necessary, for her to ogle him the way he ogled women.

"I must apologize again," he said, cutting through the silence with an impassioned tone.

Persephone pivoted to face him. He was staring at her intently, his brow still creased.

"I never should have allowed myself to be distracted downstairs. You needed my protection."

"Since I didn't particularly want it and was, admittedly,

trying to keep you from seeing me, you mustn't blame yourself." It was difficult enough to deal with his insistence on keeping her safe; she did not want to deal with him feeling guilty too. She quickly changed the subject. "If we push the four chairs together, we may be able to form a passable bed. It won't be lumpy at least."

He glanced toward the chairs near the hearth before refocusing on her. "Was that humor?"

She lifted a shoulder. "Perhaps." Moving her attention to the bed, she asked, "Should we replace your bedding with mine?" She'd no doubt hers would fit the larger bed as it had been voluminous on the narrower one back in her chamber.

A shudder tripped through her as the memory of the man pushing her onto the bed flashed in her mind. She'd been eating her dinner when she'd heard him outside her door. Fear had gripped her, the food she'd just managed to swallow roiling in her stomach. Praying the lock would hold, she'd risen on unsteady feet and looked about for a weapon before recalling the knife on her tray. However, before she could grab it, the ruffian had burst through the door, slamming it closed before seizing her with his meaty hand and throwing her to the bed.

Ice had formed in Persephone's veins as she'd realized what was about to happen. She'd tried to make a noise, and perhaps she had, but she'd felt as if she were frozen.

Then Wellesbourne had stormed in and saved her. He'd done precisely what he said he would do—keep her safe.

She couldn't very well continue to dislike him now, could she? Which didn't mean she had to welcome his advances, not that he was offering them anymore. They could, mayhap, be friends, as he'd suggested.

"There's no need to do that," the duke replied to her question about the bedding. "I'll just take the extra blanket—the one the inn provided—if you don't mind."

Glancing toward the bed, she saw that his blanket was much thicker than what was in her room. She'd been grateful for the addition of the one Wellesbourne had purchased for her. Looking back at him, she asked, "Are you sure they don't know you're a duke?"

"I didn't tell them. Why?"

"Your blanket is much more substantial than mine," she said. "But then you obviously spent more money here with your palatial accommodations." As well as the bath he'd purchased for her. No doubt, he'd had one himself too.

Chuckling, he nodded. "I suppose that makes sense."

"You must take that blanket as well as your own. I can use the one you are loaning me. I insist since you are allowing me the bed."

"Fair enough. Now, show me your chair-bed idea."

Persephone moved a wooden chair from the table to the hearth where the cushioned chairs were situated.

"How can I help?" he asked.

"Move that other chair from the table with the others," she instructed.

He joined her there and positioned the chairs in a row, with the cushioned chairs facing each other and the wooden chairs between them as the middle of the "bed."

She stood back. "You can at least lie down?"

He laughed, his dark eyes sparkling with mirth. He was really very attractive, especially when he smiled or laughed, which was often. Far more often than Persephone did. "How short do you think I am?" he asked.

Thinking of how her head tucked neatly beneath his chin if she tipped her face down, she realized he was perhaps taller than this configuration would allow. "Do you want to go back to my room and get my chair? That might do the trick?"

"It may work without that." He sat on one of the wooden

chairs and swung his legs up, then lay back. He barely fit. "Apparently, I am not as tall as I think I am." He exhaled in what she thought was mock disappointment.

She allowed a smile. "I won't tell anyone."

"Thank goodness." He pushed himself up. "But then we can't tell anyone of our adventure together."

No, they could not. Well, Persephone would tell Pandora. Or would she? Pandora would be disinclined to find any favor with Wellesbourne, just as Persephone had been. But he'd proven himself to be…different. "You are not the duke I expected."

"I'm glad to hear it. It's evident you expected someone truly awful based on the worst aspects of my reputation."

Part of her wanted to tell him all about what his horrid friend had done to Pandora, but most of her wanted to protect her sister. Persephone was still hopeful that Pandora would not be ruined, that what had happened between her and Bane in Weston would not become lasting gossip.

"Can you tell me what happened to make you so certain I am a horrid person?"

"I can't discuss it with you."

"Even though it relates to me? Or a friend of mine?"

She pursed her lips at him and gave her head a slight shake.

He threw up his hands. "All right. I shan't press you. Just know that *I* am trying to improve, and if you've anything to say that would help me do that, I would appreciate it."

She found this desire of his to change intriguing. "Why are you trying to improve?"

"Because if a lovely young lady such as yourself would rather risk danger and ruin than trust me, I must be doing something wrong."

He thought she was lovely? "I can't imagine why you have a high opinion of me. I've been rather awful to you."

"With good reason—according to you. And knowing what little I do about your circumstances, I understand why you might feel alone and defensive. Just know that you have an ally in me."

He'd made that quite clear a short while ago when he'd come to her rescue. "I don't know what I would have done if you hadn't come to my room," she said softly.

"Don't even think about it," he said quickly. "I mean it. Don't entertain such thoughts. I got there in time, and I will ensure nothing like that happens again. Whether you like it or not, you are stuck with me—at your side—until you are safely delivered home."

"And what if I don't go home?" She wished she could take that back. "Forget I said that. I'm overwrought, and I need to rest."

"I don't think you ate either."

She'd had a few bites, but she wasn't remotely hungry. Sleep sounded best. She only hoped she could find it in her current state. Indeed, she was inclined to just stay up talking with Wellesbourne. He was doing a fair job of keeping her from thinking too much about earlier. He'd even made her smile.

"We should go to bed," she said. "I'll have a clearer head in the morning, and we can discuss what I should do." Was she actually going to consult him?

That didn't sound like the worst idea anymore.

"Excellent idea." He fetched a blanket from the bed and returned to the chairs. Sitting down, he began to remove his boots.

Heat climbed up Persephone's neck and gathered in her breasts. He was only taking his boots off! She hadn't considered whether she would disrobe, but it seemed a poor idea. Since having her valise stolen, she'd slept in her chemise instead of a night rail, but tonight she would just go to bed in her gown.

She perched on the edge of the bed and unlaced her boots. "I don't snore," she said.

"That's a relief. I don't either."

"I do talk sometimes," she added as she pulled her boots off and set them together. Or at least she used to, back when she and Pandora shared a bedchamber. They still occasionally shared a bed if they were up late talking, or sometimes they would read together and one of them would fall asleep.

"How fascinating. Now, I want to stay up all night in case you say something riveting."

Persephone sat back on the bed and brought her legs onto the mattress. "I doubt you'll be able to understand anything. My sister says it's mostly gibberish."

"Pity. I can only imagine what you might say while sleeping." He gave her a suggestive look and a lopsided smile before swinging his legs back onto the chair-bed.

She didn't want to find him endearing or for his provocative manner to soften her. But she was in grave danger of exactly that happening. Better to throw up her defenses once more. "I did not give you leave to flirt with me."

"Alas, you did not. It is, I'm afraid, my nature." He arranged the blanket over himself.

Persephone lay back onto the pillow and the duke's sandalwood and amber scent filled her senses. "I fear for your wife having to put up with you doing that." *At least she'd get to smell him up close forever.*

"I should hope she will like it." He sounded like he was smiling. Persephone did not turn her head to confirm that.

"I meant you doing that with other women." She wriggled into the bedclothes and tried not to think of how she was sleeping where he'd slept. Another reason it was good that she'd left her clothes on. To have bare parts of her where bare parts of him had been would surely make her think of bare parts of them together.

"That is the second time you've mentioned that, and I took it to heart. I will *not* flirt with anyone but my wife." His impassioned response shook her from her libidinous thoughts—she was no better than he was, apparently.

"Why not? You said it was your nature. You make it sound as if you can't help yourself. How will that change once you are wed?"

"Because I've decided it will change." For the first time, he sounded almost angry.

Persephone smiled, hoping he would be able to achieve what he wanted. "I don't think you'll regret it."

He grunted in response. "I left the lantern lit. Do you want the light?"

"I don't need it, but thank you for asking."

She heard him get up, and then the lantern was extinguished. In the darkness, she somehow became even more aware of his scent on the bedclothes and the knowledge that he'd lain where she was currently.

"Good night, Miss Barclay."

"Good night, Duke."

"Wellesy or Acton, if you please."

"Wellesy?" She stifled a giggle.

"Did I hear a hint of laughter? I would be affronted that you would find my nickname humorous, but I am too delighted by the sound of your mirth. And before you admonish me for flirting, I am allowed to be delighted by you. That happens with friends, which I've decided we are. You can argue with me about that in the morning, if you wish."

She rather liked arguing with him, she realized, but she wouldn't about this. "I think I must accept you as a friend."

"Don't sound so thrilled," he said with a sardonic laugh.

Again, she giggled, but she didn't try to stop it this time. She also snorted. The idea of her laughter delighting someone, especially someone such as he, was too exhilarating to ignore. "Since we are friends, am I to call you by your first name or by the ridiculous Wellesy? What about Loxley? Wasn't that your name before?"

"For my entire life until my father died last year. Lox or Loxley. But my nurse and my governess always called me Acton." He had a vague memory of his mother calling him that too, but more often she referred to him as Loxley.

"Which do you like best?"

"I hadn't thought about it, but I suppose Acton. That's *my* name, not one I've had to share with anyone else in my family tree."

Persephone found that revelation fascinating. How odd or even overwhelming it must be to be one of a long line of something bigger than oneself. So much responsibility and expectation. She hadn't considered that before.

"I didn't mean to laugh at Wellesy. Especially since I have a nickname of my own."

"Please tell me." He sounded rather fervent.

She grinned as she thought of her sister not being able to say Persephone when she'd learned to speak. "My sister has always called me Persey."

"That is a *great* nickname. Much better than Wellesy."

"Lox isn't bad," Persephone said. "Do you have siblings? Is that what they called you?"

"Two younger sisters. They didn't call me anything. We didn't live in the same household. They resided with my mother."

Persephone felt foolish. Of course she'd known that Lady Wellesbourne had two daughters. She just hadn't put together that they were his sisters, which had been foolish. "Did you know them at all?" she asked quietly, wondering if she'd even spoken loud enough for him to hear her.

"No, so I don't really know what it's like to have siblings. I imagine it's nice."

His tone sounded flat, as if he couldn't imagine it. But perhaps he wanted to? Blast, she *had* become his friend. She was beginning to like him and to want to get to know him better. He was far more complex and caring than she'd anticipated him to be.

"My sister is my favorite person in the whole world," Persephone said.

"That's marvelous," he said softly, mayhap even wistfully.

"Good night, *Acton*," she said, though she suspected she could have continued talking with him all night.

"Good night, Persey."

Persephone was shocked she didn't tell him not to call her that name, that it was only for Pandora to use. Except it sounded, somehow, right.

~

*T*he second time he felt the movement against his leg, Acton jolted completely awake. He'd imagined the prior nudge might be Persey's hand as he'd been dreaming of her limbs entwined with his.

However, this was not Persey.

Acton kicked out his leg and heard the unmistakable skitter of rodent feet across the floorboards. Once he'd blinked the sleep from his eyes, there was just enough light from the hearth for him to see the shadow of the rat before it disappeared beneath the dresser.

Swearing, he bolted upright and instinctively rubbed his hands over his legs. Then he jumped to his feet and looked furtively around the room for any other creatures.

If only he hadn't fallen off the chair-bed, he would not have been asleep on the floor. It was somewhat of a miracle he'd found any rest on the hard surface. The blanket was off to the side, the corner hooked on one of the chairs. Acton plucked at it and was rewarded with another rat. This one was smaller but louder as it let out a piercing squeak, surprising Acton so that he threw the blanket and shouted.

"What's happened?" Persey's sleepy question came from the bed.

Acton felt like a fool for his reaction to the second rat, but he hadn't expected it to be lurking beneath his blanket. Good God, were there more of them? Were they even now trying to scale Persey's bed?

"I think you should get up," he said as calmly as possible, seeing that she was already upright as she wiped her hand over her eye. "I find that I have bedded down with rats." He shuddered to think of the two rodents snuggled beneath his blanket with him.

"Rats?" She sounded as though she might not believe him. "How did they get up on your chair-bed?"

"They didn't. I fell off. Twice. I decided to sleep on the floor. That was, evidently, a rather poor choice."

"Oh dear, I'm so sorry. And there was more than one?"

"Two," he said darkly. "So far."

"There were no rats before tonight?" she asked.

He shook his head. "No."

"This is now the second prognostication you've made that has come to pass. A man assaulted me, and now there are rats."

Acton's observation about the Black Ivy being infested with rats came back to him. He moved toward the bed. "I didn't think that was actually true. I was merely trying to illustrate what *could* happen."

"Since both have now occurred, I must wonder if you

somehow had a hand in them." She met his gaze, and it was all but impossible to even try to discern what she was thinking in the dim dawn light. "To prove your point."

He let his jaw sag. "You can't really believe that of me?" Especially the ruffian who'd manhandled her and intended to do worse. And *rats*? "What kind of beast do you think I am?" He didn't try to mask his outrage.

"No, I can't believe that of you. It's just awfully coincidental. Please refrain from offering any other ideas as to what could go wrong," she added wryly.

Acton relaxed, glad that she now seemed to trust him, at least a little. "Happily. I am as distressed as you by what has happened. Which is why I must insist we leave immediately."

"But it's the middle of the night. Where would we go?"

"It's nearly dawn, I think." Acton went to the window and moved the drape aside to look outside. Indeed, the sun was just breaking over the horizon. "I'll obtain rooms at the New Inn."

"Rooms, plural?" she asked.

"Well, a suite of rooms that are connected. I must insist we sleep in the same suite, meaning there is only one way to access the space. I will ensure we have separate chambers to sleep in, or at least separate beds."

"Before you suggest we masquerade as a married couple to avoid scandal, I prefer we pretend to be siblings. You can be my older brother. Which means we can't return to the New Inn since they know you as Wellesbourne and me as Mrs. Birdwhistle."

"Siblings? But we don't look at all alike."

"Then we can be half siblings," she said primly before leaning over the edge of the bed. "I hope there isn't a rat in my boot."

Acton hadn't considered that. The notion of a rat taking

shelter in one of his boots was an alarming thought. A raw, almost retching sound came from his throat.

"Are you all right?" Persey asked.

"Fine," he managed, though he sounded as if someone was squeezing his throat.

"Free of rats," she announced.

Acton watched, frozen, as she put her boots on. Eventually, he turned his attention to where his boots stood near one of the cushioned chairs. One had fallen over, an open invitation for a rat to make a cozy bed inside.

A moment later, he felt the air move behind him. He swung about, his gaze on the floor where he saw Persey's boots and the hem of her gown. Lifting his focus to her face, he exhaled.

"You look terrified. Did you see another rat?" she asked.

"No. Not yet." He flicked a glance toward his toppled boot. Perhaps the rodents had worked together to knock it down to create a haven.

"Are you…afraid of rats?"

"I didn't think so. But now I must reassess that assumption."

"Have you even seen rats before?"

"In London. On the streets—*certain* streets. But always from a distance. I was not sharing my sleeping space with them. Or my footwear."

Her brows arched and her eyes widened slightly. "Is there one in your boot?"

"I'm afraid I don't know. It seems possible. They were both standing upright when I retired."

"Would you like me to look?" she asked.

He appreciated her lack of teasing. This was mortifying on every level—his fear, his revelation of that to her, his dependence on her bravery. "Would you?" He shook his head sharply. "No, what if it jumps out at you?"

"I am confident it will be more afraid of me than I am of it." She moved toward his boots. "It's unlikely there is anything in there, not after the noise we've been making."

"Be careful," he warned as she bent to pick up the boot. "Perhaps you should just kick it first."

He couldn't see what she did next as she blocked the boot from his view with her body. Suddenly, she jumped and shrieked.

Acton did the same. He also moved backward until he met the side of the bed.

Persey turned. She held both his boots. Then she laughed. And laughed. Great guffaws of hilarity.

He stared at her. "Was there a rat?"

She struggled to speak between trying to breathe amidst her laughter. "No."

Frowning, he crossed his arms over his chest. "That wasn't funny." But the sound of her laughter—loud and joy filled—was making him feel better. He wished he was less rattled so he could appreciate it more.

She sobered—or at least tried to—immediately. "I'm sorry. That wasn't well done of me. I'm afraid I couldn't resist. A man of your reputation, afraid of rats…it's completely unexpected. And, if I'm honest, rather endearing."

She found him endearing? Perhaps that was worth her teasing him and him sleeping with rats. No, not the latter.

Clutching his boots, she added, "Also, it's something you may not be used to since you grew up without siblings. My sister is afraid of spiders, and I may have pulled a similar jest on her a time or two." She grimaced.

Acton sometimes thought about what he'd missed not living with his mother and sisters, more now that his mother was living in the dowager house. Mostly, he tried not to think about it, for those provoked his "softer" emotions, the ones his father had worked so hard to show him were unnecessary for men of their station.

"I suppose I can see the humor if I put myself in your... rat-free boots."

She laughed and snorted at the same time. Eyes widening, she pressed her lips together and looked away from him.

"Don't do that," Acton said. "You just laughed with joyous abandon, and it was divine. I like when you laugh *and* when you snort."

"It's not very ladylike." She glanced toward him, and he saw the self-reproach in her gaze. It seemed she'd been advised not to snort, just as he'd been counseled not to indulge any soft emotions. Except those weren't the same things. There could be no harm in snorting.

Did that mean there was no harm in allowing himself to feel sad about not having his mother or sisters around as he'd grown up?

Acton banished that thought. "I don't care if it's ladylike or not. You are my knight in shining armor for ensuring my boots are safe."

She handed him the boots. "You are the knight after saving me from that man last night."

"We aren't discussing that, remember?" But he would be happy to be her knight. "Let us collect our things, and I'll notify the innkeeper we're leaving. And that he has a rat problem."

Acton also intended to tell him about the ruffian who'd attacked Persey last night and strongly suggest the man ought to be barred from the inn. It was too bad Acton hadn't told the innkeeper he was a duke, for that would have carried a great deal of weight.

Persey went to collect her things. "What about the letter you're expecting from your mother?"

Right, that. "I'll instruct the innkeeper to have it sent to wherever we find lodgings." Acton began to pack his things from the dresser into his valise.

"Do you know where else we could go instead of the New Inn?"

"There are several fine inns on the High Street. The Traveler's Rest is a large coaching inn. I could likely book passage for us leaving from there."

"For *us*?" she asked, pausing in removing his bedclothes from the bed.

"If you think I'm letting you travel home without my company, you are sorely mistaken. After last night, I can't imagine you'd want to."

"I'm only worried about if we are seen together."

"We won't need to spend the night anywhere else. I'll make sure everything goes well." He moved quickly to finish packing while Persey was folding his bedding. They made a good team, and not just with protecting one another.

Though, he had to admit that had been his favorite part.

He'd initially come after her to Gloucester to satisfy his curiosity, but since running into her on the street, she'd commanded his thoughts as well as his need to ensure she came to no harm. He now considered it his duty and responsibility.

"Ready?" he asked.

"Yes."

Acton opened the door and guided her along the corridor toward the stairs. "What will you do after we hear from my mother about your parents?"

"I'm not sure it matters anymore, to be honest. About hearing from your mother, I mean. I've concluded that regardless of what my parents did or are doing, I will need to find a...different path." She hesitated at the top of the stairs. "I don't think I can actually go home."

Acton kept his jaw from dropping. Things were that bad?

"But you're an unmarried young woman. Where will you go?"

"I'd originally planned to stay with a friend in Bristol for a few days, but the best option for now seems to be to go to my aunt in Bath."

"Then we will leave for Bath. Today?"

"I suppose we won't need to stay at an inn?"

"Not unless you want to," he said, unsurprised when she shook her head in response.

They would likely arrive in Bath by nightfall.

Acton had never experienced such profound disappointment.

# CHAPTER 10

Though they were only patronizing the inn for a short time while they awaited their coach, the Traveler's Rest was a welcome respite after the Black Ivy. Persephone and Acton had arrived early and, after Acton had arranged for passage to Bath leaving later in the morning, ate a marvelous breakfast.

Feeling more comfortable than she had in days, Persephone allowed herself to fully relax as she curled up in the inn's cozy sitting room while waiting for the coach to be ready.

Had it really only been four days ago that she'd left her parents? It felt like a month. Part of her hoped Acton's mother's letter would arrive before they departed. Persephone would like to know if the baron and baroness had remained at Loxley Court or left after Acton did.

She still couldn't quite believe they'd gone on without her and attempted to settle the marriage contract without her present. It shouldn't have been surprising after their demand that she wed the duke and the threat that had accompanied it. In fact, their entire demeanor had changed after Pandora was compromised. They'd always been somewhat self-involved and detached, but Persephone had believed that they cared for their daughters. Until Pandora had ruined their plans for a brilliant marriage and Persephone refused to sacrifice herself to a union she didn't want.

And for what? To save their reputation and somehow bolster her father's finances? Persephone wasn't certain how that would work. She presumed he would have offered her dowry, small though it was, to Acton. Did he hope Acton would pay his debts? Or was he counting on his family connection to a duke to keep the creditors at bay? Persephone wasn't entirely sure how dire things were, but the change in their behavior—their utter desperation after what had happened to Pandora—seemed to indicate there was something serious at risk. Something beyond just their reputation.

It wasn't as if they were a prominent family. They were middling at best in Bath Society. Though her father was a baron, she suspected London would devour them whole.

Acton came into the sitting room, hat in one hand and a piece of parchment in the other. His dark auburn hair was gently tousled, making him appear more approachable and less like a duke.

"Guess what just arrived?" He held up the paper with a smile.

"Your mother's letter?"

He nodded. "Your parents left Loxley Court yesterday."

"Did she say where they went?"

"Back to Radstock Hall to oversee your recovery." He waggled his brows. "How thoughtful of them."

Persephone let out a sharp, humorless laugh. "Yes, their concern for my welfare is heartwarming." She rolled her eyes. "I'm now very glad I'm not going home." Indeed, she felt a marked relief.

"Probably for the best," he agreed solemnly. "The coach is ready when you are."

Now that Persephone had decided she wasn't returning home, she found she was eager to get to Bath. To see Pandora especially, as well as her Aunt Lucinda. She stood quickly, plucking her bonnet from the arm of the chair she'd been sitting in. "I'm ready."

"Your valise is already stowed on the coach, and I vow it will not be stolen." Acton had sent someone to secure a valise for her in which to pack the things he'd purchased for her.

"Where would I be without you?" Persephone didn't particularly want to answer that question, and she was grateful for the current situation. Things could be much worse.

"Fortunately, you don't have to contemplate that," he said, smiling as he escorted her outside.

Persephone tied her bonnet on before climbing into the coach. The interior was comfortable, with velvet cushions on the two seats facing forward and backward, windows on either side as well as the back, and a lantern that could provide illumination after dark.

They would not need the lantern as they were due to arrive in Bath before nightfall. In four or five hours, she would say farewell to Acton.

Was she really thinking of him, a duke, a rogue, an absolute scoundrel, as *Acton*?

Apparently.

How things had changed in a short time. By necessity. She'd needed him, and there was no shame or regret in it. Though, she *had* broken several of the rules she and her friends had conceived. Doing so had been necessary. Soon, she'd be in Bath, and she could put all this—and this particular rogue—behind her.

Acton climbed in and sat beside her on the forward-facing seat. He set a basket on the opposite seat. "Food for later."

"I'm not sure I'll need to eat after that breakfast," Persephone said. She was still feeling quite sated.

"Just in case." He winked at her, and Persephone's belly felt as if a butterfly had taken up residence inside.

Persephone had noticed there was a horse tied to the back of the coach. Acton had mentioned he would bring his mount along. She'd been surprised to learn his horse had been stabled at the New Inn, but then she doubted the Black Ivy could have cared for him appropriately.

She glanced out the back window just before the coach started moving. "What's your horse's name?"

"Hercules. I know, it's terribly unoriginal. But also a name like yours, from ancient stories. I take it your parents like the story of Hades and Persephone?"

"I was born in late March, so my father wanted to name me after the goddess of spring. Unfortunately, I think she's more often known as the Queen of Hell."

"I confess that is how I think of her, but not of you. Then again, you are now Persey to me." He grinned at her, and the butterfly in her abdomen flapped about wildly. "Does your sister have an ancient name?"

"Pandora."

"Was there a reason for her name too?" he asked.

"Just that it sounded pretty. My mother wanted our names to start with the same letter."

"What will your sister think of what's happened?" he asked.

Persephone had thought about that. Pandora would be livid about the way their parents had treated Persephone. "She'll be glad I didn't go through with marrying you. She didn't want me to accompany them to Loxley Court."

Thoughts of Pandora made Persephone think of what had

happened to her, which, of course, made her think of Bane, and thinking of him reminded her that he and Acton were friends. She really ought to hate Acton. She owed it to Pandora to be antagonistic.

Except Acton had done the opposite of what Bane had done—he'd stood by Persephone when she'd needed him most. Looking at Acton's profile as they bumped along in the coach, she wondered how he was such good friends with that blackguard.

Persephone steered the conversation away from Pandora. "I'm looking forward to seeing my aunt when we arrive in Bath."

"I'm glad you have someone who will give you shelter since you are uncertain you will be welcome at home." He frowned but kept his gaze straight ahead. "I am disinclined to care for your parents."

The manner in which he said that—the combination of words and tone—made her laugh. And snort. She stopped herself before she covered her mouth. It was strange to think she could be more herself with this man than with members of her immediate family.

He turned his head toward her, appearing bemused. "That was funny?"

"Probably only to me. It's just...the idea of a duke making a pronouncement like that... It struck me as terribly amusing. Particularly since it would bother them so much. They want nothing more than to elevate their position." And replenish their coffers, but she wouldn't say so. If her family became known for seeking a fortune, it would be even more difficult for her or Pandora to wed.

But if Pandora were already ruined, that wouldn't matter. Persephone sent up a silent prayer that the scandal was minimal.

Acton angled himself toward her. "What do you think

they'll do once they learn you're in Bath with your aunt? Is that your mother's or father's sister?"

"My father's sister, and I'm not sure what my parents will do. I suppose they'll try to convince me to marry you. It may be best for everyone if you sent a letter to them indicating you are not interested in making me your duchess."

His brows drew together. "If that's what you want."

"It is, thank you." Why did he seem hesitant? "Do you have any other ideas?"

He shook his head. "I don't, no. I'm sorry it has come to this for you. I'm still unclear as to why they just won't let you choose a husband."

"That, ah, hasn't been an option."

"What do you mean?"

"I've had three Seasons in Bath and no offers of marriage. It's not as if *I* can propose."

His eyes rounded. "How can that be? *Three* Seasons and you aren't married?"

She grimaced. "Ow. That stings a little."

"I'm sorry. I didn't mean to say it like that. What I meant was I can't believe you didn't have multiple marriage proposals. You're clever and funny, resourceful too. And you're certainly beautiful."

"No one has ever described me that way," she said quietly, fidgeting with her fingers and then flattening her palms against her lap.

"No one? I can't imagine why that would be." He sounded bewildered.

"The bump in my nose is wholly unattractive, and my hair can be…lackluster."

"Your hair is splendid, and that bump is incredibly enticing." Now he sounded defensive. Bless him.

"That's something my sister would say."

"Your sister is very smart. I think I'll like her."

Persephone didn't think he'd get the chance. It was best for everyone if Pandora didn't meet one of Bane's friends.

Acton yawned suddenly. He clapped his hand over his mouth and sent her a sheepish look.

"You must be exhausted," she said. "I am tired, but I have to think I got more rest than you last night. Why don't you take a nap?"

"But what if you fall asleep? I don't want to miss any of your talking."

"Did I talk last night?" she asked.

"Not that I heard."

"Well, I doubt I will sleep anyway. The last time I fell asleep in a coach, I found myself in the wrong place," she said wryly. "Granted, I had climbed into the wrong coach, but I would have noticed my mistake sooner and got out at an earlier stop."

"I am so sorry about that." He looked at her with open admiration. "Not just resourceful, but unyielding in your determination."

Persephone could get used to his compliments. And his care.

He leaned into the corner of the coach and closed his eyes, folding his arms over his chest. She would try not to watch him too closely as he slept, but it would be difficult. He was so very handsome. She realized his facial features were usually quite animated. To view him in repose was to see a different side of him. Her fingers itched to trace the angle of his cheekbone, the line of his jaw, the curve of his lips. Instead, she just stared. Then forced herself to look out the window lest he wake up suddenly and catch her enthralled.

How could she be enthralled with a man such as he? She was simply amazed that a duke had not only shown her interest but seemed to like her and find her...attractive. But then he seemed to find all women alluring. Or so it seemed. Was she really any different to him?

Probably not.

Yes, that was a better way to think of it. Safer, certainly. And easier.

Lost in thought, Persephone didn't realize the coach had slowed until they'd come to a complete stop. They were nowhere near Bath. She estimated their time in the coach at about an hour.

Acton didn't even stir. She wouldn't wake him unless it was necessary. Moving quietly to the other seat, she slid to the door. The moment she touched the handle, she froze. What if there was something wrong? Something dangerous? Perhaps they'd been stopped by a highwayman.

Wouldn't she have heard shouting or something? She shook her head and rolled her eyes at Acton. *He'd* put such thoughts in her head by warning her against things such as bad men and rats.

Still, she'd wait until the coachman came to the door.

After a moment, he did, rapping on the wood. "Your Grace?"

Now Acton did rouse, his eyelids fluttering. Blinking, he unfolded his arms and lifted his head.

"We've stopped," Persephone said. "The coachman is outside."

Acton wiped his hand over his face, then opened the door. "What's happened?"

The coachman's face was creased into worried lines. "One of the horses threw a shoe."

"Damn." Acton's face mirrored the coachman's. "Let me see." He climbed down, then offered his hand to Persephone.

"I'm not a farrier, Your Grace," the coachman said nervously. "I'll have to go to the nearest town and fetch one."

She followed them toward the front of the coach and

watched as the coachman indicated the horse. It wasn't difficult to see which one was missing a shoe since he was favoring that leg.

Acton stroked the animal's neck. "That's no good, my boy. But we'll set you to rights in no time." He turned to the coachman. "Any idea how far the nearest village is?"

"Just a few miles."

"Good thing we have my horse. You ride him into the village and find a farrier." Acton reached into his coat and pulled out several coins. "Pay him that and tell him the Duke of Wellesbourne requests his aid."

"Right away, Your Grace." The coachman went to the horse and murmured soothing words before hurrying to the back of the coach and untying Hercules, who'd been saddled in case Acton had wanted to ride part of the way. "I'll be back before you know I'm gone."

"We'll be fine," Acton said, waving as the coachman rode off. Returning to the horse, Acton whispered, "We'll get you sorted. Looks like the coachman knows what he's about. No damage done, eh?"

"The horse is all right?" Persephone asked. She knew how to ride, but was woefully uneducated in the overall care of horses.

"Seems to be. Looks as though the coachman stopped right away, so the horse wasn't shoeless for too long. That's when problems happen. I would have hated to see that." He continued to pet the horse. "He's a sweet lad, aren't you?"

Persephone couldn't help smiling at the way he coddled the horse. "You're very kind. I didn't know rogues troubled themselves with caring for horses."

"We do all sorts of nonroguish things, such as read crop treatises, discuss the latest scientific discoveries, and debate the best walking sticks."

"But you can't hem a gown," she said saucily.

"So true," he replied ruefully before grinning. "Shall we wait outside for the coachman to return since we'll be cooped up in the coach for hours?"

The coach was pulled off to the side of the road, and there was a grassy area where they could sit on a blanket. There was also a hedgerow nearby, and she envisioned armed brigands leaping out and shouting, "Stand and deliver!"

"Is it safe?" she asked.

"Why wouldn't it be?"

"I'm afraid your dire warnings about danger lurking about me has made me expect the worst. When the coach stopped, I did wonder if there might be a highwayman."

"Oh no." He pressed his lips together, and it became evident he was trying not to laugh.

She swatted his arm, and the horse neighed.

"Uh-oh, now you've upset the horse," Acton said with a teasing lilt, his eyes aglow with amusement.

Persephone stroked the animal's neck. "My apologies. This man may be nice to you, but he can be positively beastly to others. Especially women."

"That isn't at all true," Acton said with continued humor. "I am merely teasing, which is something I believe *you* know all too well, Miss There's-a-rat-in-your-boot."

Giggling, Persephone went to the door of the coach. "Touché. I'll fetch a blanket so we can sit on the grass over there. Do you want anything from the basket?"

"Perhaps some ale?"

Fetching the ale and blanket, Persephone handed him the bottle while she laid the blanket over the ground. She sat, arranging her skirt, while he lowered himself near her, but not as close as they were in the coach.

Opening the ale, Acton put the bottle to his mouth, but paused before drinking. "Are there cups, or are we just drinking from the bottle?"

"No cups," she said. "But I don't need any ale." She wasn't thirsty. But she couldn't help thinking about the implications of putting her mouth where his was now as he took a drink. Did she want that? It was probably the closest to kissing him she would ever get. Not that she wanted to kiss him.

Eager to distract her wandering thoughts, she asked, "Where will you go once we reach Bath?"

"I'll spend the night at my mother's house. I should probably return to Loxley Court tomorrow. And then I'm due at a house party next week."

"That sounds nice."

"Eh, perhaps. I'm going with my mother to meet potential brides." His gaze met hers as he quickly added. "That was the plan if I decided that you and I didn't suit. Er, *we* decided. You and I, that is."

"Well, we've done that," Persephone said, not wanting to linger on that thought. "I haven't been to a house party. What's it like?"

They spent the next half hour discussing house parties and the ridiculous games that were played as well as the various activities the hostess typically planned. The sky had begun to darken as they spoke. Acton looked up. "I think it may rain. I was going to ask if you wanted me to grab the basket so we could have a light repast, but we may need to adjourn to the coach."

Persephone tipped her head up. "It does look as though it could rain," she agreed just as a drop landed on her nose. "Oh!"

"Was that a raindrop?" he asked.

"Yes." She was already scrambling to her feet.

Acton bottled the ale and jumped up. The rain began to fall more steadily. Then lightning flashed within the clouds. He snatched up the blanket as he shouted, "Go!"

Persephone dashed to the coach and quickly climbed

inside. Acton followed, handing her the ale and the blanket before hoisting himself up. He moved too quickly, though, and hit his head as he pushed in.

"Ow." He winced before collapsing on the rear-facing seat, massaging his forehead.

Persephone set the bottle and blanket aside and moved to the other seat. "Let me see."

He lowered his hand, to reveal his reddened flesh. Persephone gently touched the area. "The skin isn't broken. But it's awfully red."

"I'm blaming that chair-bed."

Bemused, she couldn't make the connection. "Why?"

"Last night, I thought I was too tall for it. Today, I thought I was short enough to make it into the coach without hitting my head."

Persephone laughed, and his gaze met and held hers.

Their faces were so close. She could see a faint freckle at the base of his nose that wasn't really visible from a noninti-mate distance.

"I love when you laugh. It's so unreserved and…real. You aren't like other young ladies. You don't simper. Or flirt. Or pretend to be anything you're not."

"Are you real?" Persephone asked. Not just him, but the things he said to her and the way he made her feel. She'd described rogues as not being genuine, and she needed to know that he was. At least now, in this moment.

"You're touching my head," he said softly, the edge of his mouth lifting. "You tell me."

She brushed her thumb over the edge of his hairline. He was *too* real. And too close. And too…tempting.

"Move away now, or I'm going to kiss you," he whispered, his lips nearly touching hers.

Persephone couldn't retreat. She was utterly entranced by

him. Her hand caressed down the side of his face, cupping his cheek as his lips met hers.

The connection was divine. His mouth moved slowly over hers, teasing and coaxing. Soft kisses that aroused her and proved what she'd expected, that he was exemplary at this task.

His head angled, and the kisses grew longer, deeper, his lips opening against hers. She copied what he did, thinking that whatever she'd learned from past kisses was surely substandard. Then his tongue slipped past her lips, and she met it with her own. A sound reverberated low in his throat. His hand moved to her hip.

"Your Grace?"

The coachman had returned.

Persephone jumped in surprise. Acton clasped her hip. "Careful. Don't hit your head," he murmured, smiling. This was a different smile. It contained his usual amusement and cheer, but there was also a sultry quality, a promise of what could have come next had they not been interrupted.

She wasn't sure if she was disappointed or relieved. Probably both.

Acton opened the door partway as Persephone settled herself on the other seat. "Found the farrier, then?"

"I did. Hopefully, this rain will let up shortly. Then he can replace the shoe, and we'll be on our way."

"Well done, thank you." Acton closed the door and leaned back against the squab, his gaze trained on her. "I suppose now we just wait. What should we do?"

Persephone was fairly certain what he wanted. She'd glimpsed the rigid length of him in his breeches. She wasn't going to allow more kissing—or anything else. "You said you wanted to eat." She reached for the basket next to him and pulled it onto her lap. She'd ride all the way to Bath with it there as a barrier between them. "Let's eat."

"What if I'd rather continue kissing you?"

She couldn't look at him. Opening the basket, she pulled out a small hand pie. "That was a mistake. Please let's not discuss it." She shot him a dark look.

He exhaled. "I hope you won't regret that."

What a pompous thing to say.

She hoped she wouldn't regret it either.

# CHAPTER 11

*E*very moment since kissing Persey passed as if it were a week. Between that sensation and the very real delays caused by the horse losing his shoe and the subsequent rain complicating the replacement, they did not arrive in Bath until the sun had disappeared into the horizon.

It was also past dinner, not that he was hungry, because every time he thought of Persey's lips beneath his and her tongue against his, he ate something from the basket to distract himself. It was good that they'd arrived, because he was fairly certain they were out of food.

Eating also served to divert his thoughts from his roguish behavior. For all his declarations that he wanted to change, that he *would* change, when presented with the chance to make a choice other than surrendering to a kiss, he'd done what he'd always done—behaved like a rogue.

"I'm sorry for what happened earlier," he said, breaking the silence that had reigned for much of the journey. She'd barely looked at him since they'd kissed.

"You don't need to."

"I do. I behaved just as you expected, and I was trying so hard not to."

"I am equally to blame," she said, glancing at him very briefly. "Let us forget it happened."

Acton would never do that. The memory of her lips would stay with him until his dying day.

Looking out the window, Acton recognized the spires of the abbey. He hadn't spent much time in Bath, probably because his mother and sisters had lived here and his father preferred London. He knew his mother had a house in St. James's Square which was very near the Crescent where Persey said her aunt lived.

The closer they got to the Crescent, the more unsettled Acton felt. He had no idea when he would see Persey again. Or *if* he would see her again.

"May I call on you tomorrow before I leave town?" he asked as the coach pulled into the Crescent.

She glanced at him again, but quickly averted her gaze. "It's best if you don't."

"Why? Aren't we friends?"

"Yes, but I'll be busy with my aunt. I have much to discuss with her and things to decide."

He could understand that, but he sensed there was something more, that she was hiding something. She'd never been completely honest about why she wouldn't even consider marrying him. Why she would risk her reputation—and more—to avoid him? He knew what she thought of his reputation and his friends, and that one of his friends had possibly done something specific to form her aversion. Still, it hurt, especially now that he knew her.

As the coach came to a stop in front of her aunt's house, he realized he wanted to be worthy of her. He just wasn't sure how.

"I hope things go well for you," she said, sitting straighter. "At your mother's house, I mean."

He'd told Persey earlier that he'd never visited and then abruptly changed the subject to something inane. Had that been when they'd discussed their favorite syllabubs?

The door opened, and Acton climbed out of the coach. He held his hand up to help Persey. Her gaze met his—fleetingly —before she put her hand in his. The urge to pull her close, to kiss her again, was overwhelming, but she pulled from his grip as soon as her feet touched the pavement.

"I'll walk you to the door," he offered.

The coachman had her valise in hand.

"That isn't necessary," she said with a brisk nod. Taking the valise from the coachman, she thanked him for a splendid journey and congratulated him on his management of the horseshoe incident. The coachman returned to the horses, leaving Acton and Persey alone on the pavement.

She turned to face Acton, but still didn't quite meet his eyes. "I can't thank you enough for your help. I will repay you for the gifts you gave me."

He silently begged her to look at him. "I won't accept a thing, so don't even try."

"I should have known you would say that. Goodbye, Acton."

As she turned and went up the steps to the door, he said, "Good night, not goodbye, Persey."

The door opened, and Acton glimpsed a butler before it closed. Then he was alone in the night, wishing he'd said something more.

But what?

Attempting his best scowl and wondering if Droxford would approve, he went back to the coach for the short ride to St. James's Square. Acton felt strange going to his mother's house, but she'd been trying to get him to visit since coming back into his life nearly a year ago. She definitely wouldn't mind him staying there.

Still, he could go to the White Hart Inn.

The coach stopped in front of his mother's house in St. James's Square. After instructing the coachman on where to find the mews to stable his horse, Acton took his valise and walked up to the door.

He knocked, and a smartly dressed butler answered the door. Acton had expected he would wear Wellesbourne livery, but he did not. The man looked to be in his late fifties and was nearly the same height as Acton's six feet. He had light gray hair and shockingly dark, bushy eyebrows. His blue eyes surveyed Acton with extreme discernment.

"You must be His Grace."

Acton hadn't sent word ahead. But he should have. Damn, he'd been too focused on Persey. "Yes. How did you know?"

The butler very slightly pursed his lips. "There's a portrait of you in your mother's sitting room."

She had a portrait of him? "Is it recent?" Acton hadn't sat for a painting for several years.

"Recent enough that you look the same. I believe it was painted about four years ago."

Yes, that was about the last time. However, that painting had hung in his father's study in London. Acton had taken it down because it was odd to look at himself on the wall. Now, he wasn't sure where it was. Had it somehow found its way here? "Has she had it that long?" he asked.

The butler's brow wrinkled ever so slightly then smoothed immediately. "Certainly."

Were there two portraits?

"Would you care to come inside?" the butler asked, giving Acton an expectant look.

"Ah, yes. Thank you. I'm staying for the night. I hope it's

not too much trouble. I should have sent notice before arriving."

"It's no trouble at all."

"Thank you, er—" Acton had no idea of the butler's name and felt bad about that.

"I am Simmons." He inclined his head.

"It's a pleasure to meet you, Simmons. I do appreciate you accommodating me."

"It is our pleasure, sir. Your sisters are in the drawing room. I'm afraid dinner has concluded. Shall I have a plate prepared for you?"

His sisters? "No, thank you. I ate, ah, earlier." He couldn't even fit a biscuit down his gullet. "You say my sisters are here? Both of them?"

"Indeed."

"Are their husbands here too?" Acton hadn't seen his sisters in several years and thought it might be less awkward if their spouses were in attendance.

"They are not."

So much for that notion.

"Very good. Thank you, Simmons."

The butler motioned to a footman, who came and took Acton's valise. "You'll be staying on the second floor. I regret to inform you that Lady Donovan is using your mother's room, which is the largest."

"I am happy to stay wherever you put me," Acton said with a smile.

"It's in the southwest corner—the green room. If you don't mind giving us a few minutes to prepare things… perhaps you could visit with your sisters in the drawing room?"

He *should*. And he supposed he must, especially since he couldn't go directly to his room. Blast, he definitely should have gone to the White Hart. Was it too late to go?

Probably.

He forced another smile and decided he'd never suffered such difficulty with it before now. "I'll go up now."

Simmons nodded, and Acton went straight through the entry hall to the staircase hall at the back of the house. Climbing the stairs, his feet felt leaden. What did one say to sisters one hadn't seen in, what, six years? They were both married now, and he hadn't even attended their weddings. His father had gone, of course. He'd said it wasn't necessary for Acton to be there. Indeed, on both occasions, he'd sent Acton to conduct business at one of his other estates. It was as if he hadn't *wanted* Acton to be there.

Acton hadn't ever thought of it that way until now.

Taking a deep breath just outside the doorway to what he felt certain was the drawing room, he rolled his shoulders back and summoned his most charming smile. Wait, why hadn't Simmons announced him?

Ah well, it was too late now.

He stepped into the drawing room. His sisters were sitting together, each in her own chair, in a seating area near the hearth. One was doing needlework and the other was drawing. They were the perfect portrait of feminine domestic bliss.

"Good evening, sisters." The word "sisters" tasted strange on his tongue.

Their heads snapped up. Francesca, who was older and now Lady Donovan, had dark red hair and a sharp nose. He remembered her being tall and willowy, like their mother. Cecily was two years younger. She'd been an infant when their mother had taken her and Francesca away. Her hair was dark auburn like his, but with more red than he possessed. And her eyes were a stunning hazel, the green nearly overwhelming the brown.

"Loxley?" Cecily said, blinking in disbelief.

"Wellesbourne," Francesca corrected, her eyes narrowing slightly. "An easy mistake since we haven't seen him since he inherited the dukedom."

Cecily lifted a shoulder. "We rarely see him at all."

Were they speaking *to* him? He wasn't sure.

"I hope you are both well," he said evenly, wondering when it would be acceptable to retreat.

Francesca put down her needlework and fixed him with an expectant stare. "Pardon me for not prevaricating, but why are you here? We weren't expecting you."

"Er, no. I didn't send word. I didn't realize there would be anyone in residence." Why did he feel defensive? "I was, ah, traveling with a friend, and we found ourselves in Bath. Given the lateness of the hour, I thought I'd stay here tonight. I'll be returning to Loxley Court tomorrow."

"Aren't you supposed to be meeting a potential bride?" Cecily asked. She'd set her pencil down on the small angled drawing table in front of her.

They knew about that? He supposed their mother had informed them. "I was supposed to, yes, but she took ill." It was easiest—and best—to continue with the lie. He certainly wasn't going to reveal that *she* had been his traveling companion.

"It's odd to have you here," Francesca said, looking as uncomfortable as he felt.

"Well, I don't want to cause a scandal," he said with a laugh, trying to bring some humor to lighten the mood.

Cecily waved her hand. "Nothing will eclipse the current scandal sweeping through town." She cocked her head and looked directly at him. "Aren't you friends with Banemore?"

Acton's gut clenched. "What has he done? Or purported to have done, anyway."

Francesca somehow managed to look down her nose at

Acton. "He ruined a young lady and probably her entire family. I daresay there isn't anything 'purported' about it."

"Such a cad to behave like that while betrothed to someone else." Cecily shook her head.

Acton was confused. Bane wasn't betrothed. At least he hadn't been a fortnight ago. Acton had traveled with him and a couple of other friends to Weston. He'd spent the night at the Duke of Henlow's retreat, the Grove, before departing to meet another friend in Wales.

"There has to be a mistake or, more likely, this is just asinine gossip with no basis in reality." Acton knew Bane could be the worst among them when it came to taking liberties with young ladies, but he would never overstep. That wasn't precisely true. He would just hope to not be caught. Cold sweat dappled the back of Acton's neck

Francesca angled herself more fully toward him. "He was *seen*—by Mrs. Lawler—in a compromising embrace with a young woman. There is no mistake." Her voice had risen.

"But he isn't betrothed," Acton said, feeling even more defensive, and this wasn't even about him. "Perhaps Mrs. Lawler was confused, and Bane is going to marry *that* young lady. The one he was with." That made more sense. Bane wouldn't turn his back on someone if he'd been caught in a situation like that.

Cecily also pivoted to face him directly. "Banemore very plainly told Mrs. Lawler that he was *not* going to marry the woman he'd been caught with because he was already betrothed. As I said, he's a cad."

There was no way Bane would be that callous. And he wasn't betrothed! Even if he were, he would have married the woman he'd compromised instead. What a mess if that were the case. In either scenario, a young lady would be maligned by Society. Still, Acton had to think the compromised young woman would fare worse.

"There must be some explanation," Acton said calmly. He would write to his friend first thing tomorrow. Except Acton wasn't entirely sure where Bane was at present. He realized he'd see Bane next week at the house party. Or would he? Perhaps Bane wouldn't be there with all this going on. Perhaps he'd even be married? Acton would track down one of their friends—Somerton didn't live far away—and determine the truth.

"There is," Francesca stated firmly. "Bane is a blackguard."

Acton frowned. No, perhaps it was a scowl! Droxford would be proud. "You shouldn't believe everything you hear."

"Of course you would say that," Cecily said. "Your reputation isn't much better."

Francesca crossed her arms over her chest, her gaze narrowing slightly. "All you rakes stay together. Is it an organized club, or do you just flock together like libidinous birds?"

Acton's sisters stared at him expectantly. Was that supposed to be an actual question?

"Er, no. Not all my friends are rakes." He grimaced, realizing how bad that sounded.

"Give them time," Francesca said.

"Honestly, you can't believe everything you hear," he repeated. "If you got to know me, you'd see I'm a good person. I'm not a blackguard."

"We didn't say you were, but having a close friend like Banemore doesn't recommend you," Cecily said. "You know who's a good person? Miss Barclay. She didn't ask to be ruined by your friend."

"Indeed," Francesca agreed. "She is the only one in this situation who deserves sympathy."

Acton barely heard what Francesca said. His brain echoed with the name *Miss Barclay*. Good God, had Bane ruined Persey? Acton would throttle him.

This explained so much. Persey's extreme dislike of him and rejection of Acton's offers for help. Her need to marry quickly and her parents' desire to ensure that happened. Bane should be the one to marry her. Had he made up a fake betrothal to avoid doing so? Acton couldn't see him doing that, but at the moment, the only thing he could plainly see was red.

He didn't remember the last time he'd been so upset. So angry.

Yes, he did. And it was recently. When that brigand had attacked Persey. He had an overwhelming urge to return to Gloucester, hunt the man down, and drag him to the magistrate. He was quite furious with himself for not doing so. He'd just wanted to keep Persey safe, and that meant staying with her.

He didn't have that excuse now.

He could leave first thing tomorrow and find Bane. Then he'd force the blackguard to do the right thing.

So now he agreed with his sisters that Bane was a blackguard? How quickly he'd changed his mind when the young woman he'd ruined was someone he knew. Someone he cared about. Someone who deserved far better than to be tossed aside.

Cecily leaned toward Francesca and whispered, "Is he rethinking his position?"

Though she spoke softly, Acton could hear her and was certain she'd meant him to. "I am," he responded slowly. "You must excuse me. I am sorry to have troubled you this evening. I know this is awkward...being together."

Francesca clasped her hands in her lap. "That doesn't mean it's wrong. We should have been more welcoming."

Acton nodded vaguely. "I should have sent word ahead that I was coming."

"You didn't know we were here," Cecily said. "And if you

had—known we were here and sent a note—we would have told you to come." She glanced toward Francesca, who gave a slight nod.

Well, that was nice, he supposed. It wasn't that he didn't like them. He just didn't know them. And when his father had died, they were both already wed, living their own lives. While his mother had attempted to form a relationship with him, nothing had transpired between him and his sisters. Perhaps they ought to remedy that.

"As it happens, I may want to stay another day." That way, he could visit Persey tomorrow and find out what had actually happened. Then he could go in search of Bane. "If that would be all right with you."

The sisters exchanged looks, and Cecily spoke first. "That would be nice. You can show us how you are not a rake." She smiled, and Acton relaxed slightly. He really hoped they had senses of humor.

"Doubtful he can do that in a day," Francesca added wryly.

"I suppose that's true," Cecily said in agreement. "But it's a good start."

Yes, it was. "I'll see you in the morning, then." He gave them a courtly bow before departing.

He made his way upstairs to the room the butler had directed him to. Upon entering, he was struck with how much he liked it. Green was his favorite color, and the room was decorated in several hues. He felt welcome and at home. Indeed, the bedclothes reminded him of his room at Loxley Court.

There was a desk and a bookshelf in one of the corners, along with a cozy, dark green chair. He imagined sitting there reading, the nearby window offering a view of the lawn and trees in the center of the square.

Moving to the bookcase, he pulled out a few books. They

were among his favorites. There was also a carved cat. He picked it up and stroked the smooth black stone. The action triggered a memory of a black cat, of stroking its soft fur. He had dark yellow eyes. And his name had been Domino. What had ever happened to him? Acton realized the memory was from before his mother had left. Perhaps she'd taken the cat with her.

Pensive, he set the cat down and turned to survey the rest of the room. There was an armoire, a hearth with a low fire, another chair, the bed, a side table, and a dresser with all its drawers. But did they stick?

A smile would have come as he recalled his banter with Persey, but thinking of her made him agitated. He considered going back to the Crescent right now to see her.

It was too late, though, and she could very well have retired after their day of travel. Not to mention how early they'd arisen due to the rat situation.

How long ago that suddenly felt.

Tomorrow would have to be soon enough to speak with her. He would try not to arrive too early.

~

*P*ersephone did not look back toward Acton until the door to Aunt Lucinda's house was closed. Then she cast a glance toward the portal and thought of Acton on the other side, climbing into the coach and traveling the short distance to St. James's Square. He was so close, and yet he might as well have been in London.

Shaking her head as if she needed to clear cobwebs away, she handed her valise to the footman who'd answered the door. "Thank you, Davis. Are my aunt and sister still awake?"

"Certainly, miss. They're in the drawing room."

"Wonderful." She gave him a warm smile before going

upstairs. Having stayed with Aunt Lucinda multiple times each year for as long as she could remember, Persephone knew the house as well as Radstock Hall. In many ways, it was dearer to her. She and Pandora had shared a good deal of happy times with their aunt, who had no children of her own.

She paused at the threshold of the drawing room and smiled. Pandora lounged on a settee reading a book, and Aunt Lucinda was seated next to a lantern perusing a newspaper.

Stepping inside, Persephone gave a little cough. "Good evening."

"Persey!" Pandora jumped up from the settee and tossed the book aside before barreling toward her. She wrapped Persephone in a fierce hug. "What are you doing here? Tell me, what happened at Loxley Court?" She pulled away and grimaced. "Are you betrothed?" Her face paled. "Are Mama and Papa here too?"

Aunt Lucinda swept toward them. Elegant as always, with her stunning red gown and her golden-brown hair styled impeccably with ruby combs, she looked as if she were going out instead of staying at home with her niece. "Pandora, let her breathe. Persey, I can't imagine your parents are here or they'd be with you. Which raises many questions, but since your sister has already bombarded you with several, you must answer hers first." She put her arm around Persephone and gave her a squeeze. "Come, Persey." She'd started using Pandora's nickname shortly after it had been instituted. Besides Pandora, she was the only one who called her that.

And now Acton.

Or he had, when they'd been acquainted. They weren't any longer. At least, that was what she was telling herself.

"I am not betrothed." Persephone took her sister's hand, and they walked to the settee, where they sat down together.

Aunt Lucinda returned to the chair opposite the settee. "You and the duke didn't suit?"

Persephone braced herself for their reactions. "I didn't even meet him. Indeed, I didn't even make it all the way to Loxley Court."

Pandora gasped. "What do you mean?"

"I realized I couldn't marry the duke, so what was the point in even meeting him? I left Mama and Papa in Cirencester."

Again, Pandora gasped. "You just *left?*"

"I did leave them a note that I'd returned to Radstock Hall."

"And did you?" Aunt Lucinda asked. "You would have left them some days ago, and it wouldn't have taken you that long to get here."

Persephone considered telling them she had gone home before deciding to come here but decided it would be too easy for them to discover the lie.

"It's such a ridiculous tale." Persephone stalled a moment as she tried to think of what she could say. She couldn't make any mention of taking the wrong coach, her stolen valise, the violent brigand, the rats, and most certainly not the rogue.

Rogue?

Perhaps he wasn't that to her anymore. Regardless, he was in the past, and she was best off forgetting him entirely.

"Is that a new gown?" Pandora asked. "I don't remember it."

"Um, yes. I had to buy it because I left Cirencester without a thing," Persephone fibbed. "I stole away before dawn and had to be quiet as I was sleeping just a few feet from Mama and Papa."

Pandora's brow creased. "Did something happen to the gown you were wearing?"

"It got very soiled. Thankfully, I was able to have it cleaned at the inn where I stayed in Gloucester."

"That's where you went, then," Aunt Lucinda said. "Why didn't you come back here?"

"I wanted to, but I thought it best to depart on the first coach leaving Cirencester that morning, and it took me to Gloucester. Then there were issues with transportation that prevented me from arriving until this evening. It's been one thing after another," she said wearily. "Today the horse threw a shoe on the way."

"Goodness, this all sounds expensive," Aunt Lucinda surmised. "However did you pay for everything?"

"I took along my pin money." Not enough to pay for all that, but Aunt Lucinda wouldn't know. Indeed, the reason she had a decent amount of pin money at all was because Aunt Lucinda gave her and Pandora money at Yuletide and on their birthdays.

Aunt Lucinda gave her an approving smile, her slender brows slanting gently. "Such a clever girl."

"I can't believe you managed to do all that on your own." Pandora blinked. "I mean, I can believe it, but it's fortunate you are unharmed."

"I have been very fortunate." All thanks to Acton. That acknowledgment would have annoyed her a few days ago, but now she was incredibly grateful he'd come after her.

"I'm so glad you came to your senses about marrying the duke." Pandora gave her a sheepish, apologetic look. "I'm so sorry I was terrible when you agreed to go with Mama and Papa. I just didn't want you to sacrifice your future for my mistake."

"It wasn't a mistake," Persephone said vehemently. "You were swindled. You thought that blackguard loved you and had every reason to expect he would marry you. That he didn't do either of those things is *his* mistake, not yours."

"Why did you come here instead of going home?" Aunt Lucinda asked. "Not that I'm sorry to have you here. You know you are always welcome."

"Which is precisely why I came to you," Persephone said with a fleeting smile. She hated repeating what the baron and baroness had said to her, but couldn't keep it secret, not when she had to decide what to do without their support. "They told me if I didn't marry Wellesbourne that I would no longer have a place in their household. Why would I go home knowing that?"

Pandora sucked in a breath. "Oh, Persey, they are more monstrous than I ever imagined they could be. How can they treat you that way?"

There was no answer for that, so Persephone didn't even try to provide one.

Aunt Lucinda let out a soft but very unladylike curse. "My brother is a great ass. Sometimes I can scarcely believe Hugh and I are related. I'm so glad you've come here, my dear," she said to Persephone with a warm smile. "We'll sort this out. Do you know what you want to do next?"

Persephone thought of her encounter with the headmistress at the West Gloucester Day School for Girls. "Not really, but I have been considering some things."

"This isn't right!" Pandora said. "You shouldn't have to plan a future without support from our parents."

Aunt Lucinda settled her calm gaze on Pandora. "It's all right, dear. Neither Persey nor you will need to go off and find your way without help. Both of you will always have a place here."

"Thank you," Persephone murmured past the lump in her throat. She ought to have realized Aunt Lucinda would look out for them. But Persephone wondered if she was simply at a point where it was difficult to see past the pain of disappointment and lost expectation.

"I can't stay here," Pandora said sharply. She looked to Aunt Lucinda. "You are already suffering."

Persephone looked from her sister to Aunt Lucinda. "What does she mean?"

Waving a hand, Aunt Lucinda looked unconcerned, which was completely at odds with Pandora's demeanor. "Do I look like I'm suffering?" Her mouth tipped into a lopsided smile.

"You make light of it, but I'm a walking plague. No one wants to be around me, and you shouldn't either." Pandora stood and stalked from the room.

Persephone started to rise but Aunt Lucinda gestured for her to stay. "Let her be. She is not seeing things in the best light right now, which is to be expected. She's had her world turned upside down. As have you. I really could smack my brother. I suppose we should let him and your mother know you are here."

But then they would almost certainly come here, and Persephone didn't want to see them. They would likely drag her back to Loxley Court. Or somewhere else she could be forced to marry someone who would satisfy their needs.

Not wanting to think about that, Persephone scooted forward on the settee. "Tell me the truth about what's happening here with Pandora, please."

Aunt Lucinda exhaled, and right away, Persephone could see that it wasn't as rosy as their aunt would have Pandora believe. "It's not going that well, I suppose. She's only been here a handful of days, but the one time she left the house— the day after she arrived—she was given the cut direct on the street. She was, understandably, upset and hasn't left the house since."

Persephone's heart ached for her sister. "It's not fair. I'm sure no one is treating Bane like that."

"Perhaps. He's received a fair amount of criticism, particularly since he claims to be betrothed. No one knows who this other woman is, however."

"Good. No betrothed gentleman should behave as he did." Persephone couldn't see Acton doing that, once again illustrating that there was a difference among rogues. Shades of roguery, she supposed. Refocusing on her aunt, she said, "Perhaps we should leave town for a while." She thought of visiting Tamsin in Cornwall or Gwen in Bristol and immediately rejected the latter. It was too close to Bath and the gossip about Pandora was likely already there. Had it made its way to London? If so, Pandora would be well and truly ruined.

Persephone hoped Bane would suffer more than Pandora was bound to. Mayhap his betrothed would terminate their marriage agreement.

"I was thinking the same thing," Aunt Lucinda said. "I've a friend in Kent we could stay with."

"What if we went to our friend Tamsin in Cornwall?" Persephone suggested.

Aunt Lucinda's eyes lit. "That's a splendid idea. That would be good for Pandora. And for you."

"You are always so kind." Persephone stopped herself from asking why she couldn't have been their mother. "Is it true that you aren't affected by this?" Persephone would hate that. "And be honest, please."

"I wasn't lying when I said I wasn't suffering. It doesn't bother me to have fewer invitations. It also helps me see which people are my true friends." Aunt Lucinda flicked a speck of something from her skirt. "That said, there are very few who would allow me to pay a social call along with Pandora. They've suggested that time needs to pass for the gossip to settle."

But how much time? Would they need to stay away weeks or months? Years? Perhaps it was best if Persephone and

Pandora faded into spinsterhood. They could find a cozy cottage in Cornwall near Tamsin. She lived in a rather remote place. No one would have heard of Pandora's scandal.

Persephone didn't want to think of it like that. This was *Bane's* scandal.

The exhaustion of the day combined with worry about Pandora suddenly overwhelmed Persephone. "I think I need to retire. It's been a very long journey."

"Indeed it has." Aunt Lucinda rose as Persephone did and gave her a quick but warm hug. "You've endured a great deal, both from your parents and whatever happened while you were gone. I can't imagine there was *nothing* interesting or exciting to share." She arched a brow at Persephone.

"Nothing you'd want to hear about," she said cryptically. "Truly, everything went as well as one could hope. I am the same as when I left Radstock Hall."

That wasn't at all true. The time she'd spent with Acton had been singular. And the kisses they'd shared were magical. She would not think about another broken rogue rule.

Anyway, those weren't the things that mattered, and all that was behind her now. She had no hope for a future marriage and had to accept she would likely live a sedate existence in a remote locale. At least she would have Pandora.

Except that wasn't a balm. It only made Persephone feel worse, for Pandora had wanted a husband and a family more than Persephone. She deserved that.

There had to be a way to fix things for Pandora. Persephone couldn't bear to see her suffer. She'd do whatever was necessary to see her sister happy.

# CHAPTER 12

*D*espite troubling thoughts of Persey in Bane's arms, Acton managed to find rest. He'd dreamed of her, not with Bane, but with him. Acton had relived their kisses and mayhap gone a bit further than that.

He was just glad it was morning and that he could finally call on Persey. It was imperative he get to the heart of whatever Bane had done and rectify the situation. Acton was not going to allow Persey to be ruined.

He joined his sisters in the dining room and was surprised to see that Cecily was with child. Last night, she'd been seated, and he hadn't noticed. Today, as she stood and went to the sideboard to fetch another piece of toast, he noted the swell of her belly.

Should he say something? He wanted to, but he also didn't want to make her uncomfortable. It wasn't as if they had a close relationship.

"Yes, Cecily is carrying," Francesca said with a half smile. "I can see you noticed. Just as I can see that you're weighing whether to say anything."

"Aren't you astute?" he said with a quick smile. "I don't wish to overstep. But I do offer my congratulations, Cecily."

"Thank you," Cecily responded as she returned to her seat. "The baby should arrive around the new year."

Acton wanted to ask if this was her first. Shouldn't he know if he was an uncle? He suddenly felt quite awful. "It occurs to me that I have not been a good brother. I, ah—" He'd been about to say that he'd long believed they didn't care to get to know him, but he wasn't sure he believed that. His father had told him that his mother preferred to live apart, and they'd agreed it was best for the girls to be with her and for Acton to be with their father. Their parents had made the decisions, and they'd had to go along with them.

"You what?" Francesca prodded.

"I would like to know you better," he said, realizing it was true. He was glad they were here, that his surprise trip to Bath had brought them together, for however long. "I'm embarrassed to say I don't even know if either of you already has children. I think Francesca might, but I'm not certain." He lowered his gaze to his plate, which he'd filled before sitting down. He didn't want to see what was sure to be disappointment or hurt in their eyes. It occurred to him that not knowing his sisters, their husbands, or their children certainly qualified him as a rogue, at least in the way Persey had described one.

"I do have a son and a daughter," Francesca said. "He is four and she is nearly two."

"I have a daughter, Georgie, who is two," Cecily added as she spread jam on her toast.

"I'm so sorry I didn't know that. And that I haven't met them." As with his other behavior, he resolved to change that. Just because he hadn't known his sisters didn't mean he shouldn't know their children. In fact, it meant the opposite.

He should ensure he not only knew them but treated them as family. "They aren't here, are they?"

"No, my children are at home near Salisbury," Francesca replied.

"And my daughter is also at home, which is near Andover. In case you didn't know." Cecily said the last without rancor.

Sadly, he hadn't known. "I should like to meet them, as well as your husbands." Actually, he'd met Donovan in London. A few years older than Acton, he was a viscount and heir to a marquessate. Acton didn't think he'd met Fairhope. If he recalled, the man was from Yorkshire. Indeed, why were he and his wife living in Hampshire? Perhaps they owned a property there and chose it as their primary residence so the sisters could live near one another. "Do you live close to each other on purpose?" he asked.

"Yes," Cecily said. "We're very close."

Somehow, that simple statement sliced through his heart and left a terrible ache. His father's voice sounded in his brain and told him to ignore such feminine feelings.

"Are you leaving after breakfast, then?" Francesca asked before sipping her tea.

"Actually, I was hoping I might stay another day or two. If you don't mind."

"It's Mama's house, and she'd probably want you to stay." *Probably.* "We'll be here another five days or so. We just came for a week to shop and see friends."

Acton couldn't help thinking that when he got together with his friends, they played billiards and cards, typically wagering on all of it, and went out to social gatherings or clubs. There was a great deal of competition. Who would drink the most or win the most, among other things. Thinking about it, Bane, as the unofficial leader of their set, was often the driving force. Was it possible he occasionally pushed too far? Had he done that with Persey? Acton felt disgusted, not just with Bane, but with himself. He would do better. Starting with how he treated Persey.

Again, he felt badly for kissing her. And yet, she'd said they were both at fault. Was it wrong to kiss her if she wanted him to? It wasn't as if he had *no* intention of marrying her. He froze. Would he consider wedding her? He would, he realized. Just as he knew she was committed to avoiding being leg-shackled to him.

Acton was desperate to see her, to learn the truth about what had happened with Bane. "I'll just stay another day," he said. "Perhaps two. I've a few things to see to," he added vaguely, hoping they wouldn't ask him for specifics. "In fact, I need to make a call." He stood, his breakfast unfinished.

"At this hour?" Francesca asked in surprise.

It was early, but he didn't care. He couldn't wait any longer. "I need to check on my horse first, and I'll probably take a walk before paying my call. See you both later."

Acton fetched his hat and gloves and hastened from the house. But he did not go to the mews. He walked briskly to the Crescent. A compact butler with graying dark brown hair and spectacles greeted Acton.

"Good morning," Acton said. "I'm here to see Miss Persephone Barclay."

"I am sorry, but she is not receiving." The butler glanced toward a tall clock in the hall, as if to ask whether Acton knew the hour.

Yes, it was bloody early for calls. He didn't care. He smiled with all the charm he could muster through his worry. "I am the Duke of Wellesbourne."

"Be that as it may, Your Grace, Miss Barclay is not receiving." The butler spoke plainly, but with a grave authority that was impressive given his slight stature.

"Allow me to speak more clearly. I *need* to see Miss Barclay. It's a matter of urgency."

The butler's lips flattened into a thin line. He appeared utterly unmoved. However, before he could refuse Acton a third time, a woman came into the entry hall behind him.

"Who is calling at such a ghastly hour?" she asked.

"His Grace, the Duke of Wellesbourne, ma'am." the butler replied.

The woman, who had to be Persey's aunt, was elegantly outfitted from the sleek style of her light brown hair to the velvet-trimmed morning gown. Her green eyes swept over him with assessing precision. When her gaze met his, she arched a brow with open curiosity.

*Hell.* Acton hadn't considered seeing anyone but Persey. What was he going to say was the reason for his urgent call?

"I see," she murmured to no one in particular. "Duke, while it is a pleasure to see you, I must wonder why you are here and at this time."

"He has an urgent matter to discuss with Miss Barclay," the butler said.

Her finely shaped brow remained in its elevated position. "Oh? Why don't you come in for a short visit," Lucinda invited.

The butler opened the door wider, and Acton stepped inside.

"Give Harding your things," she directed before pivoting toward the stair hall.

Acton pulled off his gloves and gave them, along with his hat, to the butler. "Thank you, Harding."

Harding's expression was unreadable, and Acton was nearly certain the butler found him lacking somehow.

Following Lucinda into the stair hall, Acton scrambled to think of what he could say if Persey's aunt was going to be present for their conversation. Presumably, she would be. Their days of being alone together were behind them.

He would have to pretend he was there to see if he could

negotiate something on Bane's behalf. Except, he didn't even know what Bane had done or what Bane was doing now. Acton could very well cock things up even more.

Lucinda led him into the drawing room, a sumptuously decorated chamber that revealed the woman's exceptionally fine taste as well as her wealth. The large chandelier in the center of the room was breathtaking.

She turned to face him. "You find the chandelier attractive?"

"It's stunning."

"William Parker designed it. He also designed the ones hanging in the Upper Rooms. Perhaps you've seen those?"

He had not. "I haven't been to the Upper Rooms."

"How is that possible? A man of your stature? There are two balls each week when the Season starts in October. You should attend one or two." She gave him an assessing look. "I would think you ought to be married by now. You ought to broaden your search to Bath. But mayhap that is why you are here." Her lips curved into a charming smile.

Of course! He and Persephone were supposed to see if they would suit. "That is precisely why I've come."

Lucinda tapped her finger to her lip before holding it up briefly. "I must wonder how you even know Persephone is here?"

Well, fuck. How would he know indeed? If anything, he would think she was at home because she was ill and that was where her parents had left her. That was the answer, then. "Her parents arrived at Loxley Court without her and explained she was ill. I decided to call on her at Radstock Hall. However, she wasn't there, so I thought I would see if she was here." This all sounded completely preposterous. And it could very well conflict with whatever Persey had told her. What had he been thinking coming here?

"I'm surprised you would even think to look here,"

Lucinda mused.

"Er, my mother suggested it," he lied.

There was a long pause before Lucinda gave a single nod. It was as if she'd considered his fabrications and was trying to decide if she believed him. "That makes sense."

It might make some small modicum of sense, but he wasn't convinced she was persuaded.

Before he had to conjure more lies, Persey appeared in the doorway. She wore a pink morning gown that was a couple of years out of style. Still, she looked lovely, her dark golden hair swept back from her face but not pinned. Wearing the waves of her hair loose made her look more carefree. Or perhaps she had simply relaxed since arriving here. That would make sense.

"Aunt Lucinda?" Persey said, moving slowly into the room.

Lucinda smiled. "There you are, Persey. You've a guest this morning. This is the Duke of Wellesbourne. The man you were to meet before you became ill."

Her aunt was privy to that tale, then. Had she been part of concocting it? No, it seemed she was not of the same mind as Persey's parents.

"What a surprise to see you here this morning," Persey said, her eyes communicating far more than her words. It was as if little fires were shooting sparks at him from the depths of her blue gaze.

Acton bowed to her. "After you were unable to come to Loxley Court, I decided to visit you at Radstock Hall, but then I learned you were here in Bath. So I came to stay at my mother's house. That way, I would be closer for when you were feeling better. I must say, you look well."

"I am, thank you. My aunt has helped me regain my full health."

How long were they going to stand there and openly lie?

He had to resist the urge to laugh. Lucinda didn't seem to know anything about him other than the potential match between him and Persey. Presumably, Persey hadn't revealed anything about meeting him when she'd left her parents in Cirencester.

"Well, I suppose I should let you two get to know one another," Lucinda said. "I'll just sit out in the hall, leaving the door open, of course." She turned and inclined her head at Persey before leaving.

As soon as Lucinda was gone, Persey motioned from him to join her on the opposite side of the room. There was a settee angled in the corner. She perched on the edge, and he sat down beside her—not too close—facing his body toward her as best he could.

"What are you doing here?" she demanded, the fires in her eyes growing brighter.

"I came to help," he said in a low but urgent tone. "Why didn't you tell me the truth about what happened with Bane?"

Her jaw clenched. "You heard about that?"

"From my sisters—they are also staying at our mother's. It took everything I could do not to return and speak with you. I *had* to come this morning."

"You didn't have to, actually. What can you hope to do?"

"Bane needs to fix this." He had to work to keep his voice low. "I'm going to find him and demand he do what's right." Even if it bothered Acton to do so. The thought of her wedded to his best friend was unsettling.

She folded her arms over her chest, reminding him of the Persey he'd first met. "How can he do that if he's betrothed to someone else?"

"I'm not certain he is. At least, *I'm* not at all aware of it, and I just saw him a fortnight or so ago. He didn't mention a thing about marriage." And Acton would expect him to say something. If any of their set were headed for the parson's trap, there would likely be some sort of celebration—even if it was somewhat funerary in nature.

"You think Bane would tell you his plans?" she scoffed. "He seems to give little thought to others."

"I think he would tell his friends if he planned to marry. I've mentioned that I'm considering it."

"You've established you are different from Bane," she said quietly, glancing down at her lap.

Acton wanted to thrash his friend. And hug Persey. "I am so sorry he hurt you."

Her gaze snapped up. "He didn't hurt *me*."

Perplexed by that response, Acton wondered if he'd misheard her. "But he compromised you."

Her jaw dropped briefly before she put her hand to her mouth. A moment later, she dropped her hand to her lap and gave him a stern look. "Not me, my sister. Why did you think it was me?"

Relief poured through him, but his anger with Bane didn't dissipate. He was still outraged for Persey's sister. He was just damn glad it hadn't been Persey, that she hadn't been involved with Bane in any romantic way. That had bothered him more than he cared to acknowledge.

"My sister said he'd compromised Miss Barclay. I understood that to be you, but it seems my sister misspoke." He should have realized that was wrong. Persey had indicated that her dislike of Bane and his friends wasn't due to something that had happened to *her*. "I would still help your sister."

"How? Are you going to force Bane to marry her? I'm fairly certain she wouldn't agree to that. Not now. He's utterly ruined her—not just socially, but romantically. She is devastated by his treatment." She leaned slightly forward, her expression animated with outrage. "He told her he was desperate to be with her, that he adored her beyond all women. Then, when they were caught in an embrace, he said he was already betrothed. What sort of man does that?"

The sort who doesn't want to be trapped. And the sort who oversteps.

Oversteps?

Bane had gone way past that. He'd behaved inappropriately with Persey's sister while betrothed to someone else. Acton now saw how even embracing had been wrong if Bane had no intention of pursuing a courtship with Persey's sister. He'd been cruel and dishonest.

"I don't know," Acton said quietly, sitting with the discomfort of his own past attitude and behavior as well as that of a man he considered a close friend.

"Well, while you consider your friend's actions, just know that Pandora has been given the cut direct when she ventured from our aunt's house. And now Aunt Lucinda says she won't leave the house at all."

Acton tried to think of how he could help Persey's sister, but was at a loss. It seemed as though the damage was done in the eyes of Society.

Persey went on, "I imagine Bane won't suffer in the slightest." She muttered something more. It sounded like a curse.

"I'm going to find him and demand he answer for what he's done."

Her eyes rounded. "You're going to call him out?"

"Not that." While Bane might deserve a good thrashing, Acton wasn't going to duel with his best friend. Could a man still be his best friend if he went about ruining innocent young women? "But he must answer for his actions. Somehow."

"You don't think he's even betrothed," Persey said. "Was that a lie he concocted to avoid having to marry Pandora?"

"I don't know, but I'll find out. In the meantime, there has to be something I can do to help your sister's situation. Perhaps it would help for me to somehow indicate my support for her?"

She appeared skeptical, her eyes narrowing slightly. "How would that help?"

He lifted a shoulder. "I'm a duke. And Bane's friend. If I publicly support her and criticize Bane, it may ease the gossip."

Persey's brow darkened. "It would add to it. I'm not sure we want that. We may leave Bath anyway."

"Where will you go, and for how long?" He asked the question quickly, and perhaps with too much intensity.

"We aren't sure yet. And I wouldn't tell you. The last thing we need is for you or Bane to show up and bother us."

That stung. Acton understood them not wanting to see Bane, but him too? "I've been nothing but your staunchest ally."

"While that may be true, you are still a close friend of the devil incarnate."

"That remains to be seen," he said, surprising himself. "If he's done what you say, I'm not certain we will remain friendly."

"*If*... Do you doubt me?" Her voice rose.

"No. I just... This is not the man I thought I knew. I mean, he can be overly flirtatious and occasionally take a liberty here or there, as can I, but to be caught like that and turn his back on responsibility and honor is beyond the pale." He shook his head. "No, it's not just that he was caught. He should not have been in that situation to begin with, especially not if he was already betrothed."

"I'm surprised to hear you say that," she said softly.

"I'm learning. Trying to, anyway. Will you let me see if I can help, or are you thinking of leaving town immediately?"

"I'm sure Pandora will prefer the latter. Let me speak to Aunt Lucinda. Are you staying in Bath, then?" Persey was all business and concern for the matter regarding her sister—as she should be.

"For now." He would welcome the chance to play escort to her and her sister.

She hesitated a moment as she glanced toward the door and where her aunt was waiting in the hall. "What about our...situation? Are we going to pretend to see if we will suit?"

"That seems the best plan," he said, thinking it wouldn't be a hardship at all. Indeed, he already enjoyed spending time with her.

Was he actually considering they might suit? For real? It didn't matter. She'd made it clear she had no interest.

That was before they'd kissed, however.

"All right," she said. "I suppose I can pretend to consider marrying you for a short time." She made a sound of disgust in her throat that was not encouraging. "My parents will be thrilled," she said with great sarcasm, leading him to believe the prior noise was directed at them instead of having to feign a courtship with him. Her eyes glittered. "I shall take great enjoyment in ultimately telling them we will not marry."

That wasn't encouraging either. Perhaps their shared kisses hadn't affected her as much as they had him.

Persey went on, "I'll discuss staying in Bath and whether we want your help with my aunt—and with Pandora."

"I will do everything I can to mitigate the damage Bane has caused."

She fixed him with a sincere stare. "Just don't try to make him marry Pandora. Please."

Acton nodded. "If that's what you want."

"I'm sure that's what Pandora wants. At some point, she

did say to me that she wouldn't marry Bane if he were the last man alive."

That was inarguable, then. Still, Acton wanted to find out what his friend had done and why, as well as whether he was actually going to marry. He would return to his mother's house and send out several letters to Bane and their friends.

"You should go now," Persey said, rising from the settee.

Damn. He didn't want to leave. They hadn't even talked. At least about something other than this mess with her sister and Bane.

Acton stood, but didn't move away. "How are you? I trust you had a good night's rest after yesterday. It was a long day even if we hadn't traveled hours in a coach and been stranded for a while." He wondered if she'd thought of what had happened during that time as much as he had.

"I did, thank you, but only because I was thoroughly exhausted. I'm afraid I woke early this morning, and my mind went immediately to Pandora, which prevented me from sleeping any longer."

"I know how that can be." Because his first thoughts upon waking had been of Persey, and then he'd been eager to see her as soon as possible. He'd only forced himself to have breakfast so that he wouldn't arrive *too* early.

She tipped her head to the side. "We should plan something, I suppose. Perhaps a promenade in Sydney Gardens. Or we could meet for tea at the Pump Room?"

"Whatever you think is best. I can also consult with my sisters, since they are very familiar with Bath."

"They grew up here, didn't they?" Persey asked. At his nod, she continued, "Will they support what you're doing?"

He needn't tell them anything other than he was going to see if he and Persey would suit, as their mother had suggested they might. "Courting you? Why not?"

"Because my sister may be seen as a pariah." She flinched

as she said that last word, and Acton wished he could make the entire mess disappear.

"She won't be. At least that is our goal, and I'm taking it as seriously as I did protecting you." He held her gaze and couldn't help recalling how she'd felt in his arms. It was not going to be a chore to pretend to court her.

"Thank you." She looked away finally. "Now go." She started walking toward the door, and he had to go along with her.

"I'll send a note later with an invitation." He snagged Persey's arm just before they reached the door. "What is your aunt's surname?" he whispered.

"Barclay-Fiennes," Persey responded.

He released her arm, and Persey stepped into the hall. "Aunt Lucinda, the duke is leaving now."

Lucinda rose from a chair and looked to Acton. "Will we be seeing you again, Duke?"

"Most definitely, Mrs. Barclay-Fiennes. I shall look forward to it." Acton bowed to her and to Persey before taking himself back downstairs.

As he took his hat and gloves from Harding, he thought of the many things he and Persey hadn't discussed, namely if she had any idea what was going on with her parents. One thing was certain, they'd be delighted to discover that he was courting their daughter.

Well, not courting, exactly, for that would be too formal. Whatever they called it, the baron and baroness would be elated. Acton couldn't imagine Persey would find satisfaction in that, and neither would Acton.

But this was for Pandora. The time he got to spend with Persey was simply a happy benefit.

Perversely, he realized he had Bane and his roguery to thank for his association with Persey. Acton was still going to plant him a facer.

# CHAPTER 13

As soon as Acton disappeared down the stairs, Aunt Lucinda steered Persephone back into the drawing room. "How did things go with Wellesbourne?"

Persephone had been surprised and even annoyed that he'd called when she'd specifically asked him not to. However, after hearing that he'd thought she was the one Bane had compromised and seeing his outrage, she couldn't help but feel flattered. Or perhaps something more than that —the butterfly from the coach had reappeared in her belly.

Then, when he'd learned it was Pandora who was suffering, his desire to help hadn't lessened. He was even willing to pretend to court Persephone to elevate Pandora's standing.

Hopefully, that would work.

If not, Persephone and Pandora would leave Bath as soon as possible.

"Persey? Did he upset you?" Aunt Lucinda prodded as she sat down in her favorite chair.

Realizing she'd been chasing her thoughts about Acton, Persephone shook her head, both in response and to drive a certain rogue from her mind. She lowered herself to a settee near her aunt. "Not at all. We, ah, discussed the weather and Bath. He hasn't spent much time here."

"That's right. His mother lives here. Or lived—I understand she spends a great deal of time at the dowager house at his estate now."

"Do you know the dowager?" Persephone asked.

"Not as well as your mother, but yes, we have been friendly over the years."

She was curious about his mother. "It's sad that the duchess and his sisters lived separately from him and his father."

"I don't know if it's sad or not. The duchess always seemed in good spirits. She's been a prominent member of Bath Society, and her daughters made excellent marriages. I imagine the duke played some role in the background. It's not as if they were completely unfriendly. For as long as the duke was alive, the duchess went to London to oversee the annual ball at Wellesbourne House."

"That seems so strange to me," Persey mused. "To live separate lives, but come together for a social event. What of holidays or special occasions?"

Aunt Lucinda shrugged. "Their marriage was arranged, I believe, and it may be that they didn't particularly suit. They made the best of it. I would advise you not to do that if you can help it. Marry someone with whom you look forward to spending your life."

"Someone I love?"

"That would be ideal, but sometimes love is difficult to attain. And hold." She smiled faintly. "I think Hal and I loved each other at the start," she said, referring to her late husband. "But it didn't last. We respected and enjoyed each other, though, and I do think that's more than most have."

Persey barely remembered her Uncle Hal. He'd died when

she was eight. "I don't know that I'll have to worry about any of that," she said wryly.

"Why would you say such a thing? Just because the right man hasn't crossed your path yet doesn't mean he won't."

Acton had literally stepped into her path. Or she'd stepped into his. But that was the second time they'd met, when she'd run into him on the street. Even their first meeting was a chance occasion. If she hadn't run from her parents, they wouldn't have met.

At least not that night. They would have met, however, just at Loxley Court. Under very different circumstances. She wondered how it might have gone. Alas, she would never know.

Did she regret that missed opportunity? The chance to see if they would actually have suited?

It was hard not to consider that possibility in the aftermath of their kisses. They weren't the first ones she'd experienced, but they were, by far, the best. It made her sad to think she wouldn't get to do that with him again.

Except she was forgetting the Rogue Rules, particularly never give a rogue a chance, never doubt a rogue's reputation, and never trust a rogue to change. While she'd come to trust him and even like him, she'd do well to remember that men like him didn't just suddenly stop being rogues.

Aunt Lucinda gave her a teasing smile. "In fact, I wonder if that man crossed your path this very morning."

Persephone froze. "Wellesbourne?"

"Why not? He certainly seems interested. He was most eager to meet you. When you didn't arrive at Loxley Court, he went to Radstock Hall to see you, despite being told you were ill, and when you weren't there, he found you in Bath." As she tapped her nails on the wooden arm of her chair, her mouth turned down. "To think your parents continued on to Loxley Court instead of rushing to Radstock Hall to ensure you were home safe is positively horrid. What did they plan to do, arrange the marriage without you present? Without your consent?"

Persephone couldn't answer yes, for they would wonder how she could know. "I would guess that was their intent."

"It doesn't seem they went directly home from Loxley Court either, or at least the duke didn't mention that. Where on earth are they? Perhaps they're still at Loxley Court waiting for you and the duke to arrive," Lucinda suggested sardonically. "I will send word to Radstock Hall that you are here."

"Must you?" Persephone asked.

"Just because they are behaving awfully doesn't mean we should too. Now, when will you be seeing the duke again?"

Pandora strode into the room and joined Persephone on the settee. "What duke?"

"Wellesbourne called this morning," Aunt Lucinda said brightly. "He seems interested in Persey."

Mouth open, Pandora pinned Persephone with a horrified stare. "How could you? He's a close friend of that devil." Apparently, she wasn't saying Bane's name any longer, not that Persephone could find fault with that.

"I didn't say *I* was interested." Except she was most definitely interested in kissing him more or watching him be intrigued by her hair. She'd kept catching him staring at it earlier. At first, she'd been upset that her hair wasn't appropriately styled, but then she'd been glad since it had earned his attention. Which shouldn't have surprised her since he'd noted before that he liked it. Along with the unattractive bump in her nose.

Aunt Lucinda frowned. "I thought you might be. You'll be seeing him again. Soon. Or so he said."

"Er, yes, I thought his presence might help smooth things for Pandora."

"But he's a friend of that blackguard," Pandora said through clenched teeth.

Persephone looked at her sister with hope. "It's precisely because of their friendship that I thought it might help. Also, he's a duke. And that can't hurt."

Aunt Lucinda gave Persephone a pointed look. "Did you agree to see him again just to help Pandora?"

Glancing toward Pandora and seeing she was still agitated, Persephone hoped to show her that Acton was different. "He's aware that he's helping," Persephone answered quickly, avoiding the crux of her aunt's question. "He'd heard about what happened to Pandora and offered his assistance. Wellesbourne is most upset with Bane."

"It sounds as though you discussed far more than the weather and Bath," Aunt Lucinda noted. "Well, it would be wrong of us to refuse his help. I'm afraid I must ask if he's actually courting you or just lending his assistance? Or perhaps it's both."

Pandora made a sound of disgust in her throat. "Persephone would not enter into a courtship with the devil's best friend. Wellesbourne can be no better."

"Pandora, dear, you really mustn't weigh all men in the same manner," Aunt Lucinda advised. "Your experience with Banemore isn't the norm."

Persephone could attest to that. Acton had been wonderfully unlike Bane. Perhaps she ought to tell her sister of Acton's kindnesses, that they went beyond the help he was currently offering. Except that would mean revealing everything Persephone had kept secret thus far. Why was she hiding any of it from Pandora? They never withheld things from one another.

Until Pandora had lied about their mother chaperoning her walk with Bane. Persephone hadn't asked her about that.

Did she think Persephone would have told her not to go? Or that Persephone would have tried to stop her?

The truth was that Persephone would have done both those things. While she supported her sister trying to determine her feelings for a gentleman, she would not have endorsed her taking a promenade unchaperoned with the likes of Bane.

Pandora huffed out a breath. "I suppose I must accept whatever help I'm offered. But I do not, under any circumstances, want Wellesbourne to try to facilitate some sort of reconciliation between me and that devil. I wouldn't marry him if he were the world's last man."

"Understood," Persephone said.

Aunt Lucinda nodded once. "An excellent decision. Persephone, I do hope you will give Wellesbourne a chance. He is not Banemore. Now, you must both excuse me, for I've correspondence in need of my attention." She stood and departed the drawing room.

Pandora turned to look at Persephone. "I can't believe the duke came here. What happened? And where are Mama and Papa? Since they clearly didn't come with him."

Persephone wiped her hand over her face and pivoted toward her sister. "I would have explained everything last night, but you left upset, and I didn't want to disturb you."

"I'm upset far too much." Pandora sniffed. "I need to get over what happened. I'm trying. Now tell me everything.'"

"Where to begin?" Persephone exhaled. "Keep in mind, please, that Aunt Lucinda doesn't know any of this, and I would prefer it stayed that way." At Pandora's nod, she continued. "When I left Mama and Papa in Cirencester, I took the first mail coach I could and ended up in Gloucester. I stayed at an inn, and, this is where the story becomes almost fanciful, I met Wellesbourne."

Pandora goggled at her. "You met him at an inn?"

"Yes, but we weren't introduced. We dined together by chance, and through our conversation, I deduced his identity. Once I realized who he was, I feigned romantic interest in him, then tossed a glass of Madeira in his face."

"You didn't!" Pandora dissolved into giggles, collapsing back against the settee.

Persephone couldn't help but laugh with her.

When Pandora caught her breath, she asked what happened next.

"I left the following morning, only I took the wrong coach and ended up in Worcester. And someone stole my valise. It was an absolute disaster."

Gaping, Pandora leaned forward. "How did you manage?"

"Thankfully, my money was on my person. I had to spend it very cautiously after that. I returned to Gloucester and, if you can believe it, I ran into Wellesbourne on the street. He'd come back to Gloucester to look for me after going home to Loxley Court and learning from Mama and Papa that I was ill at home."

Pandora held up her hand. "Wait. I want to make sure I understand. The duke went home, met Mama and Papa, learned you were supposedly ill, and then came looking for you? Were Mama and Papa with him?"

"They were not," Persephone responded with a note of rancor. "After I departed their company, they continued on to Loxley Court and tried to negotiate the marriage contract without me even meeting the duke and deciding whether I would want to wed him."

Eyes narrowing, Pandora shook her head. "They are awful. I honestly didn't think they could be so thoughtless."

"I think they have plenty of thoughts," Persephone said. "They're just entirely about themselves."

"Did they send Wellesbourne after you so that you might

be compromised too?" Pandora made another disgusted noise. "I wouldn't put it past them at this point."

"Actually, Wellesbourne didn't even tell them he'd met me. They'd showed him a miniature of me, and he knew immediately who I was and that I needed saving."

Pandora rolled her eyes. "Of course he did. I hope you disabused him of that notion."

"Oh, I tried. Repeatedly." Persephone smiled as she thought back to all the ways she'd tried to push him away. "I wasn't remotely interested in his help, especially because of whom he is friends with."

"You are a loyal sister," Pandora said as she gave Persephone's hand a pat.

"He was most persistent, however, and as it happened, I did require his help. He purchased that blue gown I was wearing and paid for me to have a bath." Persephone looked directly at her sister. "It was the single greatest bath I've ever had. Still, I tried very hard to refuse. In the end, it made no sense. And I decided he could both afford to pay for those things and deserved to after all the pain and suffering men like him cause."

"Amen." Pandora wrinkled her pert nose. "I can only imagine what he demanded in return. How did you avoid his advances?"

Persephone coughed. "He didn't ask for anything in exchange." And she hadn't avoided his advances entirely. In fact, she was rather hoping he might advance again.

No, she couldn't want that. They had no future together. *Never trust a rogue to change* echoed in her brain. Pandora needed her, and until she was settled and this nightmare in the past, Persephone wouldn't abandon her.

"Absolutely remarkable," Pandora said with considerable awe. "How did you get here, to Bath?"

"I had to accept Wellesbourne's help. He hired a private coach to drive us here."

Pandora appeared aghast. "Was he with you last night?"

"He was in the coach when I arrived, yes. Then he went on to his mother's house."

"So, you were alone together for quite some time. At an inn, and again in a coach. You broke the first rogue rule. Did you break any others?"

Inwardly, Persephone cringed. Pandora had got right to the heart of things, that Acton had stolen right through Persephone's defenses. "I'm trying not to. But, he is not as roguish as I expected him to be. And the ways in which he is, he is trying to change."

Pandora studied her a moment. "You know him fairly well."

Persephone shrugged, though she felt uncomfortable. She wasn't sure what her sister might suspect, and she didn't want to reveal anything else—not the brigand's attack, or sharing a room with Acton overnight, and definitely not passionately kissing him. "Well enough, I suppose. As I said, he was fairly insistent that I accept his help because I was alone. As my potential husband, he felt responsible."

"Except he isn't your potential husband." Pandora's voice dropped to a near whisper. "Is he?"

"Absolutely not. When we parted last night, I thought I'd seen the last of him. Then he found out about what happened with you and Bane, and he came this morning to again offer his assistance."

"Not for you, but for me?"

"Yes." Persephone wondered if he would have come if he'd known from the start that Pandora had been the one his friend had compromised. Perhaps that didn't matter since he'd continued to offer his support once he'd learned the truth.

"Everything you told Aunt Lucinda is nonsense, then? He didn't come here to court you."

Persephone shook her head. "That's correct. He also told Aunt Lucinda that he went to Radstock Hall in search of me, but he didn't. Hopefully, that deception won't come to light."

"It will if Mama and Papa are there." Pandora blinked several times. "Where are they?"

"I've no idea."

"I can't believe you left them, and they just continued on to Loxley Court as if that wasn't a huge problem—as well as dangerous." Pandora smiled faintly and touched Persephone's hand again. "I'm glad the duke found you and kept you safe. It's good to know there is at least one decent gentleman out there. Though, I still can't believe someone like that would be friendly with Bane. What happens next?"

"I'm not sure, but Acton and I discussed taking a promenade in Sydney Gardens or tea at the Pump Room."

"I'm not sure I'd want to sit somewhere," Pandora said, her face going a shade lighter than it had been. "If we're in the park, I can hide or escape."

Persephone wanted to tell her that wouldn't be necessary, but she truly had no idea what would happen. Escape would be a good alternative if things went poorly. "Then I shall advocate for the gardens."

"Thank you, Persey. I don't know what I would do without you."

Persephone grinned. "Then it's most excellent that you will never have to find out."

# CHAPTER 14

s soon as Acton returned to his mother's house, he drafted and posted letters to Somerton, Droxford, Shefford, and the damnable Bane. Somerton and Droxford would likely be easy to find. Somerton's estate wasn't far from Bath, and Droxford was nearly always in residence at his house in Hampshire. The letters to Shefford and Bane had gone to their fathers' ducal residences, with express directions to forward them to Shefford and Bane if they were not present.

Hopefully, someone would know where Bane was currently or at least if he indeed planned to wed. One would think there would be an announcement in a newspaper, but Acton hadn't seen anything. Not that Acton had been looking for it. Furthermore, if there had been an announcement published, the identity of Bane's mystery bride would be on everyone's lips, wouldn't it? He'd ask his sisters about it.

First, however, he wanted to see the portrait in his mother's sitting room that the butler had mentioned. After asking for directions from the housekeeper, he made his way to her suite on the first floor at the back of the house.

Her sitting room was simply but beautifully decorated in sunny yellow and pale blue. He found it cheerful and imagined it brightened even the dreariest winter day. It fit what he knew of his mother. Since becoming acquainted with her over the past months, he'd found her almost universally pleasant. In some ways, she reminded him of himself. That seemed strange since he'd grown up away from her influence. However, perhaps some things were simply ingrained in one's blood.

The portrait was easy to spot. It hung between ones of his sisters. They all appeared to have been done around the same age—when they were in their early twenties. The resemblance between them was obvious when he looked at them together like that. He shared his eye shape with Francesca and his mouth with Cecily. The latter took the most after their mother with her smile and freckles.

The most important detail, however, was that this portrait of him was identical to the one his father had installed in his study at Loxley House. He had to have had this copy made for Acton's mother. Acton wanted to know the story behind that. Had she asked for a portrait? Had his father simply had it copied and given it to her? Were there other copied portraits? Acton had sat for at least three others in his youth, one of them at the age of eighteen with his father.

Acton had only ever heard his father's perspective regarding his wife's departure. They'd agreed it was best if they lived apart, for they simply liked different things. It had taken Acton years to realize they hadn't liked each other.

For the life of him, he couldn't recall his mother leaving. Surely a five-year-old boy would have been made distraught by that? Thinking about it now, Acton was confused as to how his mother could leave like that.

He realized he'd never spent too much time pondering it. Because his father had repeatedly told him that dwelling on such things weakened a man's constitution. In some ways, Acton agreed because the more he thought about it, which he had in recent months, the more uncomfortable he became. It was much easier—and less painful—to put it from his mind.

Turning from the portrait, Acton made his way from the sitting room and immediately encountered Simmons. "A missive has arrived for you, Your Grace." He handed Acton a folded piece of parchment.

"Thank you, Simmons." Acton opened the paper as the butler walked away.

*We would prefer to promenade at Sydney Gardens, if you are still considering a social outing. Today would suit if that is acceptable to you. If not, I will understand.*

*With gratitude,*

*Persey*

She'd signed it Persey. Acton smiled as a giddiness tripped through him. Of course he was still considering it. He was committed to helping. Or trying to, anyway. He'd already sent letters to his friends, and eagerly awaited their responses.

"Sydney Gardens it is," he murmured before making his way to the drawing room. His sisters were there; Francesca was at the desk writing and Cecily was in a chair by one of the windows reading.

"Good afternoon," Acton greeted them. "I was hoping you might promenade with me this afternoon in Sydney Gardens."

"That would be lovely," Cecily said, looking up from her book.

He couldn't not tell them about the Barclay sisters joining them. Would their aunt also accompany them? Most certainly as their chaperone.

"I confess I have an ulterior motive. The purpose of the promenade is for me and Miss Barclay, whom our mother wished for me to meet, to determine if we will suit."

"Was that your call this morning?" Francesca asked, pivoting toward him in her chair at the desk.

"It was. We decided to promenade this afternoon."

"Mama mentioned Miss Barclay in her last letter, which I just received yesterday," Francesca said. "She wrote that Miss Barclay didn't arrive at Loxley Court as expected, that she was ill."

"I imagine Mother also included the part where her parents, the Baron and Baroness Radstock *did* come to Loxley Court," Acton said.

Francesca nodded. "She did. It's all very odd. And Miss Pandora Barclay is the one Banemore compromised. I believe Cecily may have misspoken about which sister that was."

"Yes, I did reference the wrong sister," Cecily said with a faint grimace.

Francesca addressed Acton. "Honestly, you may want to cut a wide swath around the entire family."

"Why would you say that?" Cecily asked. "Mama is loyal to her friends, especially those who have been loyal to her."

"That doesn't mean Wellesbourne must demonstrate the same loyalty." Francesca shrugged. "Lady Radstock has always seemed to lack complete sincerity, in my opinion."

Acton found his sister's assessment of the baroness interesting. "I liked Miss Barclay upon meeting her this morning. I look forward to seeing if we will suit. Regardless of your opinion, the baroness is a friend of Mother's. We should be helping their family, not avoiding them."

"I suppose you are right." Francesca turned back to the desk.

"I agree, Wellesbourne," Cecily said. "Mama has always said that the baroness has been a good friend to her."

Acton was still surprised by this given what he knew of Persey's mother. He wondered what his mother found pleasing about the baroness.

"I don't think Mama is aware of the scandal," Francesca said. "I am just writing to her about it now, as she will want to know."

Cecily set her book in her lap, keeping her finger between the pages as it closed. "Yes, she will want to support them. She wouldn't want Miss Pandora to suffer unduly."

"I do feel badly for Miss Pandora, but why would anyone think walking alone with Banemore wouldn't end in disaster?" Francesca sent a look toward Acton. "I gather he's your close friend, but you can't deny his reputation is horrendous."

Acton grimaced. "Is it really horrendous?" What did that make Acton's reputation?

"It is now," Francesca said.

Now was as good a time as any to ask about Bane's betrothal. "Speaking of Banemore, have either of you seen an announcement or any news regarding his alleged betrothal?"

Cecily shook her head. "Not a word, and believe me, people are speculating. There will need to be an announcement soon, or people will think he was lying to avoid marrying poor Miss Pandora."

Which was what Acton suspected. If that was true, then Bane would truly have earned his *horrendous* reputation.

He diverted the conversation back to the promenade. "Can I count on you both to join us this afternoon, then?"

Cecily nodded. "Yes. I assume their aunt will be accompanying them? She's delightful."

"I'll come too," Francesca said. "I do enjoy Mrs. Barclay-Fiennes. And, honestly, it isn't fair that Miss Pandora will suffer so badly for her poor choices. I have no doubt Bane is entirely to blame. For all we know, he manipulated Miss Pandora into being alone with him, and his advances upon her were completely unwanted." She pursed her lips in disgust.

"That would certainly fit his reputation," Cecily agreed.

Acton couldn't hold his tongue any longer. "Is *my* reputation that bad?"

"No, but you haven't been caught in a blatant compromising position and refused to marry the woman." Francesca gave him a pointed look. "However, if you did, you would certainly be relegated to the same club."

Cecily sniggered. "The Blackguard Society."

"Don't give Wellesbourne any ideas," Francesca said with a chuckle.

On the contrary, Acton wouldn't want to be in such a club. However, it seemed he already was. And it was affecting his honest attempt at finding a bride. Persey was deterred by it, and he had to think other engaging, clever women would be too. Even more reason to ensure he changed his attitude and behavior.

"I pray my reputation will improve." Acton inclined his head toward his sisters. "Particularly with the two of you to influence me."

"One can hope," Cecily said. "It is good to have you here, I must admit."

Acton gave her a warm smile. "I feel the same. Is there a coach I can arrange for us to take to Sydney Gardens?" He'd seen a few at the mews but wasn't sure if any of them belonged to his sisters.

Francesca answered. "We each have one, but ask for Cecily's. It's newer than mine." She winked at her younger sister.

"Brilliant. I'll see you later." Acton took himself off with the intent of going to the mews personally to organize their transportation.

Anticipation began to curl in his gut as he thought of seeing Persey again. He knew that wasn't the primary reason for their promenade, but it was the part he was most looking forward to.

~

*P*ersephone was glad for the small wardrobe she had at her aunt's house, even if it was a year or two outmoded. It wasn't as if she had much of a wardrobe from the current year, just a walking dress and an evening gown, both of which she'd left in her room at the inn in Cirencester. They were supposed to win Acton's approval when they met at Loxley Court.

Somehow, she'd managed to gain his friendship in a serviceable brown traveling dress, so she didn't pay much mind to what she was wearing. Still, she couldn't help feeling lackluster beside Pandora, whose bottle-green walking dress was new. And her hat was especially jaunty, with a peacock feather and ornamental flowers.

The coach stood in the Crescent, waiting for them to climb in and travel the single mile to Sydney Gardens. However, just as Aunt Lucinda took the groom's hand to step into the coach, Pandora grabbed Persephone's arm.

"I can't," she whispered. "You both go on."

Lucinda stepped away from the groom and faced Pandora. "Nonsense. You are coming with us. You look lovely and you're going to show the world that you will not

be cowed. And that you have not been defeated by a reprobate such as Bane."

Persephone wanted to applaud their aunt's speech. "I
could not have said it better myself." She put her hand on
Pandora's back and pushed her gently toward the coach.
"Get in."

Pandora's brows pitched into a deep forehead frown,
which pulled her mouth into the same expression. "If this
goes poorly, I shan't speak to either of you for a week."

"It won't go poorly," Aunt Lucinda said with great confidence. "This will be a triumph, you'll see." She waited while
the groom handed Pandora in first. Then she sent Persephone a hopeful look and briefly crossed her fingers.

Persephone sent up a silent prayer as her aunt entered the
coach next. Soon, they were on their way. It only took a few
minutes to arrive at the gardens. The coachman stopped and
they got out nearby, Persephone linking her arm through
Pandora's before entering the gardens from Sydney Place.

"It's going to be fine," Persephone whispered as she felt
her sister shake.

"I'm so nervous," Pandora whispered back. "What if
everyone turns their backs?"

"I know at least three people who won't." At least Persephone hoped so. That depended on whether Acton was able
to persuade his sisters to come.

Suddenly, he was walking toward them, a pair of ladies to
his right. They were clearly his sisters, as there was a strong
family resemblance. But then Persephone had met them on a
few occasions in Bath Society. She'd just never seen them
with Acton before.

Acton bowed upon meeting them. "Good afternoon, Mrs.
Barclay-Fiennes, Miss Barclay, Miss Pandora."

"Good afternoon, Duke," Aunt Lucinda responded as she
dipped into a curtsey. Persephone and Pandora did the same.

Persephone noted that Pandora kept her gaze focused on the ground. That would not do. She needed to hold her head high and dare people to be offensive.

"Allow me to present my sisters, Lady Donovan and Lady Fairhope," he said. "But then I think you may have met one another at some point."

"Indeed we have," Lady Fairhope, the shorter of the two, said. She looked to be with child, and for a fleeting moment, Persephone wondered if she would ever experience that. She'd begun to think not, but things could change. She sent a surreptitious look toward Acton, only to find that he was looking at her too.

Persephone stifled a smile while her insides seemed to cartwheel. "It's lovely to see you," she said to his sisters.

"Indeed," Aunt Lucinda agreed. "Pity your mother isn't here to join us, but then I understand she is at Loxley Court."

"She is," Lady Donovan confirmed. "She was supposed to introduce Miss Barclay to our brother."

"Alas, my dear niece was ill for a few days, but she is much recovered now. Shall we take in the late summer flowers?" Aunt Lucinda gestured toward the path.

Acton walked toward Persephone and Pandora. "Ladies, I would be honored if you would allow me to escort you."

Pandora gave him a skeptical look while her lips pursed into a near frown. "Very prettily said. Your friend spoke to me like that."

"I'm sure the duke is not like his friend," Persephone said, sending a furtive look toward Acton.

"I hope not." Acton grimaced faintly. "Let us not speak of him today. The weather is fine and the company marvelous. He would only ruin it."

Persephone smiled, thinking he'd handled that well. "Hear, hear."

Still, Pandora looked uneasy. She was likely nervous. And

Persephone could see how Acton would remind her of Bane, if only because they were friends.

They began to walk—Acton between them and their aunt and his sisters trailing behind.

"That's a fetching hat," Acton said to Pandora.

Pandora kept her gaze focused straight ahead. Her features were like stone. "Thank you."

Persephone glanced about, eager to see people's reactions. There were dozens of people about, and already some seemed to be looking in Pandora's direction and talking.

Acton's arm brushed Persephone's, and she instantly turned her head toward him. He did the same, and their eyes met. She saw something new in his gaze—a vibrant expectation. Almost a...hunger. Or was she only seeing herself reflected in him?

Walking with him in public was a heady experience. She'd promenaded with gentlemen before but never someone with whom she'd shared so many intimacies, and it wasn't just the sharing of a room or kissing. He knew things about her and her family that no one else did. And she knew the same about him. But it wasn't enough. Her desire for more was nearly palpable.

"Just a moment," Aunt Lucinda called from behind them. A trio of ladies had come to speak with Acton's sisters and Aunt Lucinda. They stepped off the path to converse.

"Let's join them," Persephone said.

"Must we?" Pandora looked pale. "I'd rather not."

"I'll be right here," Acton said warmly.

Pandora cast him a dubious stare. "And how will that help?"

"I'm a duke. People like and respect me. They'll be polite to anyone I'm with."

"I suppose that would include your terrible friend too,"

Pandora said with a slight curl of her lip. "Not everyone likes or respects you just because you're a duke."

"They do to my face," he said wryly. "Except perhaps you. I don't think you like me very much."

"I am disinclined to find your company tolerable." Pandora notched up her chin.

"Yes, that's it," Persephone said with an encouraging smile. "Do more of that. Now, come look haughty and beautiful with these ladies who've stopped to converse." She nudged Pandora with her elbow.

"Fine," Pandora said through gritted teeth. To her credit, she plastered a placid expression on her face and managed to look lovelier than ever.

They exchanged pleasantries with the trio, who seemed clearly curious about what was happening. "How do your two families know one another?" one of the ladies asked.

Another of the ladies responded. "You seem to have forgotten that Lady Radstock and the Duchess of Wellesbourne are dear friends."

"Oh yes, how silly of me," the first lady said with a light laugh. Something about her demeanor said this was entirely fabricated, that this woman knew precisely how their families were connected, but was hoping for new information.

"We're delighted to find we are all in Bath at the same time," Acton said smoothly, drawing the ladies' attention.

"Does that include your parents, then?" the third lady asked.

"My brother and the baroness are not here," Aunt Lucinda answered.

"Neither is our mother," Lady Donovan put in.

They spoke with the trio for a few more minutes before taking their leave and continuing along the path. This sort of interaction happened twice more, along with one instance where the mother and daughter who'd stopped to talk had clearly wanted Acton's attention and did everything they could to ignore Pandora. Honestly, they disregarded everyone but Acton. Proof yet again that men, especially noblemen, could behave in any way they wanted and still be popular and adored.

When it was just the six of them again, Aunt Lucinda stated the outing was a success. She looked to Acton's sisters. "I can't thank you enough for supporting Pandora today. I think you've made a big difference."

"Yes, thank you," Pandora said. She still looked a little uncertain, but the fear had finally left her eyes.

Aunt Lucinda turned to Persephone and Acton. "Now, take a short walk by yourselves—so we can see you, of course —since you're also supposed to be deciding if you might suit." She gave them an encouraging smile.

Acton offered Persephone his arm. She curled her hand around his sleeve and was instantly rewarded with a delicious heat that curled through her and settled low in her belly.

"Do you agree with your aunt that this has been successful for Pandora?" Acton asked as they walked.

"I think it's early to make that assessment, but Aunt Lucinda is far more experienced in this area than I am. I am grateful to your sisters for coming today. How are you enjoying spending time with them?" She studied his profile as she awaited his response.

"It's been rather nice, actually. They have good senses of humor, and they seem interested in forging a relationship."

"Does that mean you are too?" He hadn't said he wasn't, but Persephone's impression was that they had no relationship whatsoever, and he hadn't seemed bothered by it.

"Surprisingly, yes. I didn't think I'd missed having them in my life. How do you miss what you've never known?" His gaze met hers, and she gave him a slight nod.

"I understand that sentiment."

"However, it turns out, I think I missed a great deal not having them—or my mother—in my life."

She heard a note of confusion, as if he were wrestling with that realization. "Has that been difficult to accept?" she asked softly.

"Something like that, yes. It's just…not what I expected. I only ever had my father. Now he is gone, and without them, I would have no one."

Persephone wanted to put her arms around him and assure him he would not be alone. But how could she make such promises? She was only a friend to him, and even his friends—one of them, anyway—had disillusioned him of late.

He sent her a half smile. "At least you have your sister. And your aunt. I quite like her. It's good that you have her in your life since your parents are…forgive me, I shouldn't speak ill of them."

Laughing, Persephone squeezed his arm. "Oh, please do. I've nothing kind to say about them at present. We don't even know where they *are* at this point. Are you sure they left Loxley Court? Perhaps they are still there awaiting your return."

Acton chuckled. "They will be waiting some time. I have no plans to leave Bath at the moment."

"I thought you had an engagement," she said. "A house party?"

"I'm not inclined to attend, particularly since Bane is supposed to be there. I wrote to him and a few of our mutual friends to ask about this mystery bride of his. If I find out he lied about that, I…" His jaw clenched, and she watched his pulse tick in his neck. "I'm not sure what I will do, but I will no longer call him friend."

They were walking in a circle to return to the others and had just passed the halfway point. "I was so very wrong about you," Persephone said, setting her free hand atop his arm where her other hand held his sleeve.

He paused briefly, his gaze connecting with hers. "I'm not sure you were—at least not entirely. I do hope I may be changing. I certainly feel as if my life has changed since I met you."

Persephone's heart flipped over. She felt the same, but was afraid to say so. "I hope that's a good thing."

"I think so." He smiled, and they continued walking. "My only complaint is that I no longer get to spend as much time alone with you as when we were together in Gloucester."

Persephone realized she missed that as well. "I admit it wasn't all bad," she said. "But that sort of behavior here in Bath would be ruinous."

"Probably, unless we were very careful. I've surveyed the back gardens of the Crescent, and they are largely accessible if we ever cared to meet. Alas, we will not, because I am trying to reform myself."

Shockingly, Persephone thought she might like to meet him—the rogue—in the garden. But that would break a great many Rogue Rules. She began to wonder if it might be all right to do so.

Did that make her a rogue?

"An admirable endeavor," she said, glad for his self-restraint.

His gaze smoldered. "I confess it is taking all my willpower not to propose that you meet me in your aunt's garden at, say, eleven this evening."

Heart pounding, Persephone recognized his flirtation for precisely what it was: a rogue roguing. She should be offended, even if he wasn't serious. Instead, she was incomparably thrilled by the way he was looking at her, by the singular way the sultry tone of his voice caressed her. Apparently, she could still be wooed, as she had been in her youth.

Despite those situations turning out poorly—unsatisfying physical interactions and no interest or hope for a future—here she was again actually pondering meeting a man alone. Not just a man, but a scoundrel with a terrible reputation.

"We shouldn't," she whispered unconvincingly, which surely conveyed she was considering it.

"Probably not." He sighed. "But wouldn't it be lovely if we did?"

It would be more than lovely. It would be something she chose. Something she wanted. "Will you be there?" she asked, holding her breath.

His eyes lit with surprise. "I will. And I promise we'll just talk. No kissing. You'll meet me?"

"I'll consider it." Strongly. Indeed, she would probably think of little else. Anticipation vibrated through her. She took her other hand from his arm lest she do something foolish, such as grasp him even tighter as she pressed her side to his. Anything to increase their contact. "But what if I want to kiss you?"

"All I can think about is kissing you again." He sent her a pained expression. "I do realize that makes me the worst sort of rogue—precisely the man you thought I was."

Persephone didn't want to think of how many times he might have done such things. He'd just said that meeting her had changed his life and that he couldn't think of anything but kissing her. It could all be lies and pretty persuasion, but she didn't think it was. And perhaps she'd be made a fool as Pandora had been.

"I can trust you?" She hated that she had to ask, but she'd hate herself if she didn't.

"Completely. I would never hurt you, Persey." They neared the others, and further conversation would have to wait until later.

Did that mean she was going to meet him? She wasn't

certain. The war taking place in her mind and body was going to make for a challenging evening.

Before they parted, Acton took her hand and pressed a swift kiss to her wrist just above her glove and below the sleeve of her gown. "Thank you for a lovely promenade, Miss Barclay."

The imprint of his lips on her flesh felt like a brand, but without any pain. Just a burgeoning desire. How he'd managed to find that incredibly small piece of bare skin spoke to his exceptional expertise in romantic matters. Instead of feeling unhappy that he'd honed his skills elsewhere, Persephone was thrilled to have them directed entirely at her.

They started their promenade back to the coaches. Again, Acton walked between Persephone and Pandora, and their aunt and his sisters followed behind. After a few moments, Pandora gasped. Before Persephone could even look in her sister's direction, Acton was catching Pandora in his arms.

"Are you all right?" Persephone cried as she went to Pandora. "What happened?"

"I was distracted." Pandora sounded agitated. "I tripped." She looked up at Acton. "Thank you."

"I'll set you down now." He eased her to the ground, but she immediately pulled her foot up with a pained expression.

"I think I've hurt my ankle," Pandora said. Acton moved to support her, putting his arm at her waist.

Aunt Lucinda hurried toward them. "What's wrong?"

Persephone responded as she watched her sister with concern. "Pandora tripped and hurt her ankle."

"Can you walk to the coach?" Aunt Lucinda asked, her brow creased with worry.

Pandora tested putting weight on her foot and winced. "I don't think so."

"I can carry you," Acton offered. "Ready?" Before Pandora

could respond, he'd swept her into his arms and was already making his way toward the coaches.

Persephone couldn't help noticing that people had moved closer and were staring. They were also talking and whispering. She hoped this wouldn't be bad for Pandora. But how could it be?

Aunt Lucinda hurried behind Acton and Pandora while Persephone walked with Acton's sisters. She wanted to quicken her pace to catch up to her sister, but she didn't want to leave Lady Donovan and Lady Fairhope behind.

"Go on ahead," Lady Donovan said. "If it were Cecily, I'd be rushing to be at her side." She gave Persephone an encouraging nod.

"Thank you." Persephone lengthened her stride and walked quickly after the others. She reached them just as Acton was settling Pandora in the coach.

"Should I follow you home and carry you upstairs?" he asked.

"That is most kind of you, Duke," Aunt Lucinda said. "However, one of the footmen can handle that."

Acton's sisters had now arrived. "Do let us know how you're faring," Lady Fairhope said toward the coach with a loud enough voice so Pandora was bound to hear.

"We will," Persephone said. She cast a grateful look toward Acton. "I'm so glad you were there to help. Again," she added in a murmur that only he could hear.

He smiled, and it carried a secret glow, as if he were communicating something only to her. And she supposed he was as they recalled their time together when he'd helped her.

"It was my pleasure and my honor. I hope to see you all soon," he said, though his gaze was locked entirely on Persephone.

She shivered beneath his regard, not with cold or anxiety,

but with delicious anticipation. Soon could be that very night. If she was brave enough…

Or foolish enough.

After they bid their farewells, Persephone and her aunt climbed into the coach.

"Shall I send for the doctor?" Aunt Lucinda asked.

Pandora shook her head. "My ankle is fine. I just…I needed to leave." She sounded desperate and sad. Almost afraid.

"What happened?" Persephone asked. "Did you really trip?"

"Yes, but only after I saw something awful. A young woman pointed at me and spoke to her friend. They laughed. I caught their eye, and they both glared at me, then turned their backs. I know it shouldn't bother me, but it did."

Persephone had recognized a pair of young ladies who'd followed their progress to the coach. They were girls she and Pandora had known over the years when they'd visited Aunt Lucinda in Bath. "Because you knew them," she said softly, hating that her sister had seen that, but hating those horrid young women even more.

"Later, you will give me their names so that I may skewer them," Aunt Lucinda said darkly.

Pandora shook her head. "Please don't. I just want to forget it happened. And I really don't want to go out again."

Aunt Lucinda's face creased with disappointment. "But the rest of the outing went so well. I think you should try again. Perhaps the day after tomorrow." She looked to Persephone. "You and Wellesbourne appeared to get on well."

"Er, yes. I suppose." Persephone had enjoyed her promenade with Acton, but at the moment, she was too upset about Pandora's turmoil.

"And he said he'd see you soon," Aunt Lucinda said with an encouraging smile.

"He said all of us," Persephone clarified.

Part of her wanted to tell Pandora that she was thinking of meeting him in the garden, but she couldn't. Just as Pandora had kept her walk with Bane secret, Persephone would do the same if she met with Acton tonight. She didn't want her sister trying to talk her out of it, which was undoubtedly why Pandora hadn't told her about Bane either.

Besides, Persephone didn't want to tell her sister anything yet. She wasn't certain what was happening between her and Acton. Perhaps that was the greatest reason for her to meet him—so she could find out.

# CHAPTER 15

hecking his watch, Acton saw it was five minutes until eleven. No one had seen him leave the house in St. James's Square, and he'd evaded detection as he'd made his way through the shadows, climbing three walls, to Lucinda's rear garden.

While the Crescent was uniformly constructed from the front—Ionic columns and a Palladian structure at the top—the backs of the houses were all different. One side of the rear of Lucinda's house came out farther than the other, from ground to roof. Acton wondered which window belonged to Persey's room.

Would she come?

Acton was grateful for the nearly full moon and the low number of clouds. Still, it was dark in the garden, and he wasn't sure if there was a bench or anywhere to sit. He didn't dare get too close to the house in case someone decided to look out a window. Or worse, if someone came outside.

He watched the door eagerly, the minutes crawling with the speed of a tortoise. How long would he wait?

He checked his watch again. Five minutes after eleven. He could wait much longer. Hell, he could wait all night.

But he shouldn't. Just as he probably shouldn't even have suggested this assignation—even in jest.

Assignation?

He wrinkled his nose and wiped his hand across his brow. This behavior was exactly what Persey had accused him of when they'd met. It was why she'd thrown wine in his face. And *that* had been the start of their acquaintance, which had led him to reconsider his attitude and actions. That and learning what Bane had done. There was just no excuse for endangering a lady's reputation.

Then why was he here?

Swearing under his breath, he decided he should go. He took one last look at the back door. Then it opened.

Acton was riveted to the ground. He couldn't have moved if the garden were on fire.

Persey closed the door slowly before turning and making her way into the garden. She looked about, and it took all Acton's control not to race out into the open and snatch her into his arms.

Instead, he made a sound like an owl, hooting several times. The noise drew her attention, and as her gaze settled in his direction, she walked straight toward him.

Acton's heart thundered as she neared the tree behind which he was stationed. When she was close enough, he whispered, "I'm here, behind the tree."

She found him a moment later. "Are you supposed to be an owl?"

"It was all I could think of to get your attention. And it worked."

"It did indeed, though I don't think an owl hoots with such intensity."

He smiled, glad that he could at last flirt with her without incurring her wrath. "They might if they were trying to attract a beautiful, captivating female owl."

"Is that how you see me?" she asked, and he knew the question was genuine. Little lines marred her forehead. "Or is this just something you say when you meet a woman alone in the dark?"

His smile faded. "I thought about that as I was standing here—I mean, my being here. I nearly left, but then I saw you come outside, and I was unable to move."

"Do you mean that too?" she whispered.

"With every fiber of my being. I know you've no reason to believe me. And you've every reason to think I've done this a dozen times, all with the goal of seduction."

"Only a dozen?" she teased, which helped him relax. He'd become very tense. Or nervous. This moment was unlike anything that had come before. *She* was unlike anyone he'd ever known. She stepped closer to him, so that they nearly touched. "Is seduction your goal tonight?"

"I just wanted to see you. Alone. The way we used to be."

"When I constantly refused your help, and you couldn't help but flirt with me?"

He grinned. "How did I manage to win you over?"

"I could say it was when you rescued me from that brigand. It is awfully hard to dislike a gallant hero. However, I think it was the rats that endeared you to me. It was the first time I truly saw you as a person. Not a rake or a duke or a rogue."

Her words stoked the desire that had been swirling through him all day. No, longer than that—since they'd first kissed. "But I am those things," he said quietly. "Or at least I was. Except for the duke part. I'm afraid I'm stuck with that."

She searched his face. "Is that how you feel? Do you feel trapped as a duke?"

"If I said yes, I think that would make me sound like an

ungrateful wretch. And no, I don't. It's just…I'm not sure I'm doing it…right? My father had high expectations, but he died suddenly, and I realized there are so many things I don't know."

"Such as?"

Acton lifted a shoulder. "How to persuade my peers to join with me in certain causes. I find I am often in the minority when I speak with others about issues, especially in the Lords. My father and I didn't discuss such things, at least not specifically. I think he would probably not care for some of my views. For instance, I support expanding the rules on who may vote. Many of our elections are corrupt, and I would like to see reform."

He'd become rather wrapped up in his confession and now noticed that she was staring at him, her mouth slightly open. "Did I say something wrong?"

She shook herself gently. "On the contrary, I am shocked but glad to hear such things. I'm sorry you feel as though your father didn't prepare you or wouldn't approve of you. I know that's not what you said, but it sounds as though that may be what you fear. I certainly know what it's like to not have a parent's approval. Not approval, exactly… I know what it's like to have their pity, to understand that they find you lacking."

Anger spiked through Acton. "Why on earth would you deserve that?"

"Because I'm not as pretty or as graceful as my sister."

Acton interrupted her, feeling like an ass. "Your sister! How is her ankle? I'm so sorry I didn't ask right away."

"It's all right. Her ankle is fine." Persephone appeared troubled. "A pair of young ladies we've known for years gave her the cut direct and laughed at her. Pandora did not take it well. She doesn't want to go out again."

"Who are these young women?" Acton demanded. "I will ensure they aren't invited anywhere."

Persephone laughed lightly. "You sound like my aunt. You are so kind to take up for Pandora, but I'm not sure it will help."

"It will make me feel better. Won't it do the same for you? And Pandora?"

"Probably. You must do whatever you think best, but I don't believe ruining two young women socially is the answer."

"I suppose you have a point. Perhaps I'll host a party at my mother's house and not invite them or their families. Actions have consequences." Acton thought of Bane and how he seemed to have escaped with his misbehavior. "Or they should anyway."

"Pandora is certainly paying for *her* actions and for those of Bane," Persephone said darkly. "I know she made a poor choice, but who hasn't? Look at us right now." Before Acton could respond to that, she went on. "Pandora was the one expected to make a magnificent marriage. She was to have a Season in London—if my parents could afford it."

The Radstocks did have financial challenges, then. That would explain her father's rush to secure a marriage settlement. "You have a dowry, though."

She let out a short laugh. "A small one. Did my father not tell you what it was?"

"I'm afraid our conversation didn't last that long. Once I recognized you in the miniature, I was eager to get back to you. I left Loxley Court almost immediately."

"Did you?" She sounded almost breathless.

"When I thought of you alone, without protection, I couldn't just sit there."

"I'm surprised you didn't go to Radstock Hall—didn't they tell you I'd gone home?"

"In hindsight, I wonder why I didn't. However, I had just seen you that morning in Gloucester, and that seemed the best place to start. I expected to have to search for you. But then, I wasn't sure if you were running away and if so, why."

"Right. At one point, you suspected I was going to meet someone—a gentleman." She smiled coyly. "How roguish of you to think that."

"I'm afraid I may be incurably roguish. I mean, here we are in a dark garden." He sobered for a moment. "This is exactly the ruinous behavior you accused me of."

"I know." She put her hand on his chest. "And yet here I am. Sometimes, roguery is apparently warranted."

"I don't believe there's any danger of us being caught. I would never want to put you in a compromising position." He grimaced. "Though I realize just being here is a risk. If we were seen together, I would never abandon you."

"Thank you for saying that. I should not have encouraged you to come, particularly when you are trying to redeem yourself. But I wanted this moment—with you—for me." She took his hand. He hadn't bothered with gloves, and neither had she. Indeed, she was dressed simply, in a round gown that would open down the front. That he recognized the mechanics of a woman's wardrobe only emphasized his rake status.

He groaned as she led him away from the tree to the corner of the garden where a bench sat behind a tall wall of shrubbery.

"Why are you making that noise?" she asked as she pulled him to sit down beside her.

"Because I was noting your garments and how they would unfasten. I really am a blackguard. Perhaps you should go back inside." Despite saying that, he did not release her hand.

She arched a brow. "Do you intend to disrobe me? I must

ask that you do not. While it's not cold, it's not exactly warm either. My skin will be bumpy with gooseflesh."

He envisioned that as well as what the cold air would do to her nipples if her breasts were bare. His cock, half-erect since she'd come outside, roared to full arousal.

"Persey, I am nearly mad with want for you. Please tell me I may kiss you. Now." He lifted her hand to his mouth and pressed a kiss to the back, savoring the silkiness of her skin and her delectable floral scent.

"You are kissing me," she said. "Unless you are asking to do so in a more intimate fashion."

Keeping hold of her hand between them, he used his other hand to cup her face. "Do you know what that could mean?"

She hesitated, her brow furrowing slightly. "Your mouth pressed to mine?"

"While that is more intimate, I'm afraid my roguish brain went directly to the most intimate kiss I could offer you. My mouth on your sex. Have you not heard of such a thing?"

She was slow to respond again, and he felt a faint tremor in her hand. Was she frightened? "I have. But I have not experienced such an act."

That comment made him think she'd experienced something. And she certainly hadn't shrunk from kissing him the other day. "What *have* you experienced?"

She looked down. "I'm afraid to say. I don't want you to think less of me."

He moved his hand to her chin and tilted her head back up. "You think I, a known scoundrel, could possibly fault you for anything?"

A smile curled her lips. "Well, when you put it like that, I suppose I should proudly share my exploits with you. Several years ago, I became…intimate with a young man I met in

Weston one summer. It was just the one time, and it was rather unimpressive."

"Intimate…as in you had intercourse with him?" He wanted to be sure he understood.

She nodded. "You can still leave, if you'd like. I would understand."

He stroked her jaw with his thumb as he lost himself in her eyes. "I would be a terrible hypocrite if I judged you harshly. What happened with him, if you don't mind my asking?"

"He wanted to marry me, but after we were intimate, I said I didn't want to. At first, he said he would go to my parents, but I convinced him that wouldn't turn out the way he hoped. You see, he was a poor curate. My parents would not have supported a marriage."

"You broke his heart, then?" Acton actually felt a moment's pity for the impoverished curate.

"I don't think so. We were young. I'm not sure one can know one's heart at that age. Honestly, I don't know if one ever can."

He'd stroked his hand down her neck and now rested it at the crook of her collarbone. "What does that mean? You don't believe in love?"

"I do, though I've little experience seeing it. I've accepted that I am likely never to experience it myself. Have you been in love?"

"My younger self thought I was—with the woman my father hired to 'teach' me about sex. My father explained I was merely feeling infatuation, which is common for a young man, that it would fade. He was right." He rolled his eyes. "I was also infatuated with my first mistress, before I learned it was unfashionable to have any emotional attachment to one's mistress."

Her nostrils flared. "Who told you that?"

"My father. He had the same mistress for ten years, but said he never felt more than an affinity for her. Anything more just isn't done."

She wrinkled her nose. "While I believe there is a difference between love and infatuation, your father gave you rubbish advice as to how you should feel."

Acton had begun to wonder. But he didn't want to think about that just now. He wanted to return to their discussion of kissing and the type they should engage in. "Have you considered how I might kiss you?" He moved his thumb along the bare flesh of her throat, feeling the steady beat of her pulse. It picked up speed then, as her lips parted.

"I want you to kiss me. Anywhere you like." She put her hands on his shoulders and leaned into him. "Tonight, I am yours, Acton."

"Then tonight, I am going to take what I want. But you can stop me at any moment, with the barest whisper. Understood?" He held her gaze as a primal lust streaked through him.

She dug her fingers into his flesh. "I understand. Now, kiss me."

$\sim$

*P*ersephone pulled him toward her. Since he'd asked about kissing her sex, she'd been aquiver with want. Her earlier experiences had been based on curiosity. But this was different. This was a need she couldn't ignore nor deny. A desperate desire that she felt certain only Acton could satisfy.

His hand moved to the back of her neck as his other arm circled her waist. His mouth took hers, and she met the insistent press of his lips and the subsequent thrust of his tongue. This kiss wasn't as inquisitive as their first ones had been. It didn't need to be. This kiss was about claiming one another, about conquering and submitting.

The need inside Persephone built with each sweep of his tongue. He cupped her neck, holding her in a thoroughly sensual embrace while he plundered her mouth. She pressed into him, her entire body tingling with desire.

The pulse that had started between her legs when he'd suggested putting his mouth there intensified. She wanted to feel him there. She wanted to feel him everywhere.

Suddenly, the notion of removing her clothing did not seem like a bad idea. She'd no idea of the temperature outside, just that she was burning with want.

Pivoting, she lifted her skirts so that she could straddle him on the bench. He clasped her to him as she situated herself atop his thighs. When she pressed down—her bare sex meeting the rigid length of his erection straining against his breeches—he groaned.

"Persey," he breathed before taking her mouth once more. He gripped her hip, holding her tightly against him as he thrust against her.

Moaning, she ground down, desperate for more of this sensation. Her arousal climbed as their bodies worked together. It was as if they'd been made for this moment. As wrong as this scenario might seem, nothing had ever felt so right to Persephone.

His hand moved from her neck to her bodice, plucking at the ties to lower the front.

She pulled her mouth from his. "I'm not wearing stays." She typically disposed of them by this hour of the night and hadn't thought twice about leaving them off. Perhaps some part of her had hoped this would happen.

"You are indeed a goddess." He kissed her jaw, her neck, his lips and tongue trailing down her flesh as he loosened the front of her gown.

Cool air moved over her bare, heated flesh. His mouth moved to the base of her throat, then lower to the hollow between her breasts. He cupped one of them as his lips found her nipple.

She had experienced this before, but it had been clumsy and thankfully brief. As with kissing, Acton was proving himself to be a master. He licked and sucked at her flesh, stoking her desire into a deep and demanding lust.

He held her fast around the waist while he suckled her, his free hand teasing her other breast. He brushed the pad of his thumb against her, a touch she somehow felt in her sex. Then he closed his fingers together, pulling gently on her nipple, and she cried out as everything seemed to intensify.

Wanting more of him, she rotated her hips against his. If she could unfasten his fall, she could feel him directly—flesh to flesh. Would he allow her to do that?

His mouth moved to her other breast, teasing and tormenting her. Somehow, he'd moved his hand beneath her skirts and was now stroking up along her thigh.

"Yes," she hissed. "I want you, Acton. Please."

He nipped her flesh gently, drawing a gasp from her. "I need to taste all of you." In a fluid motion, he reversed their positions, sitting her on the bench. But he didn't straddle her. He was on his knees in front of her as he pushed her skirts up to her waist. "Open your legs for me, Persey. Show me your beauty."

Indeed, Persephone had never felt so beautiful, so desirable. She did as he commanded and held her dress out of his way.

"Yes, like that, my lovely goddess. He put both of his hands on her thighs and used his thumbs on her sex, gently stroking the outer lips as he opened her. "So pretty. So perfect. Come to the edge of the bench, love."

Persephone scooted forward as his head lowered. She felt

his breath before his mouth descended to her hungry flesh. He stroked her clitoris with his thumb as he licked along her folds. Then his finger slid into her, and she arched up from the bench, eager for all he would give her.

She clutched at his head and shoulders. He pumped his finger into her and sucked at her clitoris, making her absolutely mindless as pleasure built inside her.

"Not too loud," he said, grasping her hip before he licked deep into her.

Yes, she'd been making too much noise, she realized. It was quite difficult not to shout for all the neighborhood to hear.

Biting her lip, she tried not to cry out or to completely lose control. She was so close to the edge, to a pleasure she was certain she'd never experienced. His hand moved from her hip to her backside, lifting her so he could cup her as he feasted on her.

Persephone thrust her hands into his hair, careless of whether she pulled at him too hard. She was past the point of rational thought. Her body arched and thrust, desperate for release.

His mouth and fingers pushed her over the barrier into completion. Darkness swept her into unimaginable bliss as her body twitched and quivered.

He saw her through the storm, guiding her to peace and a languid tranquility. She felt heavy and sated. Then his fingers moved over her folds once more, and she was instantly aroused again.

Pulling her skirts down, he backed away and got to his feet. She reached for him and managed to grip the fabric of his breeches.

She tugged, though her grip was feeble. "Come," she demanded.

He moved toward her, his cock level with her mouth. "I

should go now, Persey." His voice was raw, deep with unsatisfied desire.

"What about this?" She moved her hand over the length of his shaft, so clearly delineated by his clothing.

"I'll take care of that when I get home," he rasped.

"Why not here? Now?" She stroked him with her palm, her fingers moving to the buttons of his fall. "Can't I take what *I* want?"

His hand cupped her head as he groaned softly. "I don't deserve you. But yes, take what you want."

Persephone unfastened the buttons in quick succession and soon had his sex free in her palm. She stroked him slowly, relishing the way his breathing grew more rapid and his hips began to move.

"What will you do?" he asked, sounding as desperate as she'd felt a short while ago.

"What do you want me to do? You were going to use your hand, yes?" She envisioned him doing that and hoped one day she'd get to watch him reach his climax.

"Yes. You could do that."

"Or I could use my mouth as you did. Tell me what you want, Acton, or I'll do nothing." Her hand stilled.

"Take me in your mouth." He guided her head toward him. "Now. Please. I want to feel you around me."

She'd never done this, but didn't think it could be difficult. Instinct drove her to slide her hand to the base of his cock as she put her lips to the tip. She took him in slowly, loving the feel of his velvety flesh along her tongue.

When he was seated as deeply as she thought she could manage, she pulled back. She used her hand to massage his balls and grip him again before she sucked him in once more.

"Yes, Persey. God, you are amazing." His hips arced forward as he pushed into her mouth, driving as deep as before.

She grasped the rhythm, taking him in and releasing him —not entirely, but almost. Gripping his hip with her free hand, she guided the speed, urging him to go a bit faster. He needed no encouragement, his hips thrusting.

Loving this new power and the feel of him in her mouth, she grew bolder, using her hands and tongue to intensify his pleasure as he'd done to her. He lowered one of his hands to her breast, stroking and squeezing her. Moaning softly around his cock, she lost herself in the moment, giving herself over to the primal need to satisfy him, to ensure he was swept into the same sweet oblivion as her.

"I have to pull out." He pushed at her head, moaning.

Persephone held him fast. She wasn't finished, and neither was he.

"Persey, I'm going to spill inside your mouth. It's—" He cried out, then cut himself off. "I can't."

But he could. Salty liquid flooded her mouth. Persephone didn't know what was acceptable, but spitting it out seemed wrong. So she swallowed it, while using her hand and mouth to ease him through his release.

When he was spent, she withdrew, tucking his slackening cock back into his breeches. As he rebuttoned his fall, she pulled up her gown and fastened the hooks before tying the bodice more snugly.

Sucking him had been as arousing as what they'd been doing before. Indeed, she was quite ready for another climax herself, but it would be best if she went inside. No one would miss her—they thought she'd retired for the night—but if anyone decided to come outside, she and Acton would be in trouble.

She started to stand, and Acton quickly helped her, grasping her waist. He pulled her close. "You are magnificent." He kissed her softly at first, then with a deeper intensity that only increased her arousal.

Putting her hands on his upper chest, she pushed him gently. "If you don't stop, I'm going to sit you back down on that bench and lift my skirts to straddle you once more. Only this time, I'll be unfastening your breeches so I can feel you against me."

He kissed her cheek, then whispered, "If you do that, you'll be feeling me inside you."

Persephone shivered. How badly she wanted that.

"But I don't want that," he added in a low tone.

Disappointment iced her veins. "You don't?"

"Not tonight. Not here on a cold bench. When I take you in my arms and we join together, it will be somewhere special. Or at least warm."

Persephone couldn't help giggling. "I actually didn't mind the cool air. As it happened, I was rather overheated." She licked her lower lip as she thought of how, between the night air and Acton's attentions, her nipples had tightened.

"You are tempting me to continue what we've started. Only, I would bend you over the bench and take you from behind." He shook his head. "No, not for our first time together. You are turning me into a rutting beast. And before you jest that I was likely one before—aren't all rakes rutting beasts?—the answer is no. I am not a slave to my desires."

"That is encouraging to hear."

"I may, however, be a slave to you," he said softly, caressing her cheek before he pressed a kiss to her lips.

After briefly kissing him back, Persephone stepped away —far enough that he couldn't reach her. "I'm going now."

"Will I see you tomorrow?" he asked. "We could meet for tea at the Pump Room. At three?"

"I would like that, but it will depend on Pandora."

"Will you come even if she prefers not to?" His gaze was hopeful, his dark auburn hair seductively tousled from her hands. How could she refuse him?

"I'll be there," she said with a smile. "Now go!" She waved him off and started toward the house.

Looking back over her shoulder, she saw that he was gone.

She didn't know if she could talk Pandora into going, not even if she told her what had transpired with Acton tonight. Persephone was torn between wanting to share her happiness with her sister and keeping it to herself—both because she was behaving foolishly and because she didn't want her sister to feel badly. Unlike Bane, Acton wouldn't abandon Persephone.

While that might be true, what did he want? Furthermore, what did she want?

Persephone found herself contemplating the future—and not one where she worked as a governess. Could there be something between her and Acton? Something…permanent?

How her parents would love that. That nauseating thought was almost enough to make Persephone change course.

Almost.

Tonight, however, had been too wonderful to ignore.

# CHAPTER 16

At breakfast the following morning, Persephone had worked to hide her excessively wonderful mood. Not just because she didn't want to answer questions about it, but also because Pandora was still upset from the incident at Sydney Gardens the day before.

Aunt Lucinda did her best to cheer Pandora up, and when Persephone said the duke had invited them to join him for tea at the Pump Room that afternoon, she'd been delighted. Pandora, however, had declined, saying she hadn't changed her mind about not wanting to go out in public. Instead, she'd suggested it might be time for her to leave Bath. Though, she'd quickly added that she didn't expect Aunt Lucinda and Persephone to join her.

Persephone had not argued because the truth was that she didn't want to leave Bath. More accurately, she didn't want to go somewhere Acton was not.

Aunt Lucinda had argued that Pandora needed to come to tea, that she wasn't going to overcome the scandal by hiding. Pandora had then left and asked not to be disturbed.

That had been two hours ago, and Persephone was undecided as to whether she ought to barge in on her sister and try to improve her disposition. The problem was that Persephone wasn't sure how to go about that. Part of her was struggling with feeling so incredibly happy while her sister was so very *un*happy.

The other part of Persephone kept thinking of the previous night in the garden with Acton. It was most distracting. But in the best way possible.

Perhaps Aunt Lucinda might have advice on how to encourage Pandora to ignore people like those nasty young women in the gardens yesterday. Persephone walked to the drawing room but stopped short before going inside when she heard someone who wasn't Aunt Lucinda speaking. Evidently, her aunt had a visitor.

"Everyone is talking about the incident in the park yesterday," the woman said.

Persephone froze, her stomach dropping to the floor. People had noticed how those ladies had reacted to Pandora? None of this was fair. Persephone would do anything to keep her sister from finding out.

"Wellesbourne was so very attentive to Miss Pandora. And sweeping her into his arms like that to carry her all the way to the coach? So romantic."

She wasn't talking about the cut direct, then. Persephone's insides did not return to normal. She crept closer to the door to listen.

"He was simply helping my niece after she turned her ankle," Aunt Lucinda explained. "As a gallant gentleman should do."

"It looked to be more than that," the visitor responded. "Indeed, everyone is hoping for a match—the duke and Miss Pandora look splendid together."

Of course they did. He was handsome and debonair, and Pandora was incomparably beautiful. He was precisely the kind of man she'd been expected to wed.

"Except the duke is courting my elder niece, Miss Barclay," Aunt Lucinda pointed out, sounding as though she were perhaps gritting her teeth.

"Is he? Well, who knows what will happen? But everyone I've spoken to thinks a match between the woman Banemore wronged and his best friend would be delicious!" The visitor tittered, and Persephone had decided she'd heard enough.

Twirling on her heel, she made her way downstairs to get as far away from the hideous woman as possible. Only things did not improve as she descended into the staircase hall. Standing in the center of the entrance hall in front of Persephone were her parents.

Judging from the way they were removing their hats and gloves, they had just arrived.

*Blast.* Persephone tried to turn and tiptoe back the way she'd come, but her mother's voice stopped her cold.

"Persephone! Good heavens, you have given everyone a fright. Come here this instant."

Persephone hoped the gossipy visitor upstairs couldn't hear anything. To hopefully get her mother to lower her voice, Persephone hastened into the entrance hall. "Good afternoon, Mama. Papa." She smiled brightly, hoping to soothe their anger. Although, her father didn't even look perturbed. He would join with her mother soon enough, however. Of that, Persephone had no doubt.

"Don't you dare behave as if you aren't the most ungrateful, horrid daughter who ever breathed," her mother snapped. "You abandoned us in Cirencester, and apparently you didn't even go home as your note said."

"Mother, perhaps you'd care to wait to vent your spleen until Aunt Lucinda's guest has left," Persephone suggested with a sweetness she didn't remotely feel.

The baroness's eyes rounded. "You have caused us no

small amount of trouble," she whispered with a great amount of heat.

How Persephone wanted to sarcastically respond that they'd certainly made her life trouble-free, but held her tongue. There would be no point baiting her mother, not when she was already furious.

It wasn't as if Persephone hadn't expected this. She'd just hoped to delay it. She certainly hadn't been prepared to be faced with her mother and father today, not when she'd been feeling so lovely.

Voices sounded in the staircase hall behind Persephone. Aunt Lucinda and her visitor were coming downstairs.

Persephone moved to the side of the entrance hall just before her aunt and the other woman stepped into it. The other woman looked familiar, but Persephone didn't recall her name. Persephone trained her gaze on the floor lest she stare daggers at the woman.

"Oh, here are Lord and Lady Radstock," the woman said with cheerful surprise. "Does your arrival mean there will be a betrothal to announce soon?" She smiled broadly, her expression eager. It seemed she wanted to obtain the most recent information, likely so she could spread it widely and gain accolades for having the very latest gossip.

"Their arrival has nothing to do with any betrothal," Aunt Lucinda said crisply. "Thank you for visiting, Delia."

Before Delia, Mrs. Carmichael, could make her way to the door, which Harding was standing next to, ready to fling it open and hopefully toss her outside, Persephone's mother spoke. "Actually, we will have a betrothal to announce shortly," she said smugly.

Persephone shifted her gaze toward her mother. They would? Were they going to insist she wed Acton? Granted, that wasn't nearly as revolting a notion as it had once been. Indeed, she could see several benefits, not the least of which was continuing what they'd been doing in the garden last night.

"And which daughter will it be for?" Mrs. Carmichael asked breathlessly. "Lucinda and I were just discussing how marvelous the Duke of Wellesbourne and Miss Pandora look together."

"Pandora, you say?" Persephone's father asked with the most interest he'd displayed since arriving.

Aunt Lucinda shot her friend a perturbed look before addressing her brother. "I've explained that Wellesbourne and *Persephone* are spending time together to see if they will suit."

"Yes, but everyone saw the connection between him and Miss Pandora yesterday when he carried her to the coach. You can't deny when two people just seem to be perfect for one another."

She was basing that on watching, from afar, Acton carry Pandora because she was injured. Persephone could only stare at the woman.

Then, she noticed her parents exchanging excited looks. This did not bode well.

The baroness smiled. "As it happens, the betrothal we are prepared to announce does not involve the duke or Pandora." She looked at Persephone, as if she hadn't been railing at her moments ago. "It is about our dear Persephone."

It was about her, but not about Acton? Panic rose in Persephone's throat, choking her ability to speak. Not that she could think of what to say.

The next movements happened quickly. Aunt Lucinda motioned with her head toward Harding, who rapidly opened the door as Aunt Lucinda ushered Mrs. Carmichael out. "I appreciate you stopping by," she said before the butler snapped the door closed.

"Thank you, Harding," Aunt Lucinda said before

directing a glare toward her brother. "Let us remove to the drawing room so you can explain this nonsense that you just shared with one of the most prolific gossips in all of Bath."

Persephone's mother sniffed. "We don't care if she says anything. We'll be making a formal announcement shortly anyway. It's not as if people aren't supposed to know."

"But *I* don't know!" Persephone shouted, not caring who heard, but glad that Harding had left. She liked the butler, and he didn't need to be privy to their family drama. "You've betrothed me to some unknown man and shared that information with others before you even tell me?" Persephone felt sick.

"Good Lord, I hope Delia isn't listening at the door," Aunt Lucinda said. She waved them all toward the staircase hall. "Go."

Persephone turned and stalked upstairs. She had half a mind to keep going to the second floor to her sister's bedchamber and seek solace with her. But first Persephone needed to know what her parents had done. She was shaking by the time she reached the drawing room.

Aunt Lucinda followed them inside and closed the door. "Let us sit and discuss this like rational adults."

"I don't need to sit," Persephone said icily, her focus on her loathsome parents. "What have you done?"

"Come now, Persephone," her father cajoled. "Sit with us so we may tell you the good news. We've found you a husband at last."

"What happened to allowing me to decide?" she snapped. There was just no controlling her anger in this moment.

"You've had years to do so," the baroness said airily as she sat down, seeming not to have a care in the world, let alone concern for her daughter's outrage. "You need to be married. Your dashing off into the night in Cirencester is proof of that. You need a firm hand to guide you, as you are no longer listening to us."

Persephone stared at them. "You were going to force me to wed Wellesbourne, which I did not want to do." Something she would not now mind but was apparently no longer an option. "Now, you're going to force me to marry someone else? Someone I don't even know?"

"He isn't like the duke," her father said, sitting near her mother. "Your primary complaint was Wellesbourne's reputation. Your betrothed is a well-respected member of his community and in London. He's a member of Parliament. Though you won't be a duchess, you will enjoy the life of a London hostess."

As if any of that mattered to her. She'd wanted to at least like her husband, let alone know him. Oh God. She *did* know him. Or at least she thought she did. Her mother's cousin in Winchester had a son who stood for MP in the most recent election. They'd met only a handful of times, and the last occasion had been nearly five years ago. He was loud and obnoxious, and the thing he liked most was the sound of his own voice. "You can't mean Cousin Harold."

"Indeed, we do," the baroness said brightly. "He was most enthusiastic about the prospect of marrying you. Honestly, I don't know why any of us didn't think of it sooner."

They'd referred to him as her betrothed. Was there an agreement, then? Persephone managed to cross her arms over her chest. "I don't want to marry him."

"You'll come around to it," her father said with a wave of his hand. "Harold is doing great things in Parliament. This is a good marriage for you, my dear."

Persephone felt as though she couldn't breathe. "How does it help Pandora? That was *your* primary reason for wanting me to wed immediately."

"While this isn't as advantageous a match as Wellesbourne, it's good enough to keep our family in good standing."

Persephone saw no reason to ignore the subject that pricked her parents the most. "Socially or financially?"

"Mind your tongue," her mother said sharply.

"Oh, for heaven's sake, mind yours," Aunt Lucinda retorted. "You can't demand Persephone marry someone. She is of age to make her own decisions."

Surprisingly, the baron responded to his sister. "That may be, but after her actions in Cirencester, she has demonstrated an inability to make sound ones. Edith and I thought it best if we saw Persephone settled. *Immediately.*"

"I won't marry him," Persephone repeated.

"I'm afraid you have no choice," her mother said, sounding weary. "Your father has already negotiated the contract."

"And how much did Cousin Harold pay?" Persephone couldn't help the snide question. Except, the flustered expression on her father's face and the way her mother looked quickly away made Persephone's heart race. "He didn't *pay* you to marry me, did he?"

"That doesn't matter," her father said crossly.

Aunt Lucinda had sat at some point, but now she stood. "This is unconscionable." She moved to Persephone and put her arm around her shoulders. "We'll find a way to break this contract. Unlike your parents, I have the financial means to take care of this and of you." She met Persephone's gaze. "If you'll allow me to."

"Yes, please," she said softly, never more grateful for her aunt's love and concern. In hindsight, she should have left her parents and come to live with Aunt Lucinda years ago. But that had not been offered—not that Aunt Lucinda would have disallowed it. She'd often made overtures of assistance, both financial and otherwise, and Persephone's father, beholden to his ridiculous pride, had always declined them.

The baron's eyes narrowed, glittering with anger, as he looked toward his sister. "I've asked you time and again not to meddle with my family. Do not flaunt your wealth in my face. I've negotiated a favorable marriage for *my* daughter. Breaking the contract will ruin us in every way."

"That is not my concern, nor is it Persephone's," Aunt Lucinda said coldly. Persephone could feel her shaking with rage. "You should want your daughter's happiness above all else, especially your own financial comfort, which is a mess of your own making, by the way. If our father could see what you've done—" She abruptly stopped, and Persephone put her arm around her aunt's waist, giving her a squeeze.

"You'll ruin Persephone," the baroness said. "Mrs. Carmichael is even now telling everyone that Persephone is betrothed. If she cries off, she will be a pariah."

Persephone nearly laughed. She hadn't even been aware she was being betrothed, and yet *she* would pay the price.

The baroness put her finger to her lips. "But, if Pandora and Wellesbourne are truly forming a match, then all may yet be well. Still, it's best if Persephone marries Cousin Harold. It would cause strife in the family if she did not."

Persephone scoffed. "I don't think the duke will be as eager to pay you off as Cousin Harold was."

"That may be true, which is why you must marry Cousin Harold. This will settle our debts, and everyone can start fresh on happier ground." The baroness clasped her hands in her lap as if she'd just claimed victory in a game.

But that was all Persephone was to them—a pawn they could maneuver to suit their own needs. Except she wasn't going to capitulate. She had Aunt Lucinda's support. And anyway, she'd been prepared for a life of spinsterhood from the moment she'd left them in Cirencester.

"You underestimate my need to make my own choices," Persephone said quietly. "I won't let you manipulate me—or Pandora. You should just go back to Radstock Hall. Perhaps you should sell another painting, if there are any of value left." There were, of course, because the baron had been unable to part with a select number. He was an absolute slave to his pride and sense of status.

"You ungrateful chit—" The baroness began, but Aunt Lucinda cut her off.

"Please leave," Aunt Lucinda barked. "You are no longer welcome here."

The baron sputtered. "We just arrived!"

"Go on, then." Aunt Lucinda shooed at them.

Reluctantly, Persephone's parents stood. The baron fixed Persephone with a dark stare. "Think on this long and hard, my girl. You cannot undo what's been done."

"No, you cannot," Persephone said sadly. "I do hope one day you reflect back on this and realize the course you've chosen to take is one you can't return from."

His brow creased with confusion, and Persephone could see that he didn't, at least for now, understand what she was saying. They—her mother was most certainly of the same mind—didn't comprehend how they were breaking their family apart with their selfishness. *They* were the ones who would ruin the family, not Persephone and not Pandora.

They left the drawing room, and Persephone sagged against her aunt.

"We cannot go to the Pump Room now," Persephone said. "I'll send a note to the duke."

Aunt Lucinda pivoted to face her. "We could still go."

Persephone shook her head. "I'd rather not. I'm too upset. Can you really break this contract with Cousin Harold?"

"No clergyman will marry you against your will," Aunt Lucinda said firmly. "Do not even concern yourself. I will write to your mother's cousin personally and explain the error."

"But what about the gossip? Mrs. Carmichael may already have spread the news that I am betrothed."

"We must count on that, I'm afraid. But again, we'll correct the error and simply explain that she was mistaken." Aunt Lucinda faced Persephone and took her hands. "Trust me that all will work out well."

"What will work out?" Pandora asked as she walked into the drawing room.

"Oh, Pandora, you've missed quite a scene." Persephone went to her sister and wrapped her in a fierce hug.

"Whatever is wrong?" Pandora sounded most concerned.

"Your parents were here," Aunt Lucinda said darkly. Then she went on to explain what had transpired. Thankfully, Persephone didn't have to say anything.

They'd sat down before Aunt Lucinda had delivered the tale, and now Pandora was gaping at them both. She fixed on Persephone. "I cannot believe they betrothed you to Cousin Harold. Why did they give up on Wellesbourne? Didn't you tell them that you are courting?"

"We haven't discussed a formal courtship." Persephone hoped she would not turn pink as she recalled the reason they hadn't discussed such things. They'd been too busy kissing. And so forth. "Wellesbourne and I certainly don't know one another well enough to make such decisions. Anyway, Mrs. Carmichael is running about today telling anyone who will listen that Pandora and the duke are the perfect match." Persephone clenched her jaw.

Pandora paled. "She can't do that. My reputation has suffered enough. When the duke leaves Bath and there is no match, I'll be vilified again."

"I do think your parents hope that you and he will wed," Aunt Lucinda noted. "Pandora, did anything happen between the two of you while he carried you to the coach yesterday?"

"Nothing at all, save him asking how I was feeling."

"Honestly, it would be most convenient if he would marry one of you." Aunt Lucinda chuckled. "My apologies. I shouldn't jest about such things. I just want things to smooth over for both of you." She gave them a warm smile full of love and encouragement.

"You've done so much already," Pandora said softly. "We can't thank you enough."

"You've no need to thank me. And I shall insist that you both remain here with me. Pandora, this scandal with Banemore will pass, even if it takes some time. When you are ready, we will relaunch you into Society, either here or in London. *You* will decide, not your parents." Aunt Lucinda turned her attention to Persephone. "Persey, you will be safe here with no pressure to marry anyone you don't wish to. If you'd like a London Season, we can plan for that next spring."

Persephone didn't know what to say. Right now, she just wanted to send Acton a note telling him that everything was a mess, with her parents trying to marry her off and rumors swirling that he and Pandora would be making a match. She couldn't put it all in writing. She needed to see him.

Tonight.

# CHAPTER 17

$\mathcal{A}$cton wasn't entirely sure where more than half the day had gone, but he still felt as though he were floating on a cloud of bliss after last night in the garden with Persey. He could scarcely wait until he saw her for tea in just a few short hours. Less than that, even.

His sisters had commented that he seemed distracted, but he'd only shrugged. He'd mentioned that he would be meeting Persephone, her sister, and her aunt for tea. That had prompted more questions about his intentions, but he'd only said he was still considering his next steps.

That had not been a lie. Acton didn't know what Persephone wanted, but he was beginning to think she could very well be his duchess. He was mulling that thought in the library on the ground floor when his mother swept in, surprising him.

He set down the newspaper he hadn't been reading and stood. "Good afternoon, Mother. I didn't know you were coming to Bath."

"It seemed you weren't returning to Loxley Court, and I knew the girls would be here a few more days." A motherly smile curved her mouth as she spoke of her daughters, and Acton suffered a pang of envy. They shared a lifelong close relationship. He could never claim that with any of them. Even if they became close and lived the rest of their days as a family, there were so many lost years. His mother continued, "I am delighted to be here with all my children under the same roof."

"In the same room even," Francesca said as she walked into the library. Cecily trailed behind her.

The dowager beamed upon seeing her daughters. "My dearest girls." She went to them, and the three embraced together. It looked like something they'd done before. Probably all his sisters' lives. The envy returned, along with jealousy and sadness. His father would be horrified at the tumult of emotions Acton was experiencing.

When they parted, their mother glanced down at Cecily's rounded belly. "You look well. Feeling all right too, I hope?"

"Better than with Georgie, actually."

"I was the same with you," the dowager said, smiling at her younger daughter. "Each babe was a bit easier." She looked toward Acton. "You were most difficult." She said this without rancor. Indeed, she seemed nostalgic.

Acton couldn't think of what to say to that, so he remained silent.

"Would you all stand together?" their mother asked, sounding tentative.

Moving closer to his sisters, Acton asked, "Why?"

"Just seeing you all here…" Their mother clasped her hands over her heart. Her eyes glistened, and she blinked. "I've waited so very long for this. I wonder if you might humor me and sit for a portrait some time."

That reminded Acton of the portrait of him in her sitting room. He wanted to ask her about it, but not in front of his sisters. For some reason, the matter felt…private.

"I'm so glad you are here, Mama," Francesca said, sitting down in the nearest chair. "But now you won't receive the letter I sent yesterday."

"Well, you can tell me what you wrote in person." The dowager also sat, which prompted Cecily to do the same, and Acton sank back into his chair.

Francesca sent an uncomfortable look toward Acton. "I wrote to you about Miss Pandora Barclay. She was compromised by Wellesbourne's friend, Banemore."

"Oh, yes, I'd heard about that. At least a half dozen of my friends here wrote to me about it."

Acton turned toward her. "Did you know about it when you agreed for me to meet with Miss Barclay?"

"I did not, but would it have mattered?" The dowager's dark red-brown brows gathered as her forehead pleated.

"Not as far as a courtship between me and Miss Barclay; however, I would have liked to know about Bane's transgression."

"You find his behavior upsetting?" his mother asked.

"I find it repugnant." Acton hoped he would hear from Bane or one of their friends soon. "I have been trying to help Miss Pandora regain her standing in Society. She should not have to suffer because Bane led her along, then surprised her with a make-believe betrothal."

His mother gasped. "He isn't actually betrothed?"

Acton exhaled. "I don't know, but it seems unlikely in my opinion. I saw him not long ago, and he would have said something about being leg-shackled. I also can't imagine he would behave as he had with Miss Pandora if he'd already promised to wed someone else. But then that is the problem. He's behaved poorly regardless of whether he's betrothed or not."

"I'm glad to hear you say so." His mother sounded... proud? And perhaps a little surprised? She would know all about his reputation, of course. Did she believe everything she'd heard? Acton shifted in his seat, unsettled by any sense of judgment from her.

"Wellesbourne is not the reprobate we thought," Cecily said, sending Acton a smile that made him feel...odd. It was warm and conveyed support, but it was more than that. It was...familial?

"Indeed, when Miss Pandora turned her ankle at Sydney Gardens yesterday, Wellesbourne ensured she was all right and even carried her to her coach," Francesca added. "I imagine everyone is talking about that."

Their mother nodded. "They are, in fact. When I arrived a short while ago, one of the neighbors asked if I'd come to town because a betrothal was imminent. Apparently, Lord and Lady Radstock are also here."

They were? Acton tensed. He didn't like thinking of what they would say to Persey upon seeing her after she'd run away from them. He had a sudden urge to go to her. At least he would see her soon at the Pump Room.

Would her parents be there too now that they were in Bath? He hoped not. His impression of them was not good, and he preferred to avoid them if possible.

"How did you and Lady Radstock become friends?" Acton asked, thinking his mother was so much kinder and warmhearted than the baroness.

Wait, he thought his mother—the woman who'd abandoned him at the age of five—was warmhearted?

Before he could answer that alarming question, his mother responded to the one he'd asked her. "She was one of the first people to welcome me to Bath when I moved here with your sisters." She hesitated before adding, "It was a difficult time, as your father and I had chosen to live separately, and many people treated me...awkwardly."

This was the most she'd ever spoken to Acton of that

time. But then Acton had never asked. He supposed he hadn't wanted to hear about it. He'd known that she'd left him and his father, and anything else seemed unimportant. Now, he realized he wanted to learn her perspective. Perhaps he could understand why she'd left him—and let go of his residual anger that was often just beneath the surface. Even now, seeing her here in her house with her daughters, Acton was starting to feel uncomfortable, almost agitated. So many damn emotions. He didn't want *any* of them.

The dowager continued, "She was very kind to me and became a good friend. We aren't as close now, I'm afraid. She has changed somewhat over the years, becoming more distant. She seems unhappy, to be honest. However, she's always been good to me, and I will consider her a friend until that changes. I am delighted to hear that you are helping their younger daughter. That means a great deal to me."

"Mama, while it's good to support your friend's daughter, is it not also appropriate to hold Miss Pandora accountable for her actions?" Francesca asked. "She was walking alone with a known scoundrel. It seems as though she put herself in scandal's path."

"I don't disagree with you, my dear." The dowager responded with kindness and understanding. "However, have you never made a mistake?"

Francesca didn't respond, but gave a subtle nod, as if to say her mother's point was taken. Acton couldn't help thinking how their father might have responded if Francesca had asked him that question. He would have said something like "You're damned right, the chit should have known better. She has only herself to blame. Frankly, someone like that who doesn't show good judgment can't expect the heir to a dukedom to take them seriously."

Acton preferred his mother's answer.

Simmons came in and made his way to Acton's chair. "This just arrived for you, Your Grace."

Acton recognized the handwriting—it was from Persey. Knowing her parents were now in Bath, he immediately grew concerned. His pulse picked up speed as he opened the parchment and read the contents.

*I regret that I will not be able to join you for tea at the Pump Room this afternoon. My parents have arrived in town and matters have become complicated. I will explain to you in person if you could meet me in the garden again this evening at the same time.*

*Yours,*

*Persey*

*Yours.* And she'd signed with her sobriquet again.

Acton's disappointment as well as his anger toward her parents were tempered by a sense of giddy warmth. He was desperate to know how her parents had complicated things and could hardly wait to see Persey tonight.

"Good news?" his mother asked. "It's hard to tell because you frowned and then you smiled."

Refolding the letter, Acton tucked it into his pocket. "Miss Barclay is not able to meet for tea this afternoon due to her parents' arrival."

The dowager nodded. "I am delighted you were able to meet Miss Barclay here. How did you come to know she was in Bath?"

Disliking that he had to repeat the lie, Acton hesitated. "I, ah, I called on her at Radstock Hall and learned she was here in Bath."

"*That* is why you are here," the dowager said with a faint smile. "And how have things progressed between the two of you?"

"We've only met a few times," he fibbed again, thinking that he or Persey was going to forget something at some point and draw attention to their fabrications. If anyone learned the two of them had met without a chaperone and spent several days alone together, including in the same bedchamber overnight, the scandal that Pandora had endured would pale in comparison.

"With plans to meet again today," his mother observed. "I'm sorry you aren't able to go to tea. Were you meeting at the Pump Room?"

"We were."

"We met Miss Barclay at Sydney Gardens," Cecily said. "I liked her. She struck me as very sensible."

"How encouraging to hear," their mother said. "I trust she's recovered from her malady?"

"She seemed quite robust," Francesca answered.

Sensible. Robust. These were not the first words that came to Acton's mind. She was wickedly clever. Fiercely independent. Remarkably fearless.

That made him think of the rat incident. She was also in possession of a spectacular sense of humor.

And she was beautiful and seductive. Utterly irresistible.

He couldn't wait to hold her later, to soothe her anger or fear, whatever her parents' arrival had caused her to feel.

"I look forward to renewing my acquaintance with her," the dowager said. "We shall have to plan another outing."

"Or we could host something here," Acton found himself saying. "If you're amenable, of course."

"What sort of something?" Francesca asked.

"We could hold a soiree like we do during the Season," their mother said, her eyes growing animated.

"Mama's soirees are legendary," Cecily said, casting a knowing look toward their mother and Francesca. "Would you really want to have one now, before the Season has started, Mama?"

"Why not? Hosting Wellesbourne's potential bride as well as providing a public way to endorse her sister is a wonderful reason. Girls, you can help me prepare invitations, and I'll have them sent around later this afternoon."

"I can help too," Acton offered. The emotional turmoil he'd felt earlier had lessened.

Francesca arched a brow at him. "How's your handwriting?"

He lifted a shoulder. "Passable."

"You can address them, then, while Cecily and I write the details," Francesca said with a teasing laugh.

"Perfect." Their mother looked nearly ecstatic. "I'll prepare a guest list right now."

"You've only just arrived, Mama," Cecily pointed out. "Rest for a bit."

"Nonsense. This is the most excited I've been about something in a long time. I couldn't possibly take a respite." She stood. "I'll have Mrs. Hedge help me set up the table in here for us to gather around and write everything out. This will be such fun."

After she left the library, Acton's sisters pinned him with an expectant stare.

"This is because of you," Francesca said.

He blinked at his sister. "What is?"

"Her excitement about having a soiree when it isn't even the Season yet."

"Is that bad?" Acton couldn't see anything wrong with it.

"It's not bad," Cecily said. "It's just different. Please don't disappoint her in any way."

"Why would I do that?"

Francesca's eyes narrowed slightly. "Because you are our

father's son, and there was no one better at disappointing her than him."

He was? Acton had always thought—more accurately, he'd been told—that his parents' separation was mutual, that his mother had been thrilled to leave his father and have her own household away from him. That did not sound like someone who would be disappointed by the man she'd been eager to leave behind.

Perhaps the reason Acton was so good at telling lies was that he'd had a good teacher. He pushed that thought away, preferring to focus on happier things.

Such as Persey and how in a matter of hours, she would be in his arms once more.

# CHAPTER 18

*I*mpatience and anticipation drove Acton to arrive a quarter hour early for his assignation with Persey. He went to the bench where they'd been last night and sat down. Then he got up, for it was rather cold. Mostly, he needed to move as he was desperate to see her.

Though seeing her would be more difficult tonight because the sky was overrun with clouds. Acton worried it might rain.

She came out of the house five minutes later. Acton smiled, wondering if she was as eager to see him as he was her.

He stood near the bench, his body thrumming. When she came around the hedge, he snatched her into his arms as he'd wanted to do last night and kissed her.

Twining her arms around his neck, she returned the kiss. Acton swung her about, lifting her feet from the ground. She laughed into his mouth, and he set her down.

"It seems you're pleased to see me," she said breathlessly, keeping her hands on his shoulders.

"Ecstatic." He clasped her waist, unwilling and unable to

let her go. "And I'm so glad to see you smiling. I feared the worst after I received your note."

There was just enough light for him to note the darkening of her features. Or perhaps he was just that attuned to her moods after spending so much time with her. Although, it wasn't really enough time. Not since they'd reached Bath.

"My parents have made a mess of everything," she said crossly, sliding her hands down to his chest. "They've negotiated a marriage contract for me. To my mother's cousin's son, Harold."

It was as if someone had sent their fist into Acton's gut. He struggled to take a deep breath. "*What?*"

"After leaving Loxley Court, they went to my mother's cousin's and arranged this marriage. Harold is an MP, and their family is wealthy." Her eyes were wide and distressed. "He is *paying* them to wed me."

Acton actually sputtered. "This is outrageous," he finally managed. "They came to negotiate a marriage with *me* at Loxley Court. I only refused because you weren't there in person to consent. I will fight this marriage. I have first right of refusal."

She stared at him in silence for a moment. Then she laughed. And snorted.

"This isn't a joke." Acton was outraged. Her parents couldn't sell her off to the highest bidder. This was madness. In any case, he would pay more than this idiot Harold if he had to.

Wait, did he *want* to marry her? He certainly didn't want anyone else to. Not now. Not while they were…courting. Or whatever it was they were doing.

"I know." She swallowed several breaths and finally sobered, clutching his lapels. "Your anger is delightful. As is your absolutely roguish reaction. You have no claim on me— first rights or any other."

"Fine," he said tersely. "But your parents came to *me* first, and I'm a bloody duke. That they would betroth you to some nobody MP is offensive."

"My goodness, but your arrogance is on full display this evening. And here I thought you were less haughty than most rogues."

Were they having a disagreement? He didn't want to be at odds with her. "I don't mean to sound superior. It's just that your parents are ridiculous. You don't come seeking a match with a duke only to run off and arrange something else."

"I understand you aren't used to being cast aside," she said softly. "And you are right that my parents are ridiculous. They actually think you should marry my sister now. Because of the gossip that you and she are *destined* to be together." Her sardonic tone didn't take the sting from what she was saying.

Acton didn't think he could become angrier. "What rubbish is this?" He realized he was squeezing her waist and loosened his grip.

One of Persephone's golden brows arched. "You haven't heard? Shocking. I would think someone would have called at your mother's house to ask for confirmation that you and Pandora are in love. Because you look so wonderful together, you see. Your rakish good looks and her stunning beauty. It's a match made by God, to be sure."

He heard her sarcasm and thought of when they'd spoken of her attributes before. She'd mentioned things about herself that she or others found lacking. He hated that people were commenting on how he *looked* with Pandora. "Persey, please don't be hurt by these rumors. I only helped Pandora because she couldn't walk—or was acting as though she couldn't." He cupped her cheek. "*You* are the most enchanting woman I have ever known."

Now, her expression softened as she gazed up at him. "Thank you for saying that."

He dropped his hand to his side. "You're going to excuse me now, because I need to go into your aunt's house and speak with your father. He needs to understand that I have not yet decided whether we will suit."

"Acton, not only do I not want you to do that, but my parents aren't inside. My aunt wouldn't allow them to stay, so they are lodging at the White Hart."

Some of the tension released from his shoulders. "I am relieved to hear it. I was worried you would have to suffer their presence."

"That is most considerate of you. While they have complicated my life, I am just glad to not have to reside under the same roof as them. Why is family so difficult?" She briefly cocked her head. "Not all family. I could not manage without my sister, and my aunt is the parent we all deserve. What of your family? How has it been to stay with your sisters?"

"Surprisingly good. I am coming to know them. And like them," he added. "My mother arrived today. She's absolutely giddy at having all her children together. She's hosting a party day after tomorrow. You and your sister must come."

A drop of rain landed on Persey's nose. "Oh!" She brought her hand up to wipe it away.

He glanced up at the sky. "Damn, I was afraid it might rain." He didn't want their time together to be abbreviated.

"Unfortunately, we don't have a coach to run to," she said.

He swore under his breath, his mind scrambling for somewhere to go.

"Come with me." She took his hand and, as the rain picked up, pulled him quickly to a staircase at the corner of the house that led to the lower level. By pressing herself to the door and tugging him along with her, they were somewhat protected from the rain. She pursed her lips. "I thought this would keep us dry."

"I suppose I should go." Disappointment pricked through him.

"Actually, there is an unused room just inside. The scullery maid lives at home with her family, so no one sleeps there."

She opened the door before he could protest—not that he wanted to. "Are we going to sleep?"

Casting a look back at him, she rolled her eyes. "We can continue talking in there. Unless you'd rather go?"

"I would prefer to stay." And if this room had a place for sleeping, then it had a place for other activities. God, he was still thinking like a rake.

"Then close the door and come with me."

Acton didn't need to be told twice. He closed the exterior door and followed her to another door. She opened it and moved inside. The space was dark, without even a window to offer illumination.

"How are we to see one another?" he asked.

"There should be a candle. Just keep the door open a moment longer." She went to a small table in the corner, and he heard flint before the wick of a candle lit with a yellow flame. "You can close that now."

Letting the door shut behind him, Acton moved into the compact space. There was a table, one chair, and a narrow cot—with a thin mattress but no bedclothes.

She turned to face him. "I don't know that I will be able to persuade Pandora to come to a party."

It took Acton a moment to recall they'd been discussing the party before the rain had started. "Tell her she will be a guest of honor. And that the families of those young ladies who were rude to her at the gardens will not be invited." When Acton had reviewed the guest list, he'd struck off their names, explaining why. His mother had agreed wholeheartedly. She wasn't particularly friendly with the girls' mothers anyway.

"That is awfully kind of you—and presumably of your mother too," Persey said. She seemed to hesitate. "Will my parents be invited?"

Acton had also tried to remove them from the list while also expecting his mother to argue. She had insisted they be invited, citing her loyalty to the baroness. "I'm afraid so. My mother feels beholden to your mother. Apparently, she was particularly warm to my mother when she first moved to Bath."

"Warm? Are you certain that was *my* mother?" Persey quipped.

"So my mother says. She also acknowledges that your mother seems different now, but didn't elaborate." He moved to stand in front of Persey and removed his hat, tossing it on the chair. "I will do everything in my power to keep them away from you."

"It's all right. I needn't speak with them even if I do see them. I don't need them anymore. Aunt Lucinda is giving me a permanent home and I may even have a London Season next year. If I want it."

Acton kept himself from frowning. He didn't want that. The thought of her parading around London on the Marriage Mart made his stomach clench. He put one arm around her waist and pulled her tightly against him. "What if I don't want to share you with London?"

Her brows arched and her eyes rounded briefly. "'Share' me? That implies some kind of ownership or claim."

"Oh, I claim you." Acton had enough self-awareness to realize he sounded like an overbearing rogue, but he didn't possess the self-control to stop himself, apparently.

He traced his finger from her hairline to her jaw.

Tempering himself, he lowered his voice to a near whisper. "I *would* claim you."

"Tonight?" she breathed, sliding her palm up the front of his damp coat and clasping the side of his neck.

"Right this moment." He swept his lips over hers, greedily devouring her with a sudden desperate need to possess her.

She clutched him, pressing her fingers into the flesh of his neck. Her skin against his made him want to feel all of her. Would she let that happen? Could he?

This was absolutely blackguard behavior, and yet he couldn't seem to stop. Every stroke of her tongue and slant of her lips drove him deeper into an abyss of desire that he was powerless to escape.

She pushed his coat from his shoulders. Before it could drop to the floor, he caught it and tossed it toward the chair. And missed.

"You're most adept," she murmured between kisses as she tangled her fingers in his cravat. "One might think you've done this before."

"You know I have." Just as he knew she had. At least once. Did that matter? Not to him. Except he hated thinking of her with another man. Which was also beastly and exceedingly hypocritical of him. What had happened to turn him from a carefree rogue to a jealous lover?

"I've done this many times," he said darkly, suddenly overcome with lust. "And, if I may say so, I'm quite good at it." He fisted his hand in the fabric of her skirt over her backside as he cupped her neck, deepening their kisses in response to his raging need. She was wearing the same gown as last night, meaning it would be easy to divest her of it. Had she forgone the stays again? He wished he'd come in nothing but his shirtsleeves.

His cravat came loose in her hand. How she'd managed to untie it while they kissed was an erotic mystery he would solve another time—could she also tie something during the throes of passion? That would be a useful skill.

The cravat disappeared, and her hands went to the buttons of his waistcoat. Which meant they were no longer pressed together. He kissed along her jaw as she worked, using his thumb to stroke her neck. Her pulse beat strong and fast, echoing his own.

Then his waistcoat was open, and he shrugged it away intending to untie her bodice next. However, she beat him to it while he was casting his garment off. She loosened the gown and unfastened the front, letting it drop. As with last night, she was not wearing undergarments.

"One might think you dressed for this occasion."

"I was perhaps hoping for a repeat of last night. I honestly didn't anticipate *this*." Her gaze was dark, seductive, utterly captivating. Was this the same woman whose glare had nearly eviscerated him the night they'd met?

Indeed, she was the same woman, and he wanted all of her—feisty termagant, teasing charmer, and sultry siren.

"And what is *this*?" he asked softly, taking a step back. He sat on the chair, dislodging his hat without concern. Meaning to remove his boots, he hesitated.

"An assignation, wouldn't you agree?"

"I would. But I want to be clear on what you want." His gaze flicked to the cot behind her. "There is a bed."

The corner of her mouth ticked up. "And that signifies what? Are you going to ask about sleeping again?"

"Hell, no. That cot is ideal for taking our assignation to its natural conclusion."

Her eyes gleamed with sensual delight. "I can hardly wait to hear what that is. Please be specific. If you can."

She was teasing him again, and this time, he wanted more of it. Though, it was incredibly hard to focus on having an arousing conversation when her bare breasts were taunting him. Her dark pink nipples were completely erect, ready for his hands and mouth.

He managed to pull off one boot and then the other, setting them aside. Then he looked her in the eye. "How is this for specificity: you and me entwined, my cock buried inside you."

Her brow furrowed gently, as if she wasn't entirely sure she knew what he meant. Or worse, that she didn't want that. "Will there be a climax involved? I should like to have that again—with you inside me, if possible."

Acton groaned. "I will make you come more times than you can count if you'd let me."

"That sounds...overwhelming. How about three? Can you manage three?"

Launching from the chair, he clasped her against him with a growl. "Three it is. But don't blame me if I accidentally provoke four."

"Your arrogance tonight is quite something." She reached behind herself and loosened the tie of her gown. "How fortunate for you that I am finding it vastly arousing."

"I can see that." He lowered his head to her breast. "Your nipples are quite eager for me. They clearly remember me from last night and are desperate for me to pleasure them again." He blew on one, teasing her.

She sucked in breath. "*Yes.* They are most eager."

"Splendid," he murmured, blowing on the other one before lightly touching the tip of his tongue to the flesh of her breast, avoiding the nipple. He moved over her slowly, tasting her as her breathing grew more rapid. Her chest rose and fell with increasing speed.

"Now, you're being cruel. You know I want you."

"I do. And that isn't arrogance. That's just observation." Still, he couldn't help feeling cocky about it.

"Please, Acton. Deliver me from this torment."

"Lie on the bed, and I will."

She quickly moved to do as he instructed, reclining on the narrow cot.

"Hmm, I should have brought bedclothes again," he said with a wicked smile.

"I don't need those. Or anything but you. You are taking much too long to join me."

"I haven't finished with my demands." He crossed his arms over his chest, in part to try to contain his own raging lust. "Take off your gown."

"You should have asked before I got on the bed!" Huffing, she pushed the garment down and wriggled her hips free before kicking it away.

"But then I wouldn't have been able to watch your body move like that." His voice had lowered, commensurate with the lengthening of his cock. He hadn't thought he could grow harder, but he'd been wrong.

"Now, will you come?" she asked in a near whine that pushed him closer to the edge.

He shook his head. "Show me what you want. Touch yourself the way you want me to touch you."

Now she looked at him as if he'd lost all rational thought. "I can't put my mouth on my breast."

"I meant with your hands. I will put my mouth on you shortly." *Very* shortly. He was nearly at the end of his tether.

"Only if you take your shirt off," she countered.

"Saucy thing," he murmured before pulling his shirt over his head and dropping it to the floor behind him. "Better?"

Her eyes fixed on his bare chest, her lids growing hooded with desire as she perused him. Then she licked her lips, and he was done teasing.

"Show me, Persey. *Now.*"

She cupped her breasts, massaging them. He swallowed, watching the globes move in her grasp and wishing he was the one doing it. And he would be—just one more moment of delicious torture.

Her thumbs and forefingers moved to the nipples and pulled, then pinched together. She moaned softly, and he was absolutely gone.

With a primitive growl, he dropped to the floor next to the cot and replaced one of her hands with his, squeezing and stroking her. She arched up, crying out.

"Part your legs," he rasped, trailing one hand down the concavity of her abdomen. He slipped his fingers through her golden-brown curls and found the heat of her sex. She was wet and ready, as she'd been last night when he'd put his mouth on her.

She opened her thighs and rotated her hips, seeking his touch. He lowered his lips to her breast, holding her flesh as he suckled her. She bucked up into the hand between her legs as she clutched at his head.

"Acton, I need—" She gasped as he slid his finger into her sheath.

"What do you need, love?" He lifted his head to look at her face. Her eyes were closed, her lips parted. She was always stunning, but this version of her was completely disarming.

"That. More of that."

He pumped his finger into her while using his thumb to massage her clitoris. "Like that?"

"Yes, please." She moved with him, circling her hips and arching up. He could practically feel her orgasm building, and with it, his own arousal intensified.

Sucking her nipple hard, he put two fingers into her, thrusting and curving his fingers to find the spot that would send her into oblivion.

Moaning, she pulled at his hair. Her hips moved faster. He stroked his fingers deeper and pinched her nipple.

Her muscles clenched around him, signaling her release was imminent. He moved his other hand from her breast to her clitoris and pushed her into release.

Her entire body stiffened as she cried out. Then she moved again as she murmured nonsense, her head cast back leaving her neck long and exposed. Though he wanted to kiss her there, to lick every inch of her flesh, he continued pumping into her until she began to slow. Only then, did he kiss the hollow of her throat.

"That's one," he said, taking his fingers from her and clasping her thigh.

She opened her eyes. Her blue gaze was hazy with passion. "Two more to finish, then."

He laughed. "I should take off my breeches and stockings."

"What are you waiting for?" She turned to her side and pressed herself back against the wall. Gasping, she inched forward slightly. "Cold."

He watched her nipples pebble once more. "I can see that. Or are you eager for my touch once more?"

"Both."

He divested himself of the remainder of his clothing, but she stopped him before he joined her on the cot. "Would you turn around, please?" she asked. "I want to see your backside."

Slowly, he presented his back to her. Then he wiggled his arse, provoking her to laugh.

Completing his circle, he faced her once more. "Satisfied?"

"With only one climax?" She scoffed. "Not even close."

"Then I'd best get to work." Acton situated himself on the cot on his side toward her. There was just barely enough room for them both. He hesitated before taking her in his arms. "We should discuss the future. I don't want you to think this is just another tryst in a long line of affairs."

Her brows dove over her eyes, and her gaze grew serious. "Don't you dare propose to me, Acton. Promise me or you can go."

She didn't want a marriage proposal? "But you deserve that. I can't expect you to lie with me and not become my duchess."

"I am not trading my body for a title." She propped herself up with her elbow. "Perhaps you should go."

"But—" He came up on his elbow too. "I'm confused. You disdain me for being a scoundrel, and now when I am specifically trying *not* to be roguish, you won't allow me to do so."

"Because tonight I want the rogue. I don't want to think about expectations or duty or responsibility. I want to be a woman who desires a man and is desired in return. Can we just have that please?"

# CHAPTER 19

*P*ersephone watched a flurry of emotions play over his face, most of them moving too quickly for her to identify. He looked confused and surprised. And at least a dozen other things.

"I want this night with you, not the promise of a marriage neither of us particularly wants." At least not now. There was far too much going on in Persephone's life for her to consider such a monumental decision. "When I wed—*if* I wed—it will be to a man I love completely and who loves me completely in return." She hadn't realized until that moment that she really didn't want to settle for anything less.

He stared at her, and she worried he was going to say something foolish. He couldn't love her. She could never love someone like him, and no matter how much less roguish he'd turned out to be, she had to remember the rogue rule about change. At his core, he was a man who enjoyed flirting and sex. How could one woman, especially her, be enough for him?

"I don't think I know how to love," he finally said, his

voice flat while his eyes seemed to glimmer with something else. Surprise, perhaps.

"Then you are not the man for me. You are, however, the man for me right now. You owe me two more orgasms."

His nostrils flared. "You know that word?"

"I know many words. What I don't know is how to come more than once in an evening."

"Then allow me to demonstrate. One moment." Somehow, he managed to turn over. He reached for something, then faced her once more. "I needed to position my cravat closer. For later."

She arched a brow at him. "What are you going to use that for?"

"Nothing so decadent as I may want, unfortunately. I'll use it for my seed when I pull from your body. Can't have a baby now, can we?"

"Thank you." Curious, she bit her lower lip. "But what decadence do you want with a cravat?"

He positioned her beneath him. "If this bed had proper posts, I would use the cravat to tie your hands while I pleasured you. It's a delightful torment."

Persey imagined herself bound beneath him while he attended to her body. Her breasts pricked with need as her sex throbbed with renewed arousal. "That does sound decadent."

"Would you let me do it?" he asked, rising over her and sweeping his hand down her throat to her breast, where he cupped her gently.

"Yes." She was instantly breathless.

"Next time, perhaps." He gave her a wicked smile. "Ready for climax number two? I find I am nearly to my breaking point with all this talk of cravats and torment."

"I'm ready, Acton." She clasped his neck and brought his head down for a searing kiss. His hand moved down between them, finding her sex with languid strokes. Her flesh was swollen with desire, eager for more of him.

She opened her legs and lifted them, bringing her knees up.

"That's a good girl." His hand left her sex and a moment later, she felt the tip of his cock against her. "Here I come."

He eased into her, moving slowly. Almost too slowly. She wanted to feel him deep inside her, at that spot he'd found with his fingers. The climax he'd wrought had been soul altering. She hadn't known her body could come apart like that—or that it could go back together again.

She wrapped her legs around him as he pushed all the way in, filling her completely. He kissed her then, his lips and tongue caressing her mouth as his hips began to move gently.

Kissing him back, she dug her fingers into the back of his head and clasped his back, relishing the feel of his muscles going taut as he moved over her.

After nearly leaving her, he thrust back inside, creating a delicious friction. "Again," she bade him, desperate for more of the same. Faster, perhaps.

He continued with methodical thrusts, his hips snapping against hers. She clasped her legs more tightly around him, drawing him deeper as she rose up from the cot to meet him. His movements grew faster, less measured but just as precise. He kept hitting that spot inside her, expanding her pleasure. She cast her head back and gave herself over to the rhythm of him driving into her, their bodies becoming slick with sweat.

She was getting close to that second climax. It was just beyond reach.

Then his hand was between them again, his fingers pressing on her clitoris. He snagged his teeth on her earlobe and savagely kissed her neck before whispering, "Come for me, Persey." His movements on her clitoris became more frenzied as his cock dove faster and deeper. She was spinning toward the light. Or was it darkness?

Whatever it was, she was there, her body breaking apart again. She cried out his name, clutching him tightly as wave after wave of ecstasy carried her to some distant place. She was still in the throes of her release when he left her.

His pressure on her clitoris slackened. Persey opened her eyes to see him holding his cravat over his cock as he stroked himself to completion. She hadn't recalled her prior partner doing that. He'd spilled himself on her thigh and muttered an apology.

Acton grunted before rolling to the side. And onto the floor.

"Acton!" Persey rolled to the edge of the cot. He lay on the floor on his back, his eyes closed. His mouth curved into a spectacular grin. Persey's heart flipped.

Because he was unbearably handsome. Nothing more.

"Are you all right?" she asked.

Impossibly, he smiled wider. But his eyes remained closed. "Never better. This is the second occasion on which I've fallen out of bed in your presence. And this time is bliss-fully rat-free."

She couldn't help giggling. "Do you need help?"

Finally, his lids came open, revealing his dark, still-sensual gaze. "I don't think so. This floor is cold, but then I was probably overheated. Not that I minded." He gave her a wicked wink.

This was the rogue she'd tried to avoid. She could not deny, however, that being the beneficiary of his flirtations was the headiest thing she'd ever experienced. He'd chosen her when he could have anyone.

And he would have married her if she'd allowed it. Because he'd felt he must. The rogue had finally learned that there were consequences to his actions.

Persephone did not want to be a consequence.

He pushed himself up on his elbows, which made the muscles of his abdomen contract. Her body reacted, indicating that she was entirely game for a third try at a climax. So long as it involved exploring him more fully.

"When do you need to go upstairs?" he asked, perhaps reading her thoughts.

She continued surveying the marvels of his bare chest, from the dark patch of hair at the center to his intriguing nipples. Would they react as hers did when she touched them? "Not for some time," she responded.

"Excellent." He sat up fully and leaned toward her, kissing her thoroughly. She was most definitely ready for another go. He stroked his thumb along her jaw. "I should like to take my time with number three. You see, I've thought of a way to tie your hands to the legs of the cot using my stockings. If you're agreeable."

Heat pulsed between her legs. "Yes, please. But first, I want a lengthy investigation of at least your chest."

His brows shot up. "Just my chest?"

"Perhaps a bit more," she admitted with a smile.

He spread his arms wide. "I am yours to explore and conquer."

It was nearly dawn before Acton exited into the garden. Persephone smiled to herself as she carefully made her way upstairs. The night's activities hadn't eliminated the problems she faced with her parents, but she was certainly in a better mood.

But for how long?

～

*A*fter pacing a circuit around the library, Acton flung himself in a chair near the hearth. The rain had continued from last night, and the day was cool. But the weather wasn't troubling him. Persey was at the forefront of his mind.

Last night had been wonderful. Perhaps the best night of his life. He'd smiled the entire way back to his mother's house right up until he'd fallen asleep seconds after his head had hit the pillow.

Why then was he maundering about?

Because there was something off.

He should be walking on clouds, his mind firmly focused on when he would see Persey next—tonight, as they'd planned to meet in the scullery again. At midnight this time.

Wasn't that what rogues did? They enjoyed themselves without a thought for the future or any sort of permanence. Except the idea of his time with Persey being finite was making him feel somewhat…unsettled.

Though, she'd been clear that she didn't want anything permanent. She'd expressly forbade him to propose. But wasn't that the right thing to do after becoming intimate?

Not to her. She'd been intimate with someone else and hadn't married him either.

A thought occurred to him. Was she a female rogue?

Groaning, he put his head in his hand. Of course, she wasn't. She hadn't gained a reputation as a rake. Because she didn't go about sampling whatever wares might be offered from whoever was offering them. Nor did she flirt and try to actively obtain those wares. And neither did she frequent the Rogue's Den or anyplace similar. For her, there was a mutual attraction and affinity before anything physical transpired.

At least, that was how he read their situation. He

suspected it had been the same when she'd been with that other fellow years ago.

What she'd said echoed in his mind: she wanted to love someone and be loved in return. Acton hadn't lied when he'd told her he didn't know how to love. Whom had he loved?

His nurse. Until she'd been dismissed when he was seven. He'd been horribly upset, but his father had assured him that future dukes did not have nurses past the age of seven, that it was time for him to focus on his studies and manly pursuits.

He'd had a dog once. Acton recalled loving him until he'd died. Acton had been nine, perhaps? He'd also loved his first horse. Until his father had said horses were not to be loved, but appreciated and used. They did not require love, just good treatment.

Then there was the cat he vaguely remembered. Had he loved Domino? Acton was frustrated that he couldn't remember.

Acton's mother came in then, interrupting his thoughts. He looked up and met her gaze. She appeared tentative. "I wanted to speak with you, but I don't want to bother you. Should we talk later?"

"Now is fine." Acton sat up straighter in his chair. "What is it you'd like to discuss?"

She moved to a chair near his and perched on the edge of the cushion. "I've just had a visit from Lord and Lady Radstock."

Acton tensed. "What did they want?" He was careful not to reveal how much he already knew, such as the fact that they were lodging at the White Hart.

The dowager's features creased, making her appear pained. "They broached a possible marriage contract between you and Pandora. Since it seems you formed a connection the other day at Sydney Gardens when she required your assistance."

Just managing to hold in a curse, Acton snorted. Doing so reminded him of Persey. Thinking of her soothed his irritation. "I hope you informed them that no connection was formed and that a marriage between us would be absurd."

"I did not use those precise words, but that was the gist of my response, yes."

He wiped his hand over his face. "I do appreciate you managing them. Were they angry when they left?" He hoped they wouldn't retaliate against Pandora or Persey.

His mother lifted a shoulder. "I don't think so, but I would guess they wouldn't let it show if they were. Honestly, they seemed...strange. I imagine they are going through a difficult time with the scandal their younger daughter's behavior with Banemore caused. They are lodging at the White Hart, which is odd since they always stay with the baron's sister, Lucinda. And I did not receive any response from them about the party tomorrow, just a note from Lucinda confirming her attendance and that of her nieces."

"Does that mean Radstock and his wife aren't coming?" Acton asked hopefully.

His mother grimaced faintly. "I'm afraid our interview started with my asking if they were going to attend the party tomorrow night. It was obvious they weren't aware of it, but the baroness covered well by asking if their affirmative response had not yet been received. That was when she revealed they are at the White Hart—she blamed the loss of the response on their messenger boy."

Acton frowned, thinking of her loyalty to the baroness. "Did it bother you that she lied and cast blame on an innocent?"

"It did, actually. I was also put off by her—and her husband—suggesting that you marry their younger daughter when they never addressed their previous suggestion that you court their older daughter." She shook her head. "But, I suppose I understand why they've abandoned that course, since they said she has been betrothed to a distant relative. I can scarcely credit how quickly that happened when they were just at Loxley Court to negotiate a marriage between her and you."

Acton realized she was watching him closely. Hell, he couldn't act as if he already knew about Persey's supposed betrothal. "It appears the baron and baroness were simply concerned with marrying their older daughter off as soon as possible."

"Yes, I'm sure you're right. I also find that troubling. They should have been supporting their younger daughter." She clasped her hands in her lap. "I suppose that is easy for me to say as our family has never experienced such an unfortunate event."

No, because Acton's reputation and behavior were excused due to the fact that he had a cock. He felt particularly disgusted with himself at that moment.

"Was there any chance you and their older daughter may suit?" The dowager waved her hand. "Forget I asked. That is moot now."

Yes, it was. Not because she was marrying some cousin, but because she'd refused Acton before he could even ask.

Seeking to change the subject, he leaned slightly forward. "I've been meaning to ask you about something. That painting in your sitting room—Father had the exact same painting at Loxley Court."

"Yes, he did." She picked at something on her skirt, her gaze not meeting his.

"Did he have a copy made for you?"

"Yes." She looked toward him, but only for a bare moment. "Any time you sat for a portrait, a copy was made and sent to me. It was part of our…agreement."

"I see." Except he didn't really. He hadn't even known

they'd had one. All he knew was that she'd wanted to live separately, and she and his father had "agreed" that their son would live with his father while their daughters would reside with their mother.

He moved on to the other thing he'd been curious about since arriving here. "My room has my favorite books. And there's a carving of a cat. I'd forgotten we had a cat."

"I took him with me when I came to Bath."

When she'd *left*. Why didn't she use the word that was most appropriate? She'd left him.

"Your father didn't like the cat," she added. "I put those things in your room in case you ever visited." At last, she looked at him and didn't shift her attention away.

"You thought I would?"

"I hoped." Her eyes seemed to glisten, but Acton wasn't sure because the housekeeper came in then, and his mother turned her head.

"I'm sorry to intrude," Mrs. Hedge said. "We have a few questions in the kitchen about tomorrow night."

"Of course." The dowager stood and gave Acton an apologetic smile. "I'm afraid I didn't give the household much time to prepare."

"We're used to that, Your Grace," Mrs. Hedge said with a laugh. "We are more than up to the task."

"Yes, you are." Giving Acton a slight nod, the dowager turned and followed the housekeeper from the library.

Acton stared at the doorway. He felt even more unsettled than when his mother had come in. Why would she have hoped he would visit when she was the one who'd left him?

And why was a woman who'd abandoned her young son so bloody steadfast to a "friend" who lied to and manipulated those around her? Where had the dowager's loyalty been to Acton, her own child?

Acton thought of some of the things his mother had said

today. She'd taken the cat because his father hadn't liked him. Did that mean she'd also taken their daughters because he hadn't liked them either? Of course not.

Yet, he'd allowed his wife to take them. Or had it been that she'd bargained to have them under whatever "agreement" they'd made?

He wanted to know the terms of their arrangement. After twenty-three years, he deserved the full story.

# CHAPTER 20

*A*cton had come to Persephone in the scullery again last night, but he hadn't stayed as late. Or early, depending on one's perspective. He'd been pensive, perhaps even a little gruff. She'd never seen him like that.

When she'd asked him what was wrong, he'd said nothing, that he was just desperately in need of her. Then he'd stripped her bare and brought her to an earth-shattering climax with his mouth and fingers before flipping her over and taking her from behind. He'd asked first, and she'd been more than eager to try something new with him. The experience had been incredibly erotic, and even now, several hours later, her body still thrummed from his touch.

One thing he *had* mentioned was looking forward to seeing her and Pandora at his mother's soiree tonight. She'd told him Pandora wouldn't be coming, to which he'd responded that his mother thought she was because her aunt had indicated she would be in attendance.

It seemed Aunt Lucinda was hoping for the best. So far, Pandora had firmly declined—repeatedly—to accompany them. Persephone still had the rest of the day to convince her.

Aunt Lucinda was in the dining room eating breakfast when Persephone arrived. "Good morning, dear," Aunt Lucinda said. "I trust you slept well and are ready for the party tonight?"

"I am." Though she was nervous about her parents being there. However, she couldn't say so without revealing how she knew. Goodness, but it was trying having a secret affair. Persephone wasn't sure how much longer it could continue. "Please don't be upset if Pandora doesn't wish to go. I haven't had any luck convincing her."

"I know. Neither have I." Aunt Lucinda sighed. "But I can still hope. Particularly since two new gowns are being delivered early this afternoon."

Persephone stared at her in shock. "You bought gowns for us? But we only just learned of the party."

"The day after you arrived, I asked my modiste to make something up for each of you as I anticipated hosting a dinner here. However, when the dowager duchess's invitation arrived, I asked if the gowns could be done sooner. My modiste is nothing if not responsive. She will ensure you are both garbed in the latest, most arresting fashion."

"That is incredibly generous of you, Aunt Lucinda." Persephone had no doubt the gown would be the finest thing she'd ever worn. But she also hoped it would be more...flattering than what her mother typically selected for her, particularly when compared with Pandora's wardrobe. "Are the gowns similar?"

"In style, they are, but I chose a dark rose for Pandora and a stunning teal blue for you."

Of course she'd put thought into this. Persephone was nearly speechless. "Thank you."

She sent an encouraging smile toward Persephone. "I

know you haven't been given much choice in your wardrobe and that your sister has, on occasion, been outfitted to outshine you—even though she hasn't yet had a Season. You are a beautiful young lady, Persey, with many wonderful attributes, both physical and otherwise." Aunt Lucina returned her attention to the open newspaper next to her plate.

Filled with a delightful warmth, Persephone went to the sideboard and began adding items to her plate.

"Bloody hell!"

Surprised by Aunt Lucinda's outburst, Persephone dropped her plate. Eggs and kippers went flying, but the plate, miraculously, didn't break.

"Goodness gracious, I'm sorry, Persey. I didn't mean to startle you. But I may have to throttle my brother."

Persephone saw her aunt's red face and wasn't sure she'd ever seen her so angry. "What's happened?" It had to be the newspaper. What else could it be? Persephone tensed as she stepped aside for the footman to clean up the mess. She murmured an apology and thanked him.

"There's an announcement in here about your betrothal to that infernal cousin. After we told your father there would be no marriage. He can*not* sell you away like a painting or a horse!"

Pandora came in, her eyes wide. "I heard Aunt Lucinda in the staircase hall, but I couldn't catch all that she just said."

"My betrothal has made the newspaper," Persephone said, feeling strangely numb. Why wasn't she as outraged as their aunt? Because she was no longer surprised by her parents.

Pandora walked around the table to look at the paper, standing beside Aunt Lucinda.

"There's nothing much to see," Aunt Lucinda said, trying to pick the newspaper up.

"I just want to read what it says." Pandora put her hand on the paper before their aunt could pluck it from the table.

Persephone saw the deep lines furrow in Aunt Lucinda's brow and held her breath. What else did the announcement say?

The color drained from Pandora's face. She abruptly turned from the table and went to the window.

Breakfast forgotten, Persephone rushed to her aunt and looked to her in question. Aunt Lucinda pointed to the upper corner of the newspaper. There, in stark black and white, was a far more awful announcement: the betrothal of the Earl of Banemore to the Lady Isabel, daughter of the Marquess of Malton. The blackguard was engaged after all.

Persephone rushed to her sister's side and gently touched her back. "I'm sorry, Pandora."

Sending Persey a fleeting smile, Pandora exhaled. "Don't be." She glanced toward their aunt who watched them with grave concern. "I should have let you hide that from me."

"He's the worst sort of scoundrel," Aunt Lucinda said. "And he better not show his face in Bath again."

"I can't imagine he'd have any reason to," Pandora said tightly, turning from the window. She faced Persephone. "What are you going to do about your betrothal?"

"I've already directed my solicitor to send a letter to your mother's cousins," Aunt Lucinda said. "I believe it was dispatched yesterday afternoon."

"Will that really be the end of it?" Pandora asked.

"Certainly," Aunt Lucinda said briskly. "They can't force Persey to wed."

"Good." Pandora summoned a smile, but it looked quite brittle to Persephone. She absolutely ached for her sister.

"Still, I feel the need to send a note to your parents instructing them to remove themselves from anything to do with either of you. That they would put an announcement in the paper…" Aunt Lucinda's voice trailed off into a muttered curse. "I am livid with Hugh. In fact, I think I'll go to the White Hart in person and dress them down." She stood abruptly. "Excuse me, girls. I'll see you later—and I'll have a surprise for you." She directed the last toward Pandora. Persephone, of course, already knew what it was.

"What sort of surprise?" Pandora asked.

Aunt Lucinda's expression brightened. "If I tell you, it won't be a surprise. But it's something you can wear this evening." She winked at Pandora before departing.

"She bought us new gowns," Pandora said, briefly closing her eyes. "She really will be crushed if I don't go, won't she?"

"She's only trying to help you move past all this." Persephone took her sister's hand. "Which I understand is very hard to do after reading that rubbish."

"I just… I thought I loved him, Persey. And I thought he loved me. I feel like such a fool, which is bad enough, but the whole of England sees me as that too."

Persephone squeezed Pandora's hand. "You are *not* a fool. Bane is the one to blame. He led you along on a string, making promises he never intended to keep. You should go to the dowager duchess's party tonight in the new gown Aunt Lucinda purchased and hold your head high. Would it help to know that those awful girls who were rude to you at the gardens the other day—and their families—were not invited?"

A smile broke across Pandora's mouth, and it was so genuine that Persephone nearly cried out with joy. Pandora sobered quickly, but Persephone was glad for the moment of glee, no matter how brief. "How do you know that?"

"Wellesbourne sent me a note. He wanted us to know that he'd had them removed from his mother's guest list. He is really hoping you will come. I think he truly wants to help you, especially since his former friend is the reason for your distress."

Pandora wryly arched a brow. "*Former* friend?"

"Wellesbourne has indicated he does not intend to maintain his friendship with Bane. What he did was beyond the pale."

"Wellesbourne's reputation isn't much better. His support is surprising, to be honest."

"I agree wholeheartedly. I expected him to be exactly like Bane." Persephone thought back to when she'd first met Acton and how wrong she'd been about him. She had a sudden urge to tell Pandora the truth about her time with Acton—the extent of their adventures together and their current torrid affair. But she couldn't bring herself to parade her happiness, however short-lived it might be, in front of Pandora. Not right now, especially.

"You really think I can hold my head up at this party?" Pandora asked.

"The Dowager Duchess of Wellesbourne is going to publicly support your return to Society. How can you refuse such a wonderful endorsement?" Persephone held her breath. She wanted nothing more than for her sister to feel normal again.

Pandora released Persephone's hand. "I don't want to return to Society, Persey. I'd like to leave it, for a while at least. I've written to Tamsin and asked if I could go spend the winter with her."

The entire winter? Persephone didn't want her to be so far away. "That's a long time to be gone," she said slowly. "I would miss you horribly."

"Not if you come with me," Pandora said with an eagerness that tore at Persephone's heart. "I think I'll be able to face things much better in the spring. I might not want to join Society then either, but you must, whether it's here or in London. I will support whatever you decide."

How could Persephone say no? Pandora needed the time and distance to recover. Then she'd offered to come back and be here for Persephone. "Of course I'll come with you. We will always stand by one another."

"Spinsters to the end if it comes to that?" Pandora asked with a laugh.

That had been Persephone's plan. However, she couldn't deny a subtle but primal hope that things between her and Acton could continue. Regardless of what she'd said to him, the idea of permanence, of never having to say goodbye to him held a shocking appeal.

Perhaps she should have allowed him to propose.

Except he couldn't love her. And that requirement was nonnegotiable. There was also that pesky but probably true rule about rogues not changing. Persephone would much rather ride off into spinsterhood with her beloved sister than risk heartbreak with a proven scoundrel.

$\sim$

*A*fter an invigorating morning ride, Acton was feeling much more balanced than yesterday. Last night's assignation with Persey had also certainly contributed to the improvement. They had not planned to meet tonight due to his mother's party, but he hoped they would be able to steal a few moments during the soiree.

Once he'd washed the exertions of his ride away, he went downstairs to eat something more substantial than the toast and tea he'd consumed earlier. However, he was diverted from his plan by the arrival of his friends the Viscount Somerton and Lord Droxford.

He encountered them in the entrance hall as they arrived

and invited them to the library. Admitting them first, he closed the door behind himself. "I'm so very glad to see you both," he said.

Somerton was an affable fellow, slender, with wavy, dark blond hair and piercing green eyes, which ladies found irresistible, along with ridiculously long lashes. Droxford, with his perpetual scowl, somehow also managed to be sought after by the fairer sex, though he rarely paid them any attention. With his thick dark hair, brooding coffee-colored eyes, and wide shoulders, he could almost be mistaken for a brute. However, Acton had seen him laugh once or twice, and, in those moments, Droxford looked somewhat like a fresh-faced lad. It was quite the dichotomy.

"We both got your letters," Somerton said, depositing himself in a chair. "As it happened, we independently decided to come to Bath and met at the White Hart purely by chance."

Acton looked to Droxford. "You left Winterstoke to come to Bath?" Aside from attending to his duties in the House of Lords in London, Droxford only left his baronial estate a few times each year.

"You sounded distraught," Droxford responded before pulling out a chair at the round table near the window and lowering himself onto the seat.

Sitting in a chair somewhat between the other two men, Acton said, "Well, I appreciate you both responding to the call of a friend. Perhaps one of you can tell me if our other friend Bane is in fact betrothed?"

"Have you not seen the paper today?" Somerton asked.

"No, I was out riding." Acton shot out of his chair and went to the door. Opening it, he called for Simmons to bring him the newspaper. A moment later, the butler arrived with the requested item. "Thank you, Simmons." He closed the door again and returned to his seat, waving the paper. "What am I looking for?" He feared he already knew. There was an announcement about Bane's betrothal.

"Page three, I believe," Droxford said. "Announcements."

Acton flipped to the appropriate page and instantly saw it. "Who the hell is Lady Isabel? And don't say the daughter of the Marquess of Malton."

Droxford pressed his lips together while Somerton waved his hand. "Someone Wolverton wanted Bane to consider as a wife," Somerton responded. "I don't recall meeting her in London, but that doesn't mean anything. They're to wed in two weeks' time in northern England somewhere—near her father's estate. The banns have already been read."

"How do you know so much?" Acton asked, irritated that he'd known nothing, not even that Bane's father was trying to match him with some unknown lady from the north of England.

"I was with Shefford after the *incident* with Miss Pandora Barclay," Somerton said. "Sheff was privy to what happened as a result of it."

"And?" Acton prompted. "What happened?"

"I'm not entirely clear on some of the specifics, and I'm not sure Sheff is either, but Bane said he'd done something bad. He also said he'd fixed it. Then he told Sheff that he needed to go meet his betrothed."

*Fixed it.* How was that possible when he'd left a young woman ruined?

"Did Sheff ask Bane when he'd become engaged?" Acton asked. "I saw Bane not long before this happened, and he didn't say a word."

"He kept it private," Droxford said with a shrug. "Perhaps the wisest thing he's ever done."

"How is that wise?" Acton demanded.

Droxford looked at Acton as if he'd taken leave of his

senses. "Compared to what he typically does—bragging about his exploits—it seems an improvement."

Acton hadn't realized how much Bane had done that until this moment. But they'd all done their share of boasting. Well, Droxford hadn't. He'd never once uttered a word about a romantic or sexual experience.

In some ways, Droxford didn't entirely fit in with their set, and yet they regarded him as a close friend. Shefford had taken him under his wing when he'd inherited the barony, quite unexpectedly, four years ago. Acton had known him somewhat at Oxford but they hadn't become friends until Isaac Deverell had become Baron Droxford.

"So, the consummate rake is getting married," Acton said, setting the newspaper on his lap.

"Before the rest of us," Somerton noted. "My money was on Keele."

"Why, because he's more responsible than the rest of you lot?" Droxford asked.

Somerton inclined his head. "Largely, yes. You would have been my first choice, but I'm not sure you could find a woman willing to suffer your incessant brooding."

Droxford's near-frowning expression vaulted into a full scowl. "Nor am I looking."

"Exactly so." Somerton stretched out a leg and exhaled. "Alas, it is not Keele, so I'm glad I didn't place a wager." Keele was another of their friends, but far more interested in running his estates and turning profits. He'd been married before and seemed likely to do so again. "Perhaps I will for the next one. Who will that be?"

"Shefford," Acton said quickly. "His parents have been harassing him about taking a wife since the moment he left school."

"You are likely right," Droxford said. He looked to Somerton. "Don't take that bet."

"Already ahead of you," Somerton said with a chuckle. He eyed Acton. "You said you were thinking of marrying, that it was time. Perhaps you'll be next."

"I have no imminent plans." Saying that made Acton strangely upset.

His gaze drifted back to the newspaper to reread the announcement. However, before he could do so, his eye caught another name: Miss Persephone Barclay. There was a bloody announcement about her engagement too! His vague agitation vaulted to full irritation. "Fucking hell."

"What's that?" Somerton asked.

"He's just looking at the announcement again," Droxford said. "Wellesbourne, are you upset that Bane is betrothed?"

Acton managed to consider his response before he blurted anything about Persey. "Surprised, but not upset. Actually, that's not entirely true. I'm furious with him for what he's done to the young lady he ruined. In fact, I'm trying to help her regain her standing. My mother is hosting a party tonight, and she'll be there. You must both come and endeavor to speak with her. It will help her to have Bane's friends seen as supporting her."

"So, he *did* ruin someone?" Droxford asked. "That was what I suspected."

"He certainly gave it his best effort. I imagine being caught in an embrace with her was the something 'bad' he was referring to. I should like to know how he 'fixed' it, however. The young lady has suffered a great deal."

Somerton shook his head. "Carrying on like that when he was already betrothed? I confess that's rather egregious, even for him."

"It's despicable," Droxford said, with a flash of his teeth.

Somerton looked at Acton. "You're helping this young woman? Why?"

"Because it's the right thing to do. Bane treated her

poorly, and since he's not here to make amends, I will try. The lady's mother, Lady Radstock, is also a friend of my mother's."

"That makes sense," Droxford said. "It's good of you to help, though you didn't really need to. Bane's transgressions needn't be our own."

"Perhaps not, but it's come to my attention that my reputation isn't much better."

"Ah, the real reason you are helping rehabilitate this young woman," Somerton said with a knowing smile. "Your own rehabilitation."

"It isn't that." Acton tried to scowl but feared he'd never be as good as Droxford.

Perhaps it was that. At least a little. Hadn't Acton wanted to prove to Persey that he wasn't the blackguard she presumed him to be? Except he had been.

*Had.*

"I am trying to change," Acton admitted. "Bane's behavior has shown me that we are all just an ill-advised promenade away from a massive mistake." He glanced toward Droxford. "Perhaps not *all* of us."

"I wondered if we should go to northern England," Somerton said. "To support Bane."

"No. He doesn't need us." Acton was still angry with Bane, both for not telling him of the betrothal and for what he'd done to Pandora. But Acton was angrier with Persey's parents. How dare they put an announcement in the paper when their daughter had no intention of marrying this cousin?

Tossing the paper onto a nearby table, Acton stood. "I'm glad to see you both, but you must excuse me as I've an errand. You'll come tonight?"

Both men got to their feet and nodded. "So long as I'm in Bath," Droxford said without a trace of enthusiasm.

"I shall look forward to it," Somerton said with a grin. "I always enjoy a good soiree."

"Excellent." Acton saw them both out, then went upstairs to fetch his hat and gloves. It occurred to him that he was headed to the exact same place as his friends, assuming they were returning to the White Hart.

Acton intended to speak with Persey's parents. He would put a stop to their officious behavior once and for all.

~

*T*he sitting room at the White Hart was well appointed, with two seating areas and a beautifully carved marble mantel surrounding the fireplace. Being at an inn reminded Acton of the time he'd spent with Persey at the utterly terrible Black Ivy. The White Hart would never have rats or allow unsavory men.

At last, Persey's parents entered the room. They were finely dressed, as on the last occasion of their meeting, but in different garments. Knowing they lacked funds, Acton wondered how they afforded such garb. The answer was they couldn't, which explained their need to sell their daughter to the highest bidder.

Except Acton hadn't been given a chance to bid. Actually, he had. He just hadn't realized what was at stake, that if he didn't leap at the chance to marry Persey, her parents would simply betroth her to someone else.

"Good afternoon, Duke," Radstock said with a tentative smile. "What a pleasant surprise to see you. We imagine you've come to speak with us about our daughter, Pandora?"

Somehow, that hadn't occurred to Acton. But of course they would think that. "Not at all. I'm here to speak with you about leaving both your daughters alone and to instruct you to stop trying to negotiate marriages that neither of them want." The baron didn't know that Pandora wouldn't want to marry Acton, but that wasn't even an option considering his intimacy with her sister.

Radstock's face reddened. "See here, our daughters are none of your business."

Acton took a step toward them. "Aren't they? You sought to betroth me to one without her consent only to betroth her to someone else, *also* without her consent. Now, you want to betroth me to your other daughter because of some mindless gossip?"

"How do you know so much?" Lady Radstock asked, her eyes glinting with suspicion.

"I am a well-informed gentleman. And I have been spending time with your daughter—Persephone—to determine if we will suit, which was, if I recall, your original scheme." Acton turned his full attention on the baroness. "You are a friend of my mother's. I must draw upon that longtime association to beseech you to allow your daughters the freedom to choose their own husbands."

Radstock scoffed. "Your meddling is inappropriate and curious."

Acton swung his furious gaze toward the baron. "You invited my meddling when you tried to betroth me to each of your daughters in turn."

"Pandora would make you a splendid duchess," Lady Radstock said with a placid smile, as if Acton hadn't been nearly yelling at them in anger. "I understand you are seeking to help her recover from your friend's mistreatment. There can be no better resurrection for her than to become the Duchess of Wellesbourne."

Resurrection? She wasn't bloody dead. But perhaps her social downfall was as good as that to them. Acton was somehow more disgusted by them than when he'd arrived. "I regret to inform you that I have no plans to marry your younger daughter. Indeed, if I am to wed anyone, it will be Persephone!" He did yell that last part and wished he hadn't. In fact, he ought not have said that at all.

Their eyes rounded, particularly Lady Radstock's. Her lips parted, and her cheeks flushed with anticipation.

Acton moved closer until he stood directly in front of them. "I said *if*. I have no plans to marry either of your daughters, and you'd do well to remember that. If you say anything different to anyone, I will ensure you are ruined in every way possible."

"Seems I was wrong to think you were a more affable version of your father," the baron said.

"You didn't know my father." The baron might have, but it couldn't have been well. The duke had kept a very particular set of friends.

"Enough to know he was dictatorial and arrogant, always talking down to people and expecting them to do as he commanded." Radstock sniffed. "You sounded just like him then."

For a moment, the comparison stung. Or perhaps it was the man insinuating that Acton wasn't affable. He prided himself on being pleasant and charming, someone who was welcome everywhere and not just because of his title.

"How hypocritical to note someone else as commanding when you yourself are arranging marriages for your adult daughters without their consent. I would advise you to get your finances in order instead of attempting to sell your firstborn. I'm sure you'd rather people didn't hear about that."

The baroness gasped, and Acton knew he'd made his point. He pivoted slightly and stalked past them to leave the room. He would never reveal such information, but only because he cared too much for Persey and it would be detrimental to her.

As he departed the inn, he didn't feel as triumphant as he thought he would. Now he was thinking of his father, which he'd started to do yesterday after his conversation with this mother.

By the time he reached her house, he was tense with the need to talk to her again. He found her in her sitting room, which was slightly unnerving because of the portrait of him hanging on the wall.

Seated at her writing desk, she turned to face him. "I heard Somerton and Droxford called earlier. Will they be attending the party? I hope you invited them."

"I did invite them, and yes, they will be here. Why are you really having this party tonight?" That wasn't the question he'd thought he'd ask, but it had just fallen out of his mouth.

She smiled. "Because I love hosting soirees, and I wanted to help Miss Pandora. But mostly because you suggested it."

He had, and she'd eagerly agreed. "I don't understand." He shook his head and went to sit in a chair near the hearth.

She got up and followed him, standing nearby. "What don't you understand?"

He looked up at her. Though her brow was creased, her mouth was turned up in a caring smile. She was, he suddenly realized, the perfect example of motherhood. And how would he know that? It wasn't as if he'd had a mother.

But he had. For five years that he mostly couldn't remember.

Mostly.

Now, sitting here, looking up at her as if he were a small boy, several things came back to him: the way she would read and sing to him at night before he went to sleep, the way she played storm the castle with him, and the way she cuddled him when he was hurt. He recalled a specific occasion when he'd fallen from his pony on only his second ride. She hadn't been present because Cecily was only a few weeks old, but he'd run to her in the house as soon as he'd been able.

He suddenly remembered what had happened next. His father yelling at her, telling her to stop, to leave Acton alone, that he wasn't to be coddled.

"Acton?" she asked, using his name for the first time since he was a boy. He now also remembered that his father didn't like her calling him that. He had a title—Loxley—and she needed to use it.

Acton realized he was shaking. "I don't understand how a woman who seems to care so much about me could leave me." God, now he *sounded* like a little boy. His gaze met hers, and he felt the sting of unshed tears. "Why?" Dammit, his voice cracked.

She sank down in front of him and put her hands on his cheeks. "My dearest boy, I never wanted to."

"He made you?" There was no need for Acton to say who "he" was.

Nodding, she swept one hand over his brow and back down the side of his face. "It broke my heart to leave you."

"Then why did you?"

"Because your father commanded it." She said this simply and without heat, as if there could be no other explanation—or argument for it.

"Why would he do that?" Before she could answer, he said, "I know the two of you fought. I just remembered," he mumbled.

"He thought I was too soft with you, that you would grow up to be weak."

"Why didn't you fight him?" Acton's voice climbed as anger raged through him. "Why didn't you fight for *me?*"

She dropped her hands from his face. "I did try. I refused to leave, but he said I could either go and take the girls with me, or he'd say I was unstable and send me to a hospital where I wouldn't see any of my children."

Acton couldn't imagine his father being that cruel. He'd been demanding, even hard sometimes, but he'd been proud of Acton and encouraged him to do and be his best. Even so, the man hadn't been emotionally connected to his son. Or to anyone as far as Acton could tell.

The reality of what Acton had endured after she left hit him like a stone to the head. "I was devastated when you went away," he said softly. "Father wouldn't allow me to cry or speak of you. He said sadness was for lesser people, that those in our station didn't succumb to such emotion. He beat that so steadily into my head that I believed it."

She grasped his hand between hers, her eyes growing huge. "He didn't beat you, did he? I was never told about that!"

"No, not physically. I mean that he hammered it into me verbally—over and over." Acton cocked his head. "What were you told and by whom?"

Releasing him, her gaze turned sheepish. "Your nurse wrote to me secretly. After she was dismissed, the cook took over."

Acton had barely known the cook except that she baked him his favorite biscuits on his birthday and when he came home from school. She would send an entire plate to his chamber. He knew now that his father had never known about those kindnesses. Of course he hadn't. He would not have approved of such...warmth.

"That was brave of them," Acton said. "I can't think Father would have approved."

"No, he would not have."

Pain still lingered in Acton's chest. "Why did you never tell me the truth? Especially after Father died?"

"Not telling you was part of our arrangement." There was

that word. Acton understood now. "When he died, my primary goal was to find a way back into your life. That you allowed me to move into the dowager house was beyond my dreams. I thought that in time, I might tell you, but I could see how much you admired and loved your father and didn't want to take that away from you."

That was perhaps the most selfless thing Acton had ever heard. But she was wrong about one thing. "I didn't love him," Acton whispered. "Sometimes, I think I hated him. Until I learned not to feel that either." Waves of emotion flooded him.

She put her hands on his forearms. "Oh, Acton. I should have fought harder." Tears tracked down her cheeks.

He shook his head, feeling the tears he needed to shed, but could not release. "You did the only thing you could."

"I should have found a way to tell you the truth, so that you would know that I love you, that I have always loved you."

Emotion overpowered him, closing his throat. He wanted to say he loved her too, but how could he? "I don't know if I *can* love."

"Of course you can. You may not remember Domino— the cat—but you loved him very much."

Acton had thought he'd loved his nurse and his dog, but in this moment, he doubted everything he'd known. "That was a long time ago. Before Father ruined me." God, he felt so broken, and he'd just been blithely sailing through life as if nothing truly mattered. Because until now, perhaps it hadn't.

She cupped his face once more. "I never imagined your father would hurt you so badly. You *can* love. I know it. You're my son. *Mine.*" The ferocity and commitment in her voice unleashed something inside him.

At last, a tear fell down his face. She wiped it away. "Just let everything out. I'm here, my dearest. My darling, darling boy." Moving closer, she wrapped her arms around him.

He bent to hold her as more tears followed. But he wasn't sad. He felt...joy. He felt free.

"I love you, Mama," he whispered, knowing he'd said this exact thing hundreds of times as she'd held him in his arms.

"I love you too, Acton." She kissed his cheek and stroked his back.

It was a long while before they broke apart. Acton's back had stiffened. He couldn't imagine his mother was comfortable kneeling on the floor. "Can I help you up?" he offered.

"Yes, please," she said with a light laugh.

Acton guided her to stand and rose from the chair. While he was glad they'd had this conversation and knew they would certainly have more like it, he wanted to ask about something she'd said recently. "You indicated not too long ago that there were things about me you didn't like, but that you wouldn't share them. What are those things?"

"It isn't that I don't like them. I'm surprised by them—one is how unattached you seem. I worried you grew up to be too much like your father, but I could see hints of who you might be underneath. Today, you've confirmed I was right, that you are not at all like your father. The other is your reputation." She pursed her lips slightly. "I know you have not had the best role model, but I am hopeful, now more than ever, that you will not turn out like your father when it comes to love and marriage."

"Do you mean you hope I won't toss my wife and daughters aside?" Acton couldn't keep his lip from curling. Any respect he'd had for his father evaporated. "Or that I won't keep a mistress in London."

"Both of those things. For a start."

"I would never do those things." Loyalty may not have been important to Acton's father, but it was crucial to him.

When he married, he would be entirely faithful. He couldn't help but think of Persey and the ways in which she'd instigated the changes in him—changes that made him feel proud and happy. The decision to wed had come from his desire to please his father, but now it was something completely different. Persey had shown him how it felt to be with a woman who inspired and motivated him. They shared a connection he never would have imagined. Committing to a woman like her would not only be easy, it would make him happier than he ever thought possible.

This revelation about his thoughts on faithfulness prompted him to once more wonder if his mother had been loyal to his father. Acton rather hoped she hadn't. He didn't deserve that. More importantly, she deserved happiness after suffering her husband's cruelty. "Did you...have someone?"

She shook her head. "I took my vows to your father quite seriously, even if he did not. Besides, I was very busy with your sisters." A bit of color rose in her cheeks. "I may have become friendly with a gentleman in the past few years, but we did not allow our friendship to grow into something else."

"You could not be more unlike my father." Acton recalled what Cecily had said about their mother, that she possessed a soft disposition. That was the exact opposite of their father as well as being what he'd most feared his son could be. Acton wanted to feel outraged that he'd been raised by such a cold, unfeeling stone instead of the loyal, caring woman before him, and he supposed he was—a little. But he preferred to look forward, to the closeness he would share with her and his sisters in the future. He inhaled deeply, as if to cleanse the past away. "I should let you get ready for the soiree."

"I'm so glad you came to see me," she said, her expression

turning a bit shy. "I was hoping we would have this conversation someday. Do you feel any better?"

"As if a weight has been removed from my shoulders—one I wasn't even aware was there." He couldn't help but think of Persephone and the fact that he'd told her he wasn't capable of love. It seemed he was. But did he love her? Could he even recognize what that felt like?

He needed to find out.

# CHAPTER 21

*A*unt Lucinda beamed as she entered the Dowager Duchess of Wellesbourne's house flanked by her nieces. Persephone and Pandora had been delighted by their new gowns, and it had been enough to, at last, persuade Pandora to attend.

Persephone was glad. Pandora looked radiant in the dark rose trimmed with ivory lace and ribbon. Furthermore, Pandora had decided she didn't care what happened tonight. She'd hold her head up and show the world she was strong. Then, tomorrow, they would prepare to leave for Cornwall. They hadn't yet received a response from Tamsin, but expected it would arrive soon.

The line of coaches in St. James's Square was impressive, and the press of people inside the house nearly overwhelming. Persephone hadn't realized the event would be this heavily attended.

"There are so many people here," Pandora said. She looked slightly worried, her gaze darting about.

"You'll blend in more," Aunt Lucinda said but then paused to survey Pandora from head to toe. "On second thought, you are too pretty to not be noticed." She turned to Persephone. "As are you. That teal blue gown makes your eyes look like glittering jewels."

"Thank you." Persephone never had to worry about feeling as though she were less than her sister when with her aunt. Now, thanks to her, she wouldn't have to worry about it ever again, for she had no intention of returning to her parents' household. She would, however, like some of her things. She and Pandora had books and clothing and other items at Radstock Hall that they would like to claim. They feared their parents would retaliate against them by selling everything.

The dowager duchess greeted them in the staircase hall. "I'm so glad you are here." Her gaze lingered on Pandora as she gave her a subtle nod of approval. Or perhaps admiration.

"Thank you so much for inviting us," Aunt Lucinda responded before they made their way upstairs to the drawing room, which was definitely the heart of the soiree.

As soon as they stepped inside, a woman came to congratulate Persephone on her betrothal. Irritated but trying desperately not to show it, Persephone forced a smile. "I do appreciate your kindness; however, I'm afraid that was an error. I am not betrothed."

The woman's eyes rounded. "My goodness. I'm sorry to hear that. How confounding. I wonder how that happened." She looked at Persephone expectantly as if she'd asked a question and was awaiting a response.

Aunt Lucinda intervened. "Please excuse us, Mrs. Ogilvie." When they were far enough away from her, she glanced toward Persephone. "Pay her no mind."

"Should I continue to refute the announcement or simply smile, nod, and walk away?" Persephone could see how this night could become exhausting very quickly.

"You must do what you think is best," Aunt Lucinda said. "Meanwhile, I will start putting it around that this announcement was an error. I will ask my friends to ensure that is passed along."

"I am confident they will have no trouble sharing the latest on-dit," Pandora said.

Persephone laughed, and Aunt Lucinda grinned before taking herself off.

"What should we do?" Pandora asked.

"Cling to the wall?" Persephone suggested.

Pandora looked about the room. "I'm supposed to be holding my head high and daring people to give me the cut direct."

"We can do that too." Persephone almost didn't want to move. Their parents were likely here somewhere, or would be, and she'd no desire to encounter them.

Linking her arm through Pandora's, Persephone guided them to an empty space near the windows. She watched Aunt Lucinda make a circuit around the room, talking and laughing with everyone she met. Occasionally, she would look toward them—as would whomever she was talking to—and everyone would smile. Whatever she was doing, it seemed to be having a positive effect, for no one was looking at Pandora with censure or Persephone with pity.

Persephone wondered where Acton was because he certainly wasn't in the drawing room. She'd looked over every person and hadn't seen him.

A few people engaged her and Pandora in conversation, and only one mentioned the betrothal, saying she'd heard it was a mistake and how awful that must be. Aunt Lucinda's plan had worked exceedingly quickly—and effectively.

Still, Persephone was beginning to grow anxious. Where was Acton? She needed to see him, to tell him that she was leaving Bath with Pandora.

Would he be upset? Would he try to persuade her to stay? He hadn't raised the prospect of marriage again, and why would he after she'd explicitly told him not to?

Aunt Lucinda returned a short while later, and Persephone excused herself to visit the retiring room. Climbing to the second floor, she was so wrapped up in thoughts of Acton that she failed to see one of the people she'd been desperate to avoid: her mother.

They met at the top of the stairs. Persephone tried to move past her without saying anything, but the baroness clasped her elbow and drew her aside.

Perusing Persephone's gown with a narrowed eye, the baroness pursed her lips. "I see Lucinda bought you a new gown."

"Pandora too."

The baroness looked surprised. "She's here?"

"Yes, and things are going quite well. I told you the scandal would pass." Or something similar. "You only had to give it time—and solicit Aunt Lucinda's help. She wields a great deal of power here in Bath."

The baroness looked at Persephone intently. "I don't understand why you've turned so completely against us."

Persephone blinked at her. The woman couldn't be so daft. "Perhaps because you keep trying to force me to marry people I don't want?"

"It's not as if you didn't know you needed to wed. Your father and I have been patient for several years now, waiting for, as you say, the 'right' man to come along. It is apparent that will never happen without guidance." She frowned at Persephone. "You ruined a perfectly good opportunity to wed a duke. I will never comprehend why."

How Persephone wanted to tell her she'd also refused to entertain an actual proposal from that duke! But what would be the point of that besides enjoying a few minutes of gloating? Persephone didn't need that. She just wanted to be away from this toxic person.

"That is why it's pointless to explain, Mother. Because you will never comprehend why. Now, if you'll excuse me." Persephone tried to remove her arm from her mother's grip, but the baroness's fingers tightened around her.

"I will not," her mother said in a low, angry tone. "You and Lucinda have been going about the party saying the announcement of your betrothal is a mistake. You must marry him, Persephone. Your father and I will be ruined if you don't."

"I will never marry Cousin Harold."

"Then marry Wellesbourne," she pleaded, her eyes wild as she continued to squeeze Persephone's arm.

"Ouch." Persephone used her free hand to break her mother's grasp. "I won't be managed. Or manhandled. That you would continue to push me toward Wellesbourne is pathetic. You should know he is not an option."

"Isn't he? We asked him if he would wed Pandora since the two of them appeared to suit, but he said if he were going to marry anyone, it would be you."

"You're lying again," Persephone said, massaging her arm where her mother had squeezed her so tightly. "He didn't say that. When would you even have seen him?" As soon as she said that, she realized they could have encountered one another tonight already.

"He most certainly did say that," her mother said with an irritating smugness. "Earlier today when he came to see us to insist that we leave you and Pandora alone. He's quite championed your cause against us." She paused, her eyes narrowing slightly. "I must wonder why that is."

Persephone's pulse quickened. Acton had gone to see them? "Because he's a kind human being. I realize that's something you may not recognize."

"Now he's kind? I thought he was a rogue beneath contempt."

How Persephone wished she could take that back. She'd judged him entirely before knowing him at all. Granted, he had changed from the rogue he was. Or so it seemed. She recalled how he'd been when they'd first met—flirting with her and eager for an assignation. Then he'd been flirtatious with the maids at the Black Ivy as well as that other woman.

But she hadn't seen him do that since. Granted, she also hadn't seen him with other women, except at the gardens the other day, and on that occasion, he'd been entirely engaged with her and their party.

Could he really have said that to her parents? She sent her mother a cool glare. "This is another attempt at manipulation by you and Father. I doubt Wellesbourne even came to see you."

The baroness raised her chin defiantly. "Go and ask him, then. He's downstairs in the library. On the ground floor. Your father is there too, or he was a few minutes ago."

"I will." A rush of sadness hit Persephone, as if she'd just received terrible news. Except she hadn't. She was simply realizing that things would never be the same between her and her mother. "Why are you doing all this, Mama?" she asked. "Is it truly just because you need money?"

Pressing her lips together, her mother glanced away. "It is true that we are in need."

"Is it bad enough that you have forsaken your daughters and even sought to take advantage of family and friends? I understand you were very kind to the dowager duchess when she first came to Bath with her daughters. That sounds like the mother I thought I knew. What changed?"

"Nothing changed." The baroness sniffed, and she didn't sound convincing. "As I said, we are in need, and needs must."

It seemed that was all she was going to say. Persephone was left wondering if her mother had ever really genuinely sought to help Acton's mother, or if she'd been kind and supportive to the duchess because she thought it would be socially advantageous.

Heavy with disappointment, Persephone turned and went back down the stairs. She continued descending to the staircase hall, where she asked a footman for directions to the library. He escorted her there personally before bowing and taking himself off.

Persephone moved inside the doorway and scanned the room. It was not as crowded as the drawing room, but there were many people milling about. Finally, she caught sight of Acton's dark auburn head. He stood on the opposite side of the room.

Making her way around people conversing, Persephone looked toward him. When she reached the middle of the room, she had a clear line of sight to him.

He was not alone.

A beautiful woman with glittering blonde hair, creamy, luminescent skin, and sumptuous pink lips curled in an alluring smile, hung on his arm. He was entirely engaged with her, laughing and smiling. Flirting.

He looked exactly as he had with the other women at the Black Ivy. No, this was worse. He was even closer to this woman, and she was now pressing her hand against his chest. Not pressing actually, her fingertips curled beneath his lapel, as if she were holding him close to her.

Acton did not seem to mind in the slightest. On the contrary, he appeared utterly captivated. Why wouldn't he be? Indeed, why shouldn't he be? It wasn't as if he were married. He wasn't even betrothed.

He had, however, been conducting a liaison with another

woman. *Had.* Persephone now considered that activity in the past.

What if he *had* called on her parents earlier and told them he would marry Persephone? If that were true, it would only be due to the consequences of their affair. He felt beholden to make her his duchess.

Except he never had before. He'd had countless assignations and was still unwed. Persephone saw no reason for that to change. Particularly since he'd confessed to not being able to fall in love.

Suddenly, Persephone knew the awful truth—she loved him. The pain of seeing him now with this woman wasn't due to her disgust at his true nature. It was because she'd allowed him into her heart. Another rogue rule broken. With his overprotection, his obnoxious flirtation, and his commitment to helping her sister, he'd completely flattened her defenses. She'd been laid bare to him. And to heartbreak.

Dammit.

Eyes stinging, she nearly turned. No, she had something to tell him first.

Straightening her spine and notching up her chin, she marched toward him. He saw her then, his eyes widening slightly. He immediately removed the woman's hand from his lapel and stepped away from her, never appearing more like a man caught.

"Good evening, Wellesbourne," she said haughtily. "I came to thank you for including us this evening. It is a wonderful farewell as my sister and I will be leaving Bath in the next few days."

He blinked, but there was something akin to panic in his gaze? "Leaving? Where? Why?"

"We're taking a much-needed respite to the country." She wasn't about to tell him where so he could come looking for her and try to persuade her to fall into his arms again. "Good evening." Swallowing the emotion clogging her throat, Persephone spun about and strode from the room. If her father had been there, she hadn't seen him, which was just as well. Encountering him would only have made the evening an even bigger disaster.

Persephone hurried back up to the drawing room to find Pandora and her aunt so they could leave. But she encountered Pandora on the landing.

"There you are," Pandora said. "I was about to come looking for you in the retiring room. You've been gone awhile."

Taking her sister's arm, Persephone led her up the stairs to the second floor. Thankfully, their mother was no longer there. Persephone told Pandora about running into her and what she'd said about marrying Cousin Harold.

Pandora shook her head. "She finally admitted that they'll be ruined if you don't marry him? Fat lot of good that will do her. Did she understand that you aren't going to marry him?"

They walked into the retiring room, which was pleasantly empty.

Persephone released her sister and faced her. "I have no idea. She then tried to persuade me to marry Wellesbourne. Apparently, he called on them earlier to tell them to leave us alone."

"That's rather forward, isn't it? I mean, I appreciate all he's done to help me, but calling on our parents seems…inappropriate?"

It was indeed. Why would he do such a thing? Because he was a duke and thought he could order people about? "They tried to convince him to marry you, but he said if he married anyone it would be me." The emotion Persephone had tried to quash rose again. She began to shake.

"Why would he say that?" Pandora looked dubious. Then

her gaze softened. "Oh, Persey. How well have you and Wellesbourne come to know one another?"

"There is much you don't know," Persephone whispered.

Hurt flashed in Pandora's eyes. "Why?"

"Because I didn't want to talk about what was happening to you. When I met Wellesbourne—Acton—after running from Mama and Papa, he was very protective of me. Annoyingly so, but he did save me from a ruffian's attack."

Pandora gaped at her. "That's terrible! Not that he saved you, but that you were assaulted."

Persephone wrung her hands. "I grew to like him, against my better judgment. More recently, we have become close. Intimate," she added, looking away. "I've been the real fool, Pandora. At least you didn't give all of yourself to Bane. I've given Acton everything—my body, my heart, my very soul."

Pandora's brow furrowed. She seemed...confused? "But you just said he told our parents that if he married anyone it would be you? Does he not want you to be his duchess? If so, I am going to find him right now and plant him a facer."

"He was going to ask, but I didn't want to marry him just because we'd been intimate. So, I refused his proposal before he could present it." Persephone took a deep breath. "And it was the smartest thing I've done since meeting him. I knew he was a rogue, yet I allowed myself to be vulnerable to his charms. He said he wanted to change, that he was disgusted by Bane's behavior. It somehow awakened him to his own transgressions. I foolishly believed that was true."

While Pandora's features softened, she still seemed uncertain. "But it's not?"

Persephone shook her head. "I just saw him downstairs with another woman doing his typical flirtations. He can't help himself, Pandora." The emotion she'd worked to keep at bay spilled over as a tear tracked down her cheek. Persephone hastily wiped it away.

"It seems men generally can't." Pandora gave Persephone a feeble, sympathetic smile. "I'm so sorry, Persey. It's not fair that we would both fall for such scoundrels. And as much as I want to say you should have told me, I am not sure I would have wanted to hear about you being entangled with the duke. His friendship with Bane is enough to tarnish him, despite the manner in which he's helped me. It's one thing to accept the man's support and another to trust him with your heart."

That was the exact correct summation. Persephone nodded. "Just so. I am gladder than ever that we will be leaving Bath. Perhaps we could go tomorrow," she added with a shaky laugh.

"Aunt Lucinda will ask us to wait until the day after at least. I do think she is sad to see us go." Pandora took Persephone's hand and gave her a squeeze. "Shall we go find her now so we can leave this infernal party?"

"Yes, please." Persephone hugged her sister. "Thank you, Pandora. I love you so much."

"I love you too. We're going to be all right."

Yes, they were. Because they had each other.

❧

*A*cton watched in horror as Persey exited the library, her head high and shoulders back. She was angry. With him. And she had every right to be.

"Wellesbourne?" Mrs. Bertram sidled up next to him once more, pouting up at him. "Where were we before that chit interrupted us?"

"Chit?" Acton woke as if from a dream. No, a nightmare. "That was the very lovely Miss Barclay." Acton stopped Mrs. Bertram from putting her hand on him again and stepped away.

He walked toward the doorway, intending to find Persey and explain. He stopped abruptly. What, exactly, would he explain?

That Mrs. Bertram had approached him with a flirtatious manner and he'd, by habit, responded in kind? That the moment she'd clasped his arm, he'd felt a searing discomfort, something he'd never experienced before, and that he'd been in the process of trying to politely extricate himself when Persey had arrived?

Persey would never believe him. And why should she? His actions were those of the man she'd always known him to be, the man he'd thought he could leave behind: a consummate rake.

But he did want to change. He loved Persey and was ready to beg her to spend their lives together. How could he do that now? Would she even listen to him?

He had to try.

Moving toward the door once more, he ran straight into Somerton and Droxford.

Droxford inclined his head toward the corner and started in that direction. Acton didn't want to waste time with them. He needed to find Persey. "Can this wait?"

Somerton shook his head before nudging Acton toward the corner. Exhaling with frustration, Acton moved to join Droxford.

Back to the room, Somerton frowned at Acton. "Now, *you're* engaged and didn't tell us?"

What nonsense was this? "I am not, at the moment, betrothed."

"'At the moment'?" Somerton asked, brows arching.

"We've heard you are marrying the sister of the young lady Bane compromised," Droxford said. "Is that not true?"

"Good Lord, where did you hear that?" But Acton knew. Persey's parents hadn't been able to keep their mouths shut.

"It's a rumor floating about this evening," Somerton responded. "But you're saying it isn't true?"

"It is not." Unfortunately. "Though I would give anything for it to be," he admitted.

Both men stared at him in disbelief. "Have you fallen in love?" Somerton asked, appearing shocked.

"Yes."

"Congratulations," Droxford said, clapping him on the arm. "When is the wedding?"

"He's not yet engaged," Somerton interjected. "Are you planning to propose? Why is this a rumor if it has not yet happened?"

"Her parents like to spread gossip that may or may not be true. In this case, I would *like* it to be true, but it is not."

"Because you asked her, and she declined?" Somerton asked, aghast. "Is she daft?"

Droxford looked to Somerton, his scowl deepening. "You think she's somehow addlebrained because she would refuse Wellesbourne? One might think she is exceedingly clever, given his reputation."

Somerton pressed his lips together and made a sound of disgust.

"I have not asked her." Acton thought about how he'd intended to, but she'd bade him not to. And she'd been right to do so. At that moment, it would have been for the wrong reason. Now, however, asking her to marry him seemed not only right but absolutely essential.

"Then what are you waiting for?" Somerton demanded.

"She is angry with me and justifiably so."

"Make her unangry with you," Droxford said as if it were that simple.

Acton looked toward the door, worried that Persey might leave before he could speak to her. "I'm not sure that's possible, but I was about to try when you two dolts intercepted me."

"Do you need help?" Somerton offered.

"Do you know what Miss Barclay looks like? Can you stand in the entrance hall and stop her if she tries to leave while I look for her upstairs?"

Droxford inclined his head and turned toward the door. "We'll take care of it." He and Somerton moved away, and Acton followed them. Though he did not continue to the entrance hall. He went to the hidden servants' stairs at the back of the house and took them two at a time to the first floor, where he practically bolted to the drawing room in search of Persey.

Again, he was halted in his tracks, this time by his mother. "There you are, Acton. I'm afraid Lucinda and her nieces decided to leave. However, I do believe tonight was a success for Miss Pandora."

"No, they can't leave!" Glad that his friends would stop her, Acton still needed to hurry downstairs.

His mother touched his arm, her gaze darkening with concern. "What's wrong?"

"I need to convince Persey—Persephone—not to leave. Not just the party but Bath. She's going to leave me, and I don't know what I will do."

The dowager steered him to the side of the hall. "What do you want to say to her to get her to stay?"

"I'm not sure. I need her to understand that I've changed, that I'm not the reprobate everyone thinks me to be. At least, not anymore. Not since I met her."

"Is there perhaps something more…compelling you could say?" his mother prompted softly.

Realization dawned on him. "I would tell her that I love her, but I'm not sure she'll believe me. I told her I wasn't capable of that emotion."

"As we both know, you were wrong about that," she said with a smile. "Is there anything you can say or do to convince her you've changed, and that you can, indeed, love? I'd be happy to attest to that fact."

He thought about what had just transpired downstairs. He truly hadn't wanted Mrs. Bertram's attentions. She just hadn't known that yet because he hadn't told her. His reputation was that he enjoyed flirtation. Perhaps it was time to disabuse everyone of that notion.

Acton wondered how he'd made it this far in life without his mother's guidance. "Thank you, truly. However, this is something I need to do on my own." He knew precisely what he needed to say and how to say it.

For the first time, he didn't hear his father's oppositional voice in his head. The domineering duke had gone quiet at last.

# CHAPTER 22

*P*ersephone and Pandora located their aunt in the drawing room and informed her they wished to leave. While Aunt Lucinda had hoped they would stay a little longer, she understood and supported their decision.

"I should like to thank the dowager duchess before we go," Aunt Lucinda said, scanning the drawing room for their hostess. "Alas, I don't see her. Perhaps we'll encounter her on the way out." She gestured for Persephone and Pandora to precede her.

As they made their way downstairs, Persephone glimpsed their parents standing together in the staircase hall on the ground floor. They were off to the side, so she and Pandora would be able to avoid them as they continued to the entrance hall.

Still, Persephone nudged her sister on their descent and subtly inclined her head. Pandora made a face. "We don't have to speak with them."

"We most certainly do not. Tonight or ever."

"I suppose we should forget about our belongings at Radstock Hall," Pandora said with resignation.

"I'd give it all up to not have to spend another moment with them." Persephone shuddered. While she'd never felt a particularly close bond with either her mother or father, she'd still loved them, and she'd thought they'd loved her in return.

When they reached the bottom of the stairs, Aunt Lucinda came abreast of them, her body effectively blocking Persephone's and Pandora's lines of sight toward their parents. "Come, girls," she said briskly, ushering them into the entrance hall.

Persephone's heart swelled with love and appreciation for their aunt.

Their progress was abruptly blocked by two men. Persephone recognized the Viscount Somerton because he was Tamsin's cousin, but couldn't recall the name of the dour-faced gentleman beside him.

Somerton smiled broadly. "Good evening, Mrs. Barclay-Fiennes." He bowed to Aunt Lucinda. "And the Misses Barclay." He bowed to Persephone and Pandora in turn.

Persephone curtsied, as did Pandora. "Good evening, Lord Somerton." She glanced toward the other man, who was rather intimidating.

Elbowing the other man, Somerton coughed. "This is my friend, Lord Droxford. I promise he's not as terrifying as he looks."

He did indeed look slightly frightening, as if he could command a storm cloud to park over the entrance hall and drown them all. But his bow was most elegant as he bid them good evening.

"If you'll excuse us, we were on our way out," Aunt Lucinda said. "Lovely to see you, gentlemen."

Droxford seemed to grow an inch or two as he took a step toward them. "Before you depart, we simply must speak with you." He sounded rather dire.

"You *must?*" Pandora asked. "But we've only just met."

"That isn't true," Somerton said smoothly. He was far more affable than his gloomy friend. "I'm sure you've met Droxford before."

Persephone realized the baron had been in Weston for a few days when they'd first arrived at the beginning of August. She was not going to bring that up, however, since it would summon Bane to mind.

"You really must excuse us," Persephone said quickly before Somerton could say anything to spark conversation that was best left unsaid. "I am feeling unwell."

"Pers—Miss Barclay!"

The loud voice came from behind Persephone. From the staircase hall. She turned her head, knowing who'd called her name, but not believing he would do such a thing.

Acton was barreling down the staircase. He nearly knocked a gentleman over when he reached the bottom. Grasping the man securely, he murmured something before carrying on. The act reminded Persephone of when she'd run into him on the street in Gloucester.

That seemed so long ago now, and yet the memory was still fresh. Bold and searing. Thinking of it made her throat ache.

"Wait, please," Acton called as he rushed into the entrance hall. There were fewer people here than in the staircase hall, but everyone had turned to face them. Indeed, the doorways to the rooms bordering the hall became clogged with people.

Persephone turned as did her sister and Aunt Lucinda on either side of her.

"What are you *doing?*" Persephone whispered frantically. They'd made such wonderful progress tonight with putting scandal behind them. Now he was creating a new one.

"I've an announcement to make," he said in his normal voice, his gaze fixed only on her. "One that I wanted to make sure you heard before you go. My apologies for calling out your name like that."

She pursed her lips at him, but said nothing.

He looked about the hall then, his expression registering that he had a large audience. And it was completely silent, waiting, no doubt breathlessly, for whatever he planned to say.

Persephone had to admit she was a bit breathless too. What was he about?

Addressing the room—or rooms—at large, Acton raised his voice. "You all know me as a lustful libertine, a scandalous scoundrel, a rampant reprobate."

Had he practiced all that ridiculous alliteration? Persephone pressed her lips together so as not to smile. She did not want to find him amusing!

There were nods and murmurs in response to his pronouncement.

"Tonight, I renounce that reputation. I've reinvented myself, turned over a new leaf, changed for the better—I hope." He flicked a glance toward Persephone who stared at him in shock. "I am no longer the rogue I have been. I am, from this moment forward—actually from several days ago, if I'm honest—a *reformed* rake."

Somerton was gaping at Acton as if he'd suddenly sprouted a second head while Droxford had resumed his scowl. Acton, however, was smiling.

Did he think this was somehow going to make up for what he'd been doing in the library with that hussy? "How nice for you," she said, desperate to leave. Why was he doing this here, now?

Acton's face fell. He spoke more quietly now, so that only those nearest them could hear. "I need you to know that I've changed. I am not the man I was before I met you. I don't want to be that man."

Persephone's heart twisted. She loved this man so much, and yet she would be foolish to trust him. "That is most admirable. I wish you great success."

She started to turn, but he grabbed her arm. Someone gasped, and he let go immediately. "I love you, Persephone." He appeared almost...desperate. "This is not the place, but I don't want you to go. Not now, not ever. My life will be empty without you. Meaningless. I had no interest in Mrs. Bertram in the library. She latched on to me, and I was about to disentangle her when you arrived."

"You should believe him," a feminine voice said from somewhere to Persephone's right. "I tried to flirt with him tonight, and he didn't even notice."

"The same happened to me," someone else said. "Couldn't catch his attention at all."

Persephone narrowed her gaze at him. "Did you pay them to say those things?"

His eyes were wide and clear, focused only on her. "No. I don't want to flirt with anyone ever again unless her name is Persephone Barclay."

"What if her name was Persephone Loxley?" another feminine voice called out, and Persephone would have sworn it was Acton's mother.

His lips spread in that familiar, enchanting smile that never failed to make Persephone's heart race, then cartwheel about her chest. "Well, I would flirt with *her*," he said softly, moving to stand right in front of Persephone. "If she'd allow it. Marry me, Persey. Not because you should, but because you want to. Because I will spend the rest of my life making you the happiest woman alive. Because without each other, we will be despondent. Because I *need* someone to protect me from rats."

Persephone wanted to laugh, to smile, to cry out with joy.

But she simply stood there, unable to speak. Unable to do anything.

"If you don't marry him, I will," Somerton quipped.

Pandora elbowed Persephone gently. Rousing from her stupor, Persephone looked at her sister, who smiled and gave her a small nod. "He seems genuine," she whispered.

"I should have asked you in private," Acton added with a faint grimace. "I didn't do this so you would have to say yes."

"I know." Because he was genuine. She believed that he loved her. "I want to say yes. I love you too, Acton. I accept your proposal."

Instead of reacting with happiness or even relief, Acton closed his eyes and frowned, despite everyone around them cheering. He lowered himself to one knee. "I didn't even do that part right," he said, taking her hand. "Will you marry me, Persey?"

"I will."

"You believe me, right? I am reformed. The only attention I want from any woman is yours."

"No one who was as outraged by Bane's behavior as you and who has worked to help the woman Bane wronged as you have could continue to live the life of a scoundrel."

His shoulders sagged with relief as he smiled widely. He squeezed her hand, then got to his feet. "Damn, I wish I could kiss you."

"Do you really think that would be any more damaging than anything else that's happened to or been said about us in the last fortnight?" Pandora asked.

Acton sent her a nod. "Good point. I hope this is all right with you. Bane is no longer my friend."

"I don't blame you—or any of your friends—for Bane's behavior. It's past time for me to move on," she added softly, with a confident smile.

"You are a magnificent young woman, Pandora. I am glad

to call you sister." Acton turned back to Persephone and bent his head to kiss her. His lips barely brushed hers, and it was over. "That's all I dare," he whispered.

"Come now," Persephone said teasingly. "You're a duke. I should think a duke would dare anything."

"Later," he said with a soft groan. "I am already half-gone, and I'm fairly certain we are about to be mobbed with congratulations."

They were indeed, first by Somerton and Droxford, the former of whom was more effusive in his remarks. "Shocking turn of events, Acton," the viscount said. "But I couldn't be happier for you. It's obvious you made an excellent choice." Somerton took Persephone's hand and floated a kiss over the top of it.

They moved on only for everyone else who'd been watching to form a line to offer their congratulations. However, Acton's mother stepped in to redirect.

She leaned toward Acton and Persephone, speaking softly. "Do you mind if I make a formal announcement? Not that it's necessary, but I would enjoy it."

"By all means," Acton said with a smile.

Persephone saw the love in his gaze—all for his mother—and any doubt she might have had that this man wasn't capable of such emotion completely evaporated. It didn't make sense anyway. How could such an amenable, charming, thoughtful man be devoid of the ability to love?

The dowager guided Pandora and Aunt Lucinda to stand beside Persephone while motioning for Acton's sisters to join them. She gestured for them to stand on Acton's other side, and her intent became clear—she was organizing a receiving line to allow for a better flow of so many people.

Persephone caught sight of her parents on the periphery and realized Acton's mother hadn't brought them over too.

They did seem to be trying to make their way in this direction, but were having difficulty.

"Thank you," Persephone murmured to the dowager who looked at her in question. "For not including my parents here."

Her soon-to-be mother-in-law smiled warmly. "Of course, dear." She straightened and lifted her chin before loudly declaring, "It is my pleasure and honor to announce the betrothal of my son, His Grace, the Duke of Wellesbourne to Miss Barclay. May they enjoy a lifetime of joy and love." She beamed at them before taking her place at the start of the line.

"You're going to be a duchess," Pandora whispered before giggling. "Our mother will be ecstatic and perhaps even green with envy."

Persephone gave her sister's arm a squeeze as her gaze found her parents once more. They'd made progress but were now in the line that had formed to congratulate the newly betrothed couple and their families.

"Should we invite them to stand with us?" Persephone asked. "If only to quiet any gossip? I think I've had enough of that."

"You make a good point," Pandora responded with a weary sigh. "I suppose so. But make them wait in line first, then they can stand on Aunt Lucinda's other side."

Persephone grinned. "Fair enough."

A very long time later, Persephone finally had a moment alone with her betrothed. He secreted her into his mother's private sitting room on the first floor. She immediately noticed the portrait of him. "That's a wonderful painting of you. Would your mother let me steal it?"

After closing the door, Acton came up behind her and wrapped her in his arms. He kissed her neck, sending shivers of anticipation down her spine. "As it happens, the original is in London at Wellesbourne House. I just recently learned that any time I sat for a portrait, my father sent a copy to my mother. It was part of their arrangement when she left him."

Persephone turned in his arms. "They had a formal arrangement?"

He nodded. "All this time, I thought, because I'd been told, that my mother took my sisters and left his household because she preferred to be away from him. I'd buried most of my memories, but being here with her and my sisters has brought them back." His gaze held hers as he pulled her close. "Indeed, it was because of those memories that I realized I not only could love but I have. I loved my mother—*love*, as I still do—so much and I was devastated when she left. My father did everything he could to eliminate those emotions in me. He always said they made one weak, and a duke could not be weak." Acton shook his head. "I can see now that he put a great many idiotic notions into my brain, including the right of someone of my station to behave only as I want without giving a damn what others may think or say. Or *feel*."

"Acton, you do give a damn. I've seen you."

"Yes, but it apparently took a terrible situation in which a dear friend of mine was caught, and all our sins were laid bare. Then I met you, and your utter disgust with me was absolutely eye-opening. And vastly upsetting. I had to completely reevaluate myself. I'm *still* doing that and probably will be for some time. Do you know how difficult it was for me to come to you in your aunt's garden? The old Acton was more than eager and delighted of course, but the new Acton had great hesitation."

Persephone laughed. "Perhaps there are some benefits to the old Acton, provided his actions are directed entirely at me. But you've already promised that. To well over a hundred people."

He grinned. "More than that, because you know it's

already being spread throughout Bath. Which was my intent. I need everyone to know, particularly the Mrs. Bertrams out there, that I am no longer on the market in any way. The only woman I want to flirt with, touch, kiss, and take to bed is you."

"How far you've come," Persephone murmured.

"I am becoming the man I want to be, the man I think I have been all along but whom my father sought to bury. He didn't allow me to be soft or indeed feel deep emotion of any kind. And forget about attachment. That sort of nonsense is for lesser men."

Her eyes were sad for a moment, but she smiled. "I'm so glad you aren't that man. Being soft and feeling emotion makes you a greater man to me. I am also undergoing a transformation to be the woman I am meant to be, someone who snorts and laughs loudly, who doesn't live under someone else's expectations." Narrowing her eyes, she gave him a saucy look. "Turns out I *can* snare a duke."

"In every way imaginable." Acton's eyes shone with love and admiration before he kissed her. It was a deep, soul-stirring kiss that she'd been craving since he'd proclaimed his love and devotion to her. She was breathless when they broke apart. "I suppose we have to return to the party."

"We must, unless we want to arouse more gossip."

"As I told Pandora earlier, I've had enough of that."

"Will she still be leaving Bath?" he asked.

Persephone nodded. "After the wedding."

When the line had broken up finally, they'd briefly discussed a timeline with Acton's mother. The banns would be read at Bath Abbey on Sunday, and they would be married in three weeks' time. It seemed forever—longer than they'd even known one another—but there were plans to make, and Persephone was glad for that time with Pandora before she left.

"Does that upset you?" Acton asked, his gaze soft with concern.

"No. It's the right thing for her to do. But I am glad that you will get to know her before she leaves."

"I am glad for that too." He kissed her forehead. "What of your parents?" His tone took on a dark, sardonic quality.

"I told them they could attend the wedding and that was the only time I wished to see them. And I instructed them that they must send Pandora's and my belongings here, and that if they don't, you'll be forced to send someone to collect them."

"Brilliant," he interjected with a grin.

Persephone shrugged. "They seemed happy, but I don't know if that was for me or because they can now claim kinship with a duke." Persephone rolled her eyes.

"I imagine they'll be speaking to me about a financial arrangement."

Persephone put her hand on his cheek. "Don't you dare give them a shilling. Why did you visit them today anyway?"

"When I saw the announcement in the newspaper about your fake betrothal, I was livid." His gaze turned sheepish. "I couldn't stop myself from going to see them and demanding they leave you and Pandora alone. I'm afraid it's something my father would have done." He grimaced.

"And that's when you told them that if you married anyone, it would be me?"

"They'd suggested I bow to the gossip about me and your sister and wed Pandora." He shuddered. "I'd already begun to think of her in a rather sisterly fashion. Can you imagine? I could not, however, tell your parents that, so I gave them the truth. Which is that I would marry you—if you would have me. I just didn't think you would."

"I was a fool to stop you from proposing. I didn't think I could fall for a rogue as my sister did, nor did I want to. I couldn't see how that would end in anything but heartbreak, because I was convinced a rogue could never change. I'd failed to fully acknowledge that you are not the rogue that Bane is." She gave him a faux serious stare. "There are rogues and there are *rogues*."

Acton laughed. "I'm delighted to hear that my rogue status is not as egregious. I shall endeavor to continue on that path. He kissed her again, and Persephone surrendered for a moment before dragging herself away. "We need to get back."

"Yes," he said with great disappointment. "But I will find a way to see you later."

On her way to the door, she looked back at him over her shoulder with a sultry smile. "You know how to find the scullery at my aunt's house."

"I do," he said, moving to open the door for her.

She paused, turning toward him. "But tonight, I'll show you how to get to my chamber. My bed is far more comfortable. Not to mention larger."

His eyes glowed with promise. "I can hardly wait."

*A*cton drew his wife close as they snuggled into their new bed together, the day's excitement behind them. They'd married that morning and enjoyed a wonderful wedding breakfast hosted by her Aunt Lucinda, which was just ten doors down from the house that Acton had leased in the Crescent for the remainder of the Season, which was now in full swing.

They wouldn't be here the entire time, of course, because he'd have to go to London once Parliament was in session. He and Persey had already discussed their intent to avoid Cousin Harold at all costs. However, Acton had promised to meet with him regarding Parliamentary business as a means to smooth things over after the broken engagement that hadn't even really been an engagement.

"You're sure you're looking forward to London?" he asked his new wife. Persey said she was excited to see London for the first time, especially with him, but he knew she'd been through a great many changes of late. She was no longer associated with her parents, as evidenced by the scant number of words they'd exchanged after this morning's ceremony at the abbey. And they had not been invited to the breakfast that followed.

Persey had expected them to complain about not being included, but what she didn't know was that Acton had paid them to leave Persey—and Pandora—alone. He'd settled their debts and informed them that there wouldn't be any more financial assistance. Ever. He'd also advised them to keep to themselves for a while, that their meddling and deception had not endeared them to anyone.

Time would tell if they would listen.

"I would look forward to rowing to America if it means I'm with you," she said sweetly, kissing his neck.

Acton laughed. "That sounds abominable."

She snorted. "Doesn't it?"

How he loved her snort. He'd learned that very day that it was snorting that had brought Persey and her dear friend Lady Minerva together. Acton had discovered many things about his bride in the past few weeks, namely that she had a delightful group of friends that included Shefford's sister, Minerva, Somerton's cousin, Tamsin, with whom Pandora had departed following the breakfast, and several others. Pandora had stitched something called Rogue Rules, but Acton hadn't had a chance to look at it closely.

"What was that Pandora stitched for you?" he asked. "I thought I saw the words 'Rogue Rules'?"

He was rewarded with another snort. "It is my favorite gift, if I'm being honest. After Bane was seen compromising Pandora, we all came up with a list of rules for rogues. How to avoid falling for their wicked charms, that sort of thing."

"I see. Were they useful to you?"

"Clearly not," she said with a laugh. "Since I find myself married to one!" Persey sobered. "They are still important. Too many young ladies have fallen prey to men who think they are above reproach or consequence."

"I couldn't agree more," he said sincerely. "I will do everything I can, as a reformed rogue, to further your cause."

"I don't know that we have a *cause*. But I do think you serve as proof that a rogue *can* change and that for some, the rules may be broken." She seemed to think a moment, her brow creased. "On second thought, Pandora might have a cause. She has said on more than one occasion that she will help other young ladies avoid the trap she fell into."

"I will miss Pandora," Acton said, stroking Persey's shoulder. "Do you think she will consider joining us in London for the Season? Your aunt seemed to greatly favor the idea."

Persey exhaled. "I doubt it. And not because she's concerned about people shunning her. She simply has no desire to consider marriage. I did try to persuade her to come for a fortnight, just to visit and see the sights. But I am not sure she'll want to. She does plan to spend August in Weston as we have done the past several years." She tilted her head to look at him. "Will you mind terribly if I go for a week or two?"

"Not at all. I adore Weston. I will lease a cottage, if that suits you."

"That would be splendid." Her gaze turned serious. "However, you mustn't interrupt my time with my friends. This sojourn together is very important to us."

He put his hand over his heart. "I vow I will relegate myself to the periphery. You won't see or hear me unless I am summoned. Except at night." He tipped his head toward hers. "Then, you are *mine*."

Persey's lips curved into an alluring smile. "If you insist."

Pressing his lips to her neck, he kissed along the underside of her jaw to her ear. "I'll beg if I have to. I am not above that. If you had not said that you loved me in return, I was prepared to prostrate myself before you until you could find a way to summon the emotion."

"And if I could not?" she teased.

"I would have had to consult someone for a potion or some spell that would make you fall in love with me." He groaned. "That is something Rake Acton would do."

Persey laughed. "I am fairly certain Minerva mentioned such a potion."

"She would use such a thing?"

"We were discussing it in terms of questioning why there wasn't a potion for repelling men."

Acton flung himself to his back as he roared with laughter. A moment later, Persey moved over him, her body blanketing his.

"You find that amusing?" she asked, straddling her legs around him and instantly awakening his cock with her movements.

"I find it utterly endearing." He swept his hand along her jaw and cupped the back of her head as her golden hair tumbled over his fingers and caressed her cheeks. "How deeply I love you, my beautiful wife."

"Show me now, my darling husband. And I will tell you again and again that I love you—no beseeching required."

"We have an accord." He pulled her head down to his, their lips nearly touching. "I will, however, be using certain… techniques to ensure your undying devotion."

Her eyes glittered above his. "Challenge accepted."

**Join Persephone, Pandora, and all their girlfriends in Weston in August 1815 when perennially cheerful Tamsin Penrose attempts to turn Baron Droxford's permanent frown upside down. But Isaac Deverell's grumpiness hides a dark past he would prefer stayed buried…no matter the cost. Preorder BECAUSE THE BARON BROODS today!**

Would you like to know when my next book is available and to hear about sales and deals? **Sign up for my VIP newsletter** which is the only place you can get bonus books and material such as the short prequel to the Phoenix Club series, INVITATION, and the exciting prequel to Legendary Rogues, THE LEGEND OF A ROGUE.

**Join me on social media!**

Facebook: https://facebook.com/DarcyBurkeFans
Instagram at darcyburkeauthor
Pinterest at darcyburkewrite

And follow me on Bookbub to receive updates on pre-orders, new releases, and deals!

**Need more Regency romance? Check out my other historical series:**

**The Phoenix Club**
Society's most exclusive invitation...

Welcome to the Phoenix Club, where London's most audacious, disreputable, and intriguing ladies and gentlemen find scandal, redemption, and second chances.

**Matchmaking Chronicles**
The course of true love never runs smooth. Sometimes a little matchmaking is required. When couples meet at a house party, provocative flirtation, secret rendezvous, and falling in love abound!

**The Untouchables**
Swoon over twelve of Society's most eligible and elusive

bachelor peers and the bluestockings, wallflowers, and outcasts who bring them to their knees!

### The Untouchables: The Spitfire Society
Meet the smart, independent women who've decided they don't need Society's rules, their families' expectations, or, most importantly, a husband. But just because they don't need a man doesn't mean they might not *want* one…

### The Untouchables: The Pretenders
Set in the captivating world of The Untouchables, follow the saga of a trio of siblings who excel at being something they're not. Can a dauntless Bow Street Runner, a devastated viscount, and a disillusioned Society miss unravel their secrets?

### Wicked Dukes Club
Six books written by me and my BFF, NYT Bestselling Author Erica Ridley. Meet the unforgettable men of London's most notorious tavern, The Wicked Duke. Seductively handsome, with charm and wit to spare, one night with these rakes and rogues will never be enough…

### Lords in Love
More books from me and Erica Ridley set in the world of Marrywell, England! For those in want of a husband or wife, there is no better time or place to find one's true love than the annual May Day Festival in Marrywell. Princes and paupers alike fall head over heels, sometimes with the person they least expect…

### Love is All Around
Heartwarming Regency-set retellings of classic Christmas

stories (written after the Regency!) featuring a cozy village, three siblings, and the best gift of all: love.

## Secrets and Scandals
Six epic stories set in London's glittering ballrooms and England's lush countryside.

## Legendary Rogues
Five intrepid heroines and adventurous heroes embark on exciting quests across the Georgian Highlands and Regency England and Wales!

If you like contemporary romance, I hope you'll check out my **Ribbon Ridge** series available from Avon Impulse, and the continuation of Ribbon Ridge in **So Hot**.

I hope you'll consider leaving a review at your favorite online vendor or networking site!

I appreciate my readers so much. Thank you, thank you, *thank you*.

## ALSO BY DARCY BURKE

**Historical Romance**

### *Rogue Rules*

If the Duke Dares

Because the Baron Broods

As the Earl Likes

When the Viscount Seduces

### *The Phoenix Club*

Improper

Impassioned

Intolerable

Indecent

Impossible

Irresistible

Impeccable

Insatiable

### *The Matchmaking Chronicles*

Yule Be My Duke

The Rigid Duke

The Bachelor Earl (also prequel to *The Untouchables*)

The Runaway Viscount

The Make-Believe Widow

### *Lords in Love*

Beguiling the Duke by Darcy Burke

Taming the Rake by Erica Ridley

Romancing the Heiress by Darcy Burke

Defying the Earl by Erica Ridley

Matching the Marquess by Darcy Burke

Chasing the Bride by Erica Ridley

### *The Untouchables*

The Bachelor Earl (prequel)

The Forbidden Duke

The Duke of Daring

The Duke of Deception

The Duke of Desire

The Duke of Defiance

The Duke of Danger

The Duke of Ice

The Duke of Ruin

The Duke of Lies

The Duke of Seduction

The Duke of Kisses

The Duke of Distraction

### *The Untouchables: The Spitfire Society*

Never Have I Ever with a Duke

A Duke is Never Enough

A Duke Will Never Do

### *The Untouchables: The Pretenders*

A Secret Surrender

A Scandalous Bargain

A Rogue to Ruin

***Love is All Around***

*(A Regency Holiday Trilogy)*

The Red Hot Earl

The Gift of the Marquess

Joy to the Duke

***Wicked Dukes Club***

One Night for Seduction by Erica Ridley

One Night of Surrender by Darcy Burke

One Night of Passion by Erica Ridley

One Night of Scandal by Darcy Burke

One Night to Remember by Erica Ridley

One Night of Temptation by Darcy Burke

***Secrets and Scandals***

Her Wicked Ways

His Wicked Heart

To Seduce a Scoundrel

To Love a Thief (a novella)

Never Love a Scoundrel

Scoundrel Ever After

***Legendary Rogues***

Lady of Desire

Romancing the Earl

Lord of Fortune

Captivating the Scoundrel

**Contemporary Romance**

Prefer to read in German, French, or Italian? Check out my website for foreign language editions!

# ABOUT THE AUTHOR

Darcy Burke is the USA Today Bestselling Author of sexy, emotional historical and contemporary romance. Darcy wrote her first book at age 11, a happily ever after about a swan addicted to magic and the female swan who loved him, with exceedingly poor illustrations. Join her <u>Reader Club newsletter</u> for the latest updates from Darcy.

A native Oregonian, Darcy lives on the edge of wine country with her guitar-strumming husband, incredibly talented artist daughter, and imaginative, Japanese-speaking son who will almost certainly out-write her one day (that may be tomorrow). They're a crazy cat family with two Bengal cats, a small, fame-seeking cat named after a fruit, an older rescue Maine Coon with attitude to spare, an adorable former stray who wandered onto their deck and into their hearts, and two bonded boys who used to belong to (separate) neighbors but chose them instead. You can find Darcy in her comfy writing chair balancing her laptop and a cat or three, attempting yoga, folding laundry (which she loves), or wildlife spotting and playing games with her family. She loves traveling to the UK and visiting her cousins in Denmark. Visit Darcy online at <u>www.darcyburke.com</u> and follow her on social media.

facebook.com/DarcyBurkeFans

instagram.com/darcyburkeauthor

pinterest.com/darcyburkewrites

goodreads.com/darcyburke

bookbub.com/authors/darcy-burke

amazon.com/author/darcyburke

threads.net/@darcyburkeauthor

tiktok.com/@darcyburkeauthor

Made in United States
North Haven, CT
15 February 2024